Also by Michelle I. Mason

Your Life Has Been Delayed

My Second Impression of You

MICHELLE I. MASON

BLOOMSBURY

NEW YORK LONDON OXFORD NEW DELHI SYDNEY

BLOOMSBURY YA
Bloomsbury Publishing Inc., part of Bloomsbury Publishing Plc
1385 Broadway, New York, NY 10018

BLOOMSBURY and the Diana logo are trademarks of Bloomsbury Publishing Plc

First published in the United States of America in September 2022 by Bloomsbury YA

Bloomsbury books may be purchased for business or promotional use.
For information on bulk purchases please contact Macmillan Corporate and
Premium Sales Department at specialmarkets@macmillan.com

Library of Congress Cataloging-in-Publication Data
Names: Mason, Michelle I., author.
Title: My second impression of you / by Michelle I. Mason.
Description: New York : Bloomsbury Children's Books, 2022.
Summary: Sixteen-year-old Maggie thought she knew everything about her friends and
boyfriend—until she relives her "best day ever" and discovers she had it all wrong.
Identifiers: LCCN 2021062835 (print) | LCCN 2021062836 (e-book)
ISBN 978-1-5476-0412-8 (hardcover) • ISBN 978-1-5476-0413-5 (e-book)
Subjects: CYAC: Dating (Social customs)—Fiction. | Friendship—Fiction. |
Interpersonal relations—Fiction. | LCGFT: Romance fiction.
Classification: LCC PZ7.1.M3762 My 2022 (print) | LCC PZ7.1.M3762 (e-book) |
DDC [Fic]—dc23
LC record available at https://lccn.loc.gov/2021062835

Book design by Jeanette Levy
Typeset by Westchester Publishing Services
Printed and bound in the U.S.A.
2 4 6 8 10 9 7 5 3 1

To find out more about our authors and books visit
www.bloomsbury.com and sign up for our newsletters.

For Luke and Anna, the ultimate triple threats:

Brilliant. Compassionate. Weird.

Always and forever your biggest fan.

1

Wardrobe is vitally important not only on the stage but in life as well.

As the incomparable Kristin Chenoweth once said, "A nice pair of Jimmy Choos never hurt anyone."

Not that I could afford Jimmy Choos. More like a pair of Jessica Simpsons from the clearance rack at DSW. Or, today, because it's so unseasonably warm for March, the rhinestone-embellished flip-flops my friend Alexis Santiago gave me because it turned out her mom bought the wrong size and she couldn't return them. Win for me!

Second win: both my *A Midsummer Night's Dream* rehearsal *and* Theo's golf practice were canceled today. Totally unprecedented. And instead of just asking me to meet him at the driving range or his basement for a make-out session, Theo suggested Starbucks.

I can't remember the last time we went out for real. Thus the sparkly flip-flops instead of my more practical Vans or ballet flats. I also swapped out the Metro Theater Arts tee and leggings I wore to school for black ankle pants and a hunter green off-the-shoulder peasant top. Too much for coffee? Maybe. But prom is around the corner; this could be big. Theo stepped up the setting; I'm stepping up the costume and I'm ready for an important moment.

Glancing around the parking lot, I decide my car is the best background option. I snap a picture of myself and send it to my best friend, Rayna Fuentes. Do I look promposal-worthy?

Prom is 6 wks away, she replies. And he's already your boyfriend. He probably assumes you're going together.

She doesn't add an eye-roll emoji, but I can see her doing it while she types. I start walking along the row of cars while I respond.

33 days! Like she doesn't know I have a countdown. It's tacked on my wall beside the daily calendar entry I saved from when I met Theo. My grandma started buying me these tear-off calendars years ago (my favorite featured quotes from famous Broadway stars). Last year's was a word-of-the-day theme, and that particular day was "genesis: the origin or mode of formation of something." I'd already marked it with a star in red pen because I was expecting the casting announcement for my theater troupe's fall production of *Frozen* that day. After meeting Theo, I added a heart and kept it as a memento because it turned out to be the best day ever, the start of a wonderful relationship *and* a fun role.

But the point is, I know the exact number of days until prom. It's one of the benefits of dating a junior. Most sophomores don't get asked to the prom. Though I'm anxious for Theo to make it official.

Prom isn't even on Rayna's radar. *Her* wall features prints of famous female scientists. We have very different priorities, but in general she still supports mine, so I assure her, Will keep you posted!

I've reached the edge of the parking lot. After stowing my

phone in my pants pocket, I dash across the street that separates it from the strip center and up the steps toward the Starbucks entrance. As I'm about to reach for the door, it swings out, emitting Carson Lockwood. *Ugh.* My lip curls, as it generally does when Theo's best friend is around. What's he doing here, at the scene of my potential promposal?

I instinctively step backward, putting space between us. Carson exits the coffee shop completely, tugging his gray baseball cap low over his forehead.

"Maggie," he grunts, without a split second of direct eye contact.

Talk about a character study—his body language is one hundred percent "Get away from me." The feeling is mutual.

But you know what? He's not spoiling today for me.

"Have a great afternoon, Carson!" I say brightly, and sail past him inside.

I'm still smiling with satisfaction over Carson's startled expression when I spot Theo at a cozy table in the corner. He hasn't seen me yet; he's looking at his phone. But there he is, the most perfect boyfriend ever. He once told me his last name, Kallis, is Greek for "best," and I believe it. He's so handsome, with his olive-toned, year-round tan and dark, wavy hair. Sometimes I get lost in his rich brown eyes. And he dressed up too! He always trends preppy, but today he's wearing an untucked plaid button-down shirt with the sleeves rolled up so his forearms show. I love his forearms.

A warm feeling tingles through me, like when he draws me close for a kiss. I'm right. I know I am. He's planning to ask me today!

I weave quickly through the tables and lean down to kiss his cheek, since we're in public and all. "Hi!"

He startles and fumbles his phone. "Hey. Didn't see you come in."

A little underwhelming. Oh well. I sit across from him and pick up the drink waiting for me. "Is this a mocha cookie crumble Frappuccino?"

"Yep." He leans forward, propping his elbows on the table with his spine all straight like he's nervous. A good sign!

"Here." He pushes a paper bag toward me. "I got you a chocolate chip cake pop too."

"Aww, that is so sweet!"

"It's no big deal," he says.

But it totally is. Either he has an amazing memory or possibly keeps a Maggie note of all my favorites (drinks, ice cream, flowers), because he's a model boyfriend when it comes to knowing what I like.

"No, really. You're so thoughtful!" I suck in a strawful of delicious chocolate and caffeine and start giving him a mental costume change, picturing our big night. Theo is very traditional, so I'll never get him to wear anything too trendy, like a retro velvet jacket (so soft to cuddle against!) or a pop of color. Hmm. He'd look fantastic in a slim fit suit with the slightest sheen to it. "How do you feel about a nice charcoal?"

"Charcoal?" Theo blinks his beautiful brown eyes. "Are you planning a barbecue? Were you even *listening* to me?"

Um. He was talking? I bite my lip. "Sorry. The caffeine went straight to my head. What were you saying?"

I better not have missed him asking me to the prom.

4

"Just—" He heaves a distinctly *un*romantic sigh. "I think it's time for us to break up."

His lips keep moving, but I don't hear a word. Like that moment when you're on a plane, trying to get your ears to pop. There's nothing—no whir of machines as the baristas make drinks. No hum of conversation from other customers. No steady thump of my heart in my chest.

And then it all snaps back. *Pop!*

". . . too much drama. I just can't handle it anymore. I'm sorry, Maggie."

"WHAT?" I shriek. I'm laser-focused on Theo, but I can tell from the way his panicked gaze moves from side to side that half the coffee shop is now focused on *us*. And our *drama*. "You're breaking up with me? I thought you were going to ask me to prom!"

"Um. Maggie." He looks like a cornered animal. "I really care about you, but no. We're—" He takes a steadying breath, like I'm about to go all *Carrie* on him. "We're done."

We can't be. Not when I came here expecting us to plan out the ultimate prom evening. I dressed up for him! There has to be some *reason*.

"Is there someone else?" My voice is still about three ticks higher than usual, but all my acting training has gone out the window. I have absolutely no control over my vocal cords.

"No." He shakes his head vigorously, still nervously watching the people around us. "No one else. I have to go."

And then he's up and running out of Starbucks. Running away. From me.

2

I sit there, stunned, staring after Theo. The nearby patrons who were so avidly following the destruction of my dreams a few moments ago are now looking anywhere else.

He broke up with me.

Theo *broke up* with me.

My eyes well with tears as my throat closes up. How *could* he? I don't get it. I thought Theo was the one. Or at least the one I'd be with until he graduated, and now he's ruined it by dumping me more than a year early. Everything was going so perfectly.

The tears spill over as I gather the mostly full Frappuccino and uneaten cake pop and toss them in the trash before I leave the scene of the heart crime. What a waste. Just like my carefully chosen outfit.

Tears course unchecked down my cheeks as I exit Starbucks and fumble with my phone, typing the words I wouldn't have believed possible twenty minutes ago.

He dumped me.

It seems so final to hit Send, but how else will Rayna know to show up at my house with chocolate and a stack of *People* and *Us Weekly* so we can focus on the even sadder lives of celebrities?

My feet propel me toward the parking lot as Rayna's last text stares back at me, assuring me Theo already assumes we're going to prom together. Just as my thumb connects with the arrow making it all real, I step into nothing. My phone flies from my hand as I cry out and try to find solid ground. I twist sideways, tilting forward as the outside of my right foot hits the edge of the concrete step. I sit hard on the step above it, and a jolt passes through my entire body.

"Are you okay?" A lady rushes over, tugging along a young girl with adorable pigtail braids in her wake. An older white gentleman runs up behind them with an iced Starbucks cup in his hand. Their eyes are wide as they stare at me, sprawled out on the steps. At least my wardrobe choice didn't include a miniskirt.

"I think so?" I can't tell. I feel sort of numb. But I also don't want to move and find out. My eyes are completely dry now, and my skin is all tingly.

I don't think I'm okay.

I peer into the parking lot, searching for Theo, but he's long gone. He couldn't leave fast enough, and now I'm here on the steps with a growing group of strangers gawking at me. I usually like an audience, but not like this.

"What's your name?" the mom asks, releasing her daughter to crouch in front of me.

Name. My name. Why can't I remember my name?

"Maggie!" a familiar male voice answers.

That's it. Maggie. Maggie Scott.

"Maggie!" the voice repeats, and then its owner is kneeling beside the mom.

It keeps. Getting. Worse. "Carson? What are you doing here?"

Surely he should have left by now. He was clearly in there with

Theo before I arrived, probably getting the scoop on Theo's plans and then patting him on the back and saying, "About time." Maybe he stuck around to see the fallout.

Carson reaches a hand toward my foot and then draws it back again, almost like he's afraid. "Are you hurt?"

I scan the crowd behind him. It's grown to about ten people now. I call on all my acting skills, but the most I can muster is a grimace. "I think I'm fine. Just startled."

Carson looks down at my foot in concern but turns to the rest of the gathering with a reassuring smile. "I'll take care of her. She's a friend."

I stifle my snort—because contradicting him won't make everyone else go away, and I definitely don't want them watching when I pick myself up.

"Are you sure?" the mom asks.

The little girl points down. "There's a dent in your foot."

"What?!" She's right. About halfway up the outside of my foot, there's a small indentation. I look at my other foot—no dent. This is not good. My breath shortens.

"Don't worry, I'll take care of her," Carson repeats. He keeps talking, but I don't hear what else he says to convince them all to go away because THERE'S A DENT IN MY FOOT, AND THAT'S NOT NORMAL.

Why, oh why, did I wear flip-flops today? It was so unseasonably warm all I could think was that my feet could finally be free (and how cute the flip-flops were). But if I'd been wearing Vans or boots like I normally would in March, they would have protected my feet. Or maybe, if I'd followed Kristin Chenoweth's advice and somehow lucked into "never hurt anyone" Jimmy Choo flip-flops instead of Alexis's castoffs, I wouldn't have a dent in my foot now!

"What are you muttering about? Are those really Jimmy Choos?" Carson says, leaning close. He smells like freshly mown grass, and I realize he's never been near enough for me to smell him before. But also, his remark reminds me why he's on my list of the Most Annoying People to Grace the Stage of Life—a list that also includes my older brother, Adam, and Katelyn Saverin, who's always competing with me for the best roles.

"Of course they're not." I didn't realize I was saying all of that out loud. "I'm fine. You can go."

He looks up enough that I can actually see his face fully under his cap. His light blond eyebrow arches into the shadow of the brim, his pale blue eyes skeptical. "I just assured all those people I'd take care of you, and I will. But that kid called it. Your foot is dented. Let's see if you can stand."

He holds out his arm, but I don't want to touch Carson. I don't want anything to *do* with Carson. Until this very moment, the only remotely kind thing he ever said to me was "Nice sweater," and it might have been sarcastic (even though it was my most flattering, soft pink cashmere sweater that I only wear for special occasions because it has to be dry-cleaned). So instead of taking Carson's arm, I place my palms firmly on the same step where my butt landed and push up, putting all my weight on my left foot. There's a brick post to my left, and I place my hand against it for support. It's only once I'm standing there with my right foot swinging in the air that I realize I lost my flip-flop.

I hate to ask him for help after I just told him I didn't need it, but I don't see any other option. "Um. Could you . . . ?"

Surprisingly, Carson doesn't smirk as he leans down and retrieves my shoe from the pavement. He fits it onto my foot—which is starting to seriously throb—like a regular Prince Charming.

Nothing is right in my world today.

I take a deep breath. Carson stands on the sidewalk at the base of the steps—there are only four—braced like he expects me to topple over as soon as I put weight on my right foot. I gently step down, and pain radiates sharply from the dent up the side of my leg. I quickly shift most of my weight back to my left foot, but it's bad. It's really bad. I bite my lip to keep from crying out.

There's no way I can walk to the car by myself. "Carson?"

I'm staring at the ground, and his feet shuffle closer. "What do you need?"

I jerk my head toward the parking lot. "My car." My voice is strangled, a knot caught at the base of my throat. It's not so much that I don't want to cry in front of him. More that I'm afraid if I start crying from the pain, I won't be able to stop and I'll be trapped here. "Can you help me get over there?"

Carson comes around to my right side and loops an arm around my back and under my left armpit, stooping in an awkward bent-over position but taking most of my weight. "Is that your phone?"

My gaze follows his finger to my phone, seemingly undamaged on the concrete. The whole reason I wasn't looking where I was walking. They say don't text and drive. Where's the warning about walking?

"Yeah."

"I'll get it." He reaches for it effortlessly while still holding on to me. "Ready?"

No. Even standing here is excruciating, but at least if I go home I can take some ibuprofen and put some ice on it. "Let's go."

We hobble across the street to the parking lot, and with every step, pain jolts through my foot. White light fills the edges of my vision, and I'm afraid if Carson weren't holding on to me I'd collapse in the middle of the parking lot. My stomach doesn't feel great either, not exactly like I'm going to throw up but like I'm about to take a huge test and I haven't studied at all. By the time we reach my car, I'm shivering, but there's sweat beading along my hairline.

As I unlock the door, I turn to Carson. "Thanks," I mumble, knowing I need to say it but not really wanting to because it's him.

His brows are crinkled as he studies me. Do I look like I'm about to pass out?

"No," he says.

Despite the pain, I straighten. Maybe that wasn't the most gracious "thanks" ever, but still. He's rejecting it? "What's your problem?"

"You shouldn't drive," he says. "It's your right foot."

Weirdest of all, he doesn't sound defensive in response to my tone or display any of the *you are a horrible human* vibes I usually get from him. It's confusing, and I don't like it.

I lift up the foot and wiggle it back and forth, holding back a wince as the muscles along the outside stretch and burn. "It'll be fine for driving. I just need to move it back and forth, see? My ankle is okay."

"What about pushing on the pedal, though?"

Why won't he just give up? This concerned act is very out of character. In my normal reality, the only way Carson would have helped me is if Theo had asked him to. Instead, Theo's nowhere to be found and Carson's hovering like we're old friends.

"Carson, you've done your good deed for the day. I don't need you anymore. Just go!"

He steps back, stricken at my harsh tone, and I feel a tinge of remorse. But I have got to get out of here. "Please," I say more softly.

He looks down at my foot again and grimaces. But then he squares his shoulders and looks back up at me, determined. Carson's much more leanly built than Theo, and sometimes he comes across seeming younger, especially wearing a ball cap all the time, but when he gives me that *I mean business* stare, I believe it.

"It's not safe," he says. "I should drive you."

Ugh. That's more like the Carson I know. He's made it clear before he doesn't trust my intelligence—apparently even when it comes to my own well-being.

Like I'd ever get in a car with him. "No, thanks."

"Or you can call Theo? He's probably still nearby."

"Talk about kicking a girl when she's down."

He frowns. "What do you mean?"

My laugh sounds more like a sob. "Theo just broke up with me. Like right before this happened."

"Oh." Carson looks around the parking lot—at an abandoned shopping cart in the next spot over, at a pebble near his shoe, at a light pole—before finally focusing on me again. "I'm sorry."

He doesn't *sound* sorry. Probably because he's never thought I was good enough for Theo. But also, how could Carson have been with Theo right before he dumped me and not know about it?

"I'll call my mom," I say.

"I'll wait."

Of course. For seven months, he didn't want anything to do with me. Now, he won't go away.

"Fine. Whatever."

3

I open my car door and gingerly lower myself into the seat, letting out an audible sigh. The whiteness at the edge of my vision and the nausea go away almost instantly once I'm off my foot. Maybe it's not so bad.

But then I look down to assess the situation and have to admit Carson's right. Driving would be an issue.

I think there's something seriously wrong with my foot, but I'm not yet willing to put a name to it. If I don't, then every plan I have for the next few months doesn't have to be ruined.

I glance up toward the car ceiling, and as I do my eyes catch on the rearview mirror. Carson may have walked away to give me privacy for my call, but he's lingering at the row of cars behind me, watching.

He never lets things go—like the first time I came to a golf tournament. Carson snapped at me to shut up while they were hitting. I'd never been to a golf tournament or even watched one on TV, so I didn't know we were supposed to stay quiet. I definitely kept my mouth clamped after that, but he still watched me suspiciously the whole time, like he expected me to burst into show tunes at any moment.

What does he think now, that I might ignore him and drive

off anyway? I'm tempted to try it, just to see if he'd jump behind my car. Not gonna lie—running over Carson has crossed my mind before.

Might as well get this over with. I dial Mom. Normally Dad's the better parent to call in case of an injury, but he's out of town on business. I'm surprised at the distinct wobble in my voice when she answers.

"What's wrong?" she asks in a laser-focused tone.

I explain to her about Theo and my fall and describe what's happening with my foot. I peek down. "I actually can't see the dent right now. Do you think that's a good thing?"

"No, I do not. It's probably swelling," Mom says firmly. "I'm going to leave work now, but Adam should be at home, so I'll send him to get you, and I'll meet you at urgent care."

"No!" I shout, imagining Adam's mockery over my inability to walk down steps.

"Maggie—" Mom starts, exasperated. Then, in a quieter voice, "Where are you now?"

I tell her.

"Okay," she says like she's trying to keep herself calm. "I'll be there as fast as I can. I love you."

"I love you too."

After she hangs up, I wave Carson over. "My mom's on the way."

"Good." He tugs his cap off and runs a hand through his short, pale blond hair. Everything about Carson is pale, which I've always thought strange considering how much time he spends outside golfing. He must wear a ton of sunscreen.

My phone buzzes in the seat beside me. I pick it up and wave it around. "So I'm good now."

"Right." Carson backs away, taking the hint. "Well, let me know what happens."

As if he really cares. Besides, it's not like I ever talk to him outside of Theo.

I return to my phone, filing Carson's help away as another unexplainable part of my completely rotten day. I'm expecting an updated ETA from Mom, but it's Rayna.

He DUMPED you? Did he say why? Where are you now?

Theo. He seems both all-important and completely insignificant right now. I snap a picture of the ever-expanding lump on my foot and send it to Rayna with an explanation about waiting in the parking lot for my mom to take me to urgent care.

Her reply is almost instantaneous: WHAT HAPPENED?

Isn't it obvious from the picture? But I start typing out the story, starting with Theo's seemingly perfect promposal setup. Rayna often tells me she doesn't need every little detail, but as an actor, I believe all the little nuances are important. But now that I'm typing them all out, I see they're proof Theo's also learned something about setting the scene—in this case, the scene of our breakup. He was trying to—what—let me down easy? A particularly strong pulse of pain shoots through my foot, and I'm reminded of how my stupidity extended beyond that coffee shop.

A knock on my window startles me. Without waiting for a response, Mom opens my door and sticks her head in, bringing with her a cloud of Calvin Klein Euphoria, her signature scent. "Maggie, sweetheart, let me see."

My phone buzzes again, but Rayna will have to wait.

"You got here fast!" And I find I'm really grateful she did. I pivot my leg out of the car and hold my foot up for her inspection.

She tries to mask it, but her wide eyes and shaky indrawn breath say it all.

"Do you think it's broken?" I ask quietly, finally giving voice to my worst nightmare.

Because a broken foot means I can't try out for the summer production of *Footloose* (cue the jokes) next week. A broken foot means the part I already have in the spring play will probably be given to my understudy. A broken foot means—

"Let's not get ahead of ourselves." Mom brushes a strand of hair behind my ear. "We don't know for sure until the doctor checks you out."

Her words leave wiggle room for a possibility that doesn't destroy all of my plans for the immediate future, but the doubt in her voice sounds like "It looks bad, kid."

.+ .+ .+ .+.

The next hour passes in a haze of driving to urgent care, filling out paperwork, repeating my story, and X-rays. Mom sits in a chair off to the side while we wait for the doctor to come in with my results. "Your dad's in a meeting, I think, but I texted him, so he might call to see how you are. I also let Adam know what's going on."

I snort. "Like he'll care."

Mom tilts her head to the side, a disappointed twist to her lips. But before she can say anything, her phone rings, and she quickly answers. "Yes, she's here. Just a second."

She hands me the phone, and my eyes are already welling up even before Dad says a word. "Hey, Maggie Mae, what's going on?"

"Um. I think I broke my foot? And my life is ruined?"

"Maggie, your life isn't ruined. Even if it is broken—and you don't know that yet—it will heal. Bones are amazing that way. Remember when Adam broke his arm a few years ago?"

I grunt.

"And he's all back to normal now."

"Dad, that took *months* to heal, plus he had to do rehab. I don't have months before the *Footloose* tryout. It's next week!"

"Maggie—"

The door opens, and an older white guy in a doctor's coat comes in.

"Dad, I have to go. We'll call you after we get the final verdict."

He sighs. "Okay, sweetheart. I love you."

"Love you too," I grumble, then hang up and hand the phone back to Mom. So much for Dad being the better parent in a crisis.

"Hello, I'm Dr. Vandermark. You must be Margaret."

He holds out his hand, and I begrudgingly shake it.

He turns to Mom. "And Mrs. Scott?"

"Yes." Mom's smile is tinged with worry. "I hope you have good news for us."

"Well, let's see what we have here." Dr. Vandermark sits on a padded stool in front of me, then pulls a tablet out of his front pocket. A few taps later, a side X-ray of my foot appears. He points to a dark spot in the bone. "So, you definitely broke it."

Way to ease into the good news, Dr. Vandermark.

4

I can't believe a split second could wreak so much havoc. Six to eight weeks in a huge, ugly boot.

By the time we get home, it's after five, and Adam's car is in the driveway. Perfect.

We haven't gotten along since . . . actually, I can't remember us ever getting along, but there are pictures of us playing together when we were very young. By the time I started retaining my memories, though, he'd decided it was his mission in life to torment me. He gave all my Barbies decidedly *un*attractive pixie cuts. He spread a rumor around grade school that I was a bed-wetter—in fourth grade (not true). And his soccer friends all call me Shaggy Maggie thanks to a picture he took of me with crazy bed hair and my mouth open in horror. He's the absolute worst.

I hobble inside, and he's waiting at the counter, eating some sort of disgusting energy bar. He swallows and gestures at my foot with the wrapper. "I wonder if they'll give you bonus points at the audition for literally making your foot loose."

My hands ball into fists, but a reaction is exactly what he wants, and I've given it to him too many times before.

"Aw, cheer up, Mags; I bet you get off school tomorrow."

I inhale slowly, trying to center myself and praying Mom comes in soon.

"Or maybe—" The door from the garage opens, and he smiles sweetly at me. "Hey, Maggie, let me help you over to the couch."

And with that, as soon as Mom's within view, Adam's beside me, practically carrying me into the living room.

"Does this mean I don't have to go watch your boring play next week?" he says close to my ear as he deposits me on the couch. He straightens and looks down on me with false concern.

"Adam," Mom calls, "could you get an ice pack for Maggie?"

"Sure thing, Mom!"

He winks at me as he strides off. Ugh.

The way I'm positioned, my phone is digging into my butt, so I lean over and pull it out. I snap a quick shot of the boot and compose a post, remembering my thought from earlier:

Note to self: Texting and stairs don't agree. #brokenfoot #donttextandwalk #newboot #worstdayever

For good measure, I add it to my stories too. I want Theo to know what happened. He has to be sorry once he sees it, right? Then he'll call and say he didn't mean any of it and ask what he can bring me to make up for it.

As if on cue, my phone blares "My Shot" from *Hamilton*, but instead of Theo, it's Rayna. Even though I'm completely miserable and she'll get that, I still paste on a smile as I answer the video call. "Hey!"

"You broke your foot?" she practically yells at me.

Adam drops an ice pack in my lap and sticks his face in front of mine. "Rayna. Looking good."

He's constantly making comments about Rayna, who has always been self-conscious about her appearance. Especially how her left eye seems slightly bigger than her right. I think it makes her more interesting. When she smiles, a dimple pops in her right cheek, and somehow this evens everything out. Rayna inherited her rich brown coloring from her Dominican dad, but she owes her clear complexion to her fair, Irish mom who swears by a multi-step skincare regimen (that woman gives amazing tips!). Rayna keeps her curly black hair shoulder length so it's long enough to pull back—like it is now.

Adam's attention used to annoy Rayna (she was positive he was mocking her), but lately she's gotten much better at ignoring him.

Not so me.

"Argh, go away!" I push him with my free hand, and he smirks at me as he saunters off. "He's so awful. He's already made multiple jokes about the audition."

I remind myself I only have to endure another year and a half, and then he'll be off to college.

"Oh, Maggie." Rayna's face falls. "That sucks. Can you try out for a part that doesn't involve dancing? Or volunteer or something?"

"What would be the point?"

"To at least still be involved?"

She doesn't understand. From the moment my parents took me to see *Annie* at the Muny the summer I was eight, I pictured myself on that stage, belting out "Tomorrow" in front of thousands of people. Or even dancing and singing in the ensemble. That looked like a blast! Everything I've done since then has been geared toward a future musical theater career—acting, dance, and voice lessons. Sitting on the sidelines, watching everyone else do what I should be out there doing myself . . .

"I love the theater because the theater is alive. The audience is right there."

Rayna raises her eyebrows. "Who said that?"

She knows me too well. "Chita Rivera."

"And it's not worth it if you don't have an audience?"

I have to think about that a moment. "I guess it's not everything, but I love the thrill when the audience gets into a performance. Like a jolt of adrenaline straight to my core."

I unscrew the pump on the boot, causing air to whoosh out. The ripping sound the Velcro makes as I undo the straps is extra satisfying. I let the boot drop to the floor with a *thump*.

"How does it look?" Rayna asks tentatively.

I twist the phone toward my foot; thanks to the swollen ball where the break occurred, the whole thing is listing awkwardly to the left.

Rayna sucks in a loud breath, and I turn the phone back to my face.

"It looks really *painful*," she says.

"It is." I asked Mom if we could pick up the pain meds the doctor prescribed on the way home, but she was nervous about letting me take something that strong and instead gave me three ibuprofens. It helped some, but it's a broken foot, not cramps.

"Maggie, do you need a towel for that ice pack?" Mom calls.

I glance toward her. "Please."

I refocus on Rayna and start filling her in on the breakup. "Honestly, it's kind of a blur. I was *so sure* it was a special day. He didn't just text me about it. He found me at school and asked me *in person* to meet him there."

Rayna wets her lips. "Maybe he was just trying to be a standup guy about the whole thing?"

"By getting my hopes up and dumping me in public?" I whimper, in both emotional and physical pain. "You have no idea how embarrassing it was."

"I have a mental picture of how it might've gone down," Rayna says knowingly, but adds a comforting smile.

I lean back against the couch, waiting to continue until Mom finishes adjusting the ice pack and returns to the kitchen. "There I was, imagining us at prom together, when he dumped me. He said something about too much drama? I don't get it! I've been the model girlfriend!"

Rayna hesitates.

"What?"

"I don't suppose you reacted . . . dramatically?"

"Maybe a bit?" I pinch my finger and thumb together. "But it came out of nowhere!"

"I know. I didn't anticipate this either."

"But, Rayna, you know that's really not me. I have *not* been a drama queen in our relationship. Only on the stage. Wait!" Is it possible . . . ? "Do you think he meant *literal* drama? Like I have too many drama activities in my life?"

Rayna shrugs uncertainly. "You do have a lot of drama-related commitments. Dance classes and your theater group, and you're always trying out for another show. Maybe it was too much for him."

I try to recall Theo's breakup speech, but it's mostly a complete blank. Maybe the problem was that he felt neglected.

"If he did mean my drama activities, maybe something good will come out of this broken foot. I definitely won't be doing any shows while I'm in this boot." For the first time, I see a glimmer of hope. "This might be just what my relationship with Theo needs! I can focus entirely on him."

"Uh, Maggie." Rayna bites her lip. "I'm all for looking on the bright side, but do you really want Theo back after he caused this in the first place?"

I wave a hand. "I'm the one who wasn't looking where I was going. I could've been texting about anything."

"O-kay," Rayna drags out. "But let's consider this. *If* that's what Theo meant, sure you could make him the center of your universe while your foot heals—which, by the way, sets back feminism about a century—but what about after?"

I shake my head. "It won't matter by then. And I don't really mean he'd be my *only* focus."

Though, what else do I have?

"Will you be at school tomorrow?" Rayna asks.

I blink at the abrupt subject change.

"No." I explain that Mom's taking me to a foot specialist for a second opinion. We talk a few minutes more before signing off.

As soon as we do, I pull up my story to see who's watched it so far. Forty-five views. Lots of friends from school and my theater group. Including Katelyn Saverin, who's probably jetéing across the floor to celebrate. Also Carson, who I didn't realize followed me. Guess I don't have to let him know I'm okay.

I click over to my texts. There's a weird one from an unknown number.

Worst day ever? Can you remember your best day ever?

What a weird question. But even so, August 6 of last year pops into my head. The day I met Theo. I only remember the exact date because of that saved calendar page on my wall. Was it my best day ever? It's kind of hazy now, but it seemed so magical, meeting Theo at the Bridgeport Days festival, finding out I landed the part of Oaken in *Frozen*. I feel like there were other good things too. I wouldn't say it was my best day *ever*, but it was pretty fantastic.

Wait, why am I thinking about this? It's scary how marketers can even get into your text messages these days. I delete it and return to messages from people I know.

My other good friend from school, Clara Doyle, texts to see if I'm okay and if she can bring me anything. She's so sweet. Alexis, from my theater troupe and also the original owner of the flip-flops, asks if I'll be better in time for the *Footloose* audition. I send her a crying GIF, and she hits back with a Boomerang shaking her head no, her coppery-brown high pony whipping from side to side. Her dark eyes look super big and sad, and tears drip down the perfectly applied blush on her brown cheeks (they don't make tracks—definitely a filter—but it still makes me smile for a brief moment).

Until I see the panicked message from Riley Saengchan, my understudy for *A Midsummer Night's Dream*. I'm supposed to be Helena, but it's pretty hard to chase after Demetrius with a bad foot. Maybe I should've notified a couple of people *before* I posted. Oops. I don't reply to that one for now.

But even as more views and responses pop up, there's nothing from the person I most want to hear from. Even if he isn't clicking on it because of our breakup, surely someone (even Carson) has told him by now and he'd be worried enough to check on me. After seven months together?

The fact that he could ignore me so completely when he must know I'm physically hurt is like being dumped all over again. I just want to curl up in a ball and die.

Worst day ever indeed.

5

First thing the next morning, we're sitting in an exam room at the offices of Dr. Christine Rowland.

"Dr. Rowland comes highly recommended," Mom says. "She fixed Mrs. Gova's bunion, and she raves about her."

"Ew." I scrunch my nose. Although, is there any sort of foot condition that isn't disgusting?

While Mom attends to paperwork, I check my phone again. Still nothing from Theo. Unfortunately, there's an email from Mrs. Pintado, my school drama teacher, asking if it's true I've been injured. It seemed so fortuitous when rehearsal got canceled yesterday. I've been putting off thinking about what to do about today, and I can't even think about tomorrow evening, when I have rehearsal for my Future Stars Troupe. We still have our end-of-year concert. I guess I can sing, but I won't be able to do any of the choreography, which sucks.

I rub my thumb along the rubber phone case. Yesterday I was sure I couldn't perform in the boot, but *A Midsummer Night's Dream* doesn't involve any dancing. Maybe I could make it work. It would be a little clunky, but it's still better than having to put in my understudy. I hold on to the small bit of hope.

A quick knock signals Dr. Rowland's arrival, and she's quite a surprise. With her foot fetish, I expected her to be a drab older lady, but she looks like she could be on one of those doctor shows on TV, with porcelain skin, perfect makeup, and glossy black hair pulled back in a low ponytail. After the normal introductions, she sits to examine my foot, pressing carefully around the bump with her gloved fingers.

I can only handle the silence for about one minute. "Please tell me that other doctor was wrong and it's not really broken."

Dr. Rowland leans back, and I can already tell from her compressed lips that she is *not* going to give me the news I want. She turns her laptop toward us, an X-ray of my foot pulled up. "Typically if you have a break two millimeters or less, we can be confident the bone will grow back together on its own. Your break"—she points at the screen, where I can actually see a gap in the long bone along the outside of my foot—"is nearly four millimeters."

"What does that mean?" Mom asks.

"It means Maggie here is an overachiever," Dr. Rowland says. Ha. *Not.*

"Because it's connected to this tendon"—she points to a spot along the outside of her ankle and leg—"if we don't fix it and the bone *doesn't* grow back, it could have ramifications for the use of the foot down the line."

"What?" I'm trying to process all of that about tendons and bone growth and whatever, but what gets through most clearly is that my foot might not work properly. "Are you saying I need surgery or something?"

She nods. "I recommend putting in a screw to ensure the bone will grow back together properly."

That sounds *horrible.* "How long will *that* take to heal?"

Since *Footloose* is out no matter what, I was hoping I might be healed in time for another audition in late April. Then there's my dance recital in early June. I'm in four numbers, and we already ordered the costumes. Does surgery mean that's out too?

"No weight on it for at least two weeks; then you can walk with the boot for—"

"Wait, what do you mean, no weight? How am I supposed to walk?"

Dr. Rowland folds her hands in her lap. "It's really safest if you have a knee scooter, but crutches are another option."

"A *knee scooter*?" I've seen people—*old* people—going around on those things. No way I'm getting one of those, no matter how much safer it is.

"We'll figure it out." Mom pats my shoulder. "When do you recommend doing the surgery, Dr. Rowland?"

She looks down at my foot. "I'm headed out on vacation next week. I can see if my partner's available instead. Or, Fridays are my usual surgery day, so we could try to schedule it then."

A moan builds in the back of my throat. "This Friday? But I have a play next week. I can't be Helena on crutches! Can we do it after your vacation?"

Dr. Rowland shakes her head. "I'm sorry, Maggie, but I wouldn't advise performing either way. Regardless of when we schedule the surgery, you really need to keep weight off your foot before as well, to ensure you don't incur additional damage. That would be quite challenging on a stage."

"So if I put off the surgery, I'll have to do this no-weight thing even longer?"

She nods.

"Argh!" I don't even care how rude it is to shout my frustration in her exam room.

"Maggie . . . ," Mom says warningly.

"Sorry, Dr. Rowland, but this broken foot is really messing up my life."

"I understand. If you need some time to discuss it—"

"No, I don't need time. I want it fixed as soon as possible." The sooner she puts that screw in, the sooner I'll be back to my normal activities. "Right, Mom?"

"Yes, Dr. Rowland. Please move forward with the preparations for surgery this Friday."

Mom gets Dad on the phone, Dr. Rowland explains everything all over again, and there's more paperwork.

No *Footloose*. No *A Midsummer Night's Dream*.

And I am literally getting screwed on Friday.

6

By the time we get home, I want to throw my new torture devices into the street and watch the next car that drives by mangle them. Unfortunately, I have to settle for tossing them on the living room floor. "Why haven't they come up with something better than those?"

After we finished all the paperwork, Dr. Rowland sent us downstairs to a physical therapists' office to get me fitted for crutches. I had to endure a thirty-minute lesson on how to use them—everything from how to walk to how to go up and down stairs and lower myself into a chair.

Mom bites her lip. "We could always get you a scooter."

I can think of at least three boys who would find it hilarious to steal a scooter and race it down the halls, leaving me stranded in class. But seeing how hard Mom's trying, I muster a smile. It's not her fault. "No thanks. I'll survive."

"I know you will." She strokes my hair before walking away. "I'll get your laptop so you can check your assignments."

I barely hold in the sarcastic retort that springs to my lips— that homework's the perfect cure to all this. Mom's been so great, and she's handling it all while Dad's out of town. She doesn't need me piling on a bad attitude.

I resignedly accept my backpack. "Sorry this foot thing has created so much drama."

She leans over to kiss my temple. "Life throws unexpected things at us. We just have to roll with them."

"That sounds like something Julie Andrews once said."

"And what was that?" Mom humors me.

"Life knocks you about and pushes you over boundaries. But be ready . . ." I pause, suddenly realizing the rest of the quote.

"Is there more?" Mom asks, catching on.

"Yes." I sigh. "Do your homework; that's all I can say."

Mom laughs, and I can't help joining her.

"Got caught in your own Broadway quote!"

"Sure did." I gesture at the laptop. "Guess I'll get to it."

Now that I'm having surgery on Friday, I can't put off my response to Mrs. Pintado anymore. There's no scenario in which I can still perform next week. I send off an explanation, copying my understudy. She's a freshman, but she's pretty good. She wouldn't get a chance at a role like this otherwise. I also update Yvonne, my Future Stars director. She replies right away, saying I should take a few weeks off, practice at home, and they'll rearrange the choreography without me. It's a bummer, because I really loved the dance sequence for "Seize the Day."

I spend the next couple of hours doing homework like Mom suggested. Less than fifteen minutes after school lets out, the doorbell rings. Mom gets up from her makeshift office at the kitchen table to answer.

"Where's the Wicked Witch of the West?" Rayna calls.

Although Rayna wouldn't get anywhere near a stage herself, she does like going to shows, and *Wicked* is her favorite.

"Ouch. What kind of best friend are you?" I call back.

Rayna comes into the living room holding a reusable grocery bag. "The kind who knows what a crabby patient you are."

Fair. "Well, if I were Elphaba, I wouldn't *be* a patient because I would've enchanted my shoes to make this all better."

"Based on that picture you sent me, you aren't putting on any kind of shoes."

"Only this super-stylish boot." I gesture at the clunky thing. "It comes in black and black."

"Nice." She sits facing me on the couch. "So what did the doctor say?"

Tears well up as I give her the rundown. She passes me the bag; inside are chocolate and magazines.

"Bless you!" I hug her tight. "You always know exactly what I need."

She squeezes me back. "At least the doctor can fix it. Isn't it better to know how bad it is than keep walking around and making it worse?"

"No," I say stubbornly. She purses her lips until I relent. "Fine. Yes. It just really sucks. New topic: Did anyone ask about me today?"

Rayna picks up a movie-theater-size box of M&M's and rips it open. She pours out a handful and offers them to me. "As a matter of fact, yes."

I knew it! Theo feels guilty about how he dumped me and doesn't know how to apologize. I wouldn't mind a bit of groveling.

I pick out a few M&M's and lean toward her, a smile itching to break free. "Go on."

Rayna pops several candies into her mouth, chews, and

swallows. "Well, basically everyone knew about your foot, so almost every person I talked to today asked about you."

I grab more M&M's. She's stalling, and I'm not feeling so confident now. "That's it? Just everyone?"

"Oh!" Rayna sits up. "Carson came up to me at lunch. That was weird. He seemed really concerned about you."

I scrunch my nose. "Eh. He helped me to my car when it happened, refused to let me drive *my own vehicle*, and then stood around like a stalker until Mom showed up."

"What?" Rayna jumps on the couch, causing the M&M's to spill. We both start digging them out from between the cushions. "You didn't mention that detail yesterday."

Guess I skipped straight from the breakup to the break. "Because I wanted to forget it. You know how Carson is."

Except he was different yesterday. It freaked me out how nice he was, basically coming to my rescue. It seemed like he cared. Typical Carson, messing with my head.

"I do," Rayna says. "But he wasn't himself today. I thought he was going to take my phone away and check our message thread to make sure you were okay."

"Weird." Maybe he has some sort of savior complex that got activated when he saw me sprawled on the concrete steps.

"Tell me everything you skipped yesterday," she says.

I reluctantly do, even admitting Carson was nice the whole time.

"Huh." Rayna twists a curl around her finger. "I can't believe he stuck around, knowing Theo was about to dump you."

Actually . . . I'm not a hundred percent sure he knew about

the breakup. He seemed genuinely surprised when I mentioned it. Regardless, seven months of the Mr. Hyde version of Carson make me inclined to believe that's the real Carson rather than the Dr. Jekyll side I met yesterday. "I'm tired of talking about Carson. What about Theo? Did you talk to him today?"

Rayna stuffs more M&M's in her mouth. "Uhhhn," she says, which I take as a negative.

"Really? I can't believe Theo would be so indifferent. He's always been very thoughtful. Like when I had the flu on New Year's Eve, he dropped off a cute stuffed bear. Remember? This just isn't like him. Even if he feels bad that I broke my foot right after he— Oh! I get it now. He must have sent Carson over to ask you about me instead of doing it himself."

Rayna shakes her head vigorously and holds up her finger. I have to wait a good thirty seconds for her to chew up her mouthful of candy. "I really don't think so. Theo wasn't paying any attention to us."

"What do you mean?"

Her eyes dart to the side before refocusing on me. "It was during lunch when Carson came over to me, and Theo was busy laughing with . . . other people."

I don't like that pause or what I think she's implying. I asked Theo point-blank if there was someone else and he said no. But an uneasiness in the pit of my stomach prevents me from asking Rayna the same question outright. "He probably just didn't want you to know and was pretending."

She shakes her head again. "Maggie, I really don't think so. I think you need to let Theo go."

"Let him go?" I set my jaw. "Now that even *A Midsummer Night's Dream* has been taken from me, getting him back is the only thing I have to focus on."

"Don't you still have a concert for Future Stars?" she asks.

I wave a hand. "That's not the same at all. I'll be off to the side on a chair or something."

Rayna stares at her knees. "But what if he's already moved on?"

"After one *day*?" I study her incredulously until she looks back up at me.

"Never mind," Rayna says. "Let's just watch something. Clara told me about a new show on Netflix that's supposed to be good. How about that?"

I'm supposed to be at rehearsal right now. Instead, my understudy is running after Demetrius, probably loving her opportunity to step into the spotlight. I can't fix my foot—at least not in time to do any of the things I really want to do—but maybe I can fix whatever went wrong with Theo. I'm not going to let Rayna's doubts sway me. I have to be able to control *something* in my life. Theo doesn't realize what he's given up yet.

He'd better get ready, because I'm gearing up to make him fall for me all over again.

But in the meantime, I might as well get lost in a good binge.

7

Apparently Dr. Rowland told Mom there's no reason I have to stay home from school, unless my pain is unmanageable.

It isn't.

I protest that I could get jostled and further injured. Mom counters that with the boot on, my foot is well protected, and she'd rather I get a couple of days of school in before surgery since I'll probably miss next week recovering.

As soon as we arrive, Adam hands me my crutches from the back seat, waits for me to close the passenger door so he can lock the car, and jogs away with an unconcerned "See ya."

Yep. That about sums up our relationship. I prop the crutches against the passenger door while I adjust my backpack straps. Once I have them tight enough, I grab the crutches and start swinging toward the door. Adam has already disappeared inside. We haven't ridden together since I got my driver's license in December. As a sophomore, I don't have an assigned spot and have to park in one of the neighborhoods near the school, but the extra walk is worth it to avoid *non*-quality time with my brother.

I focus on moving across the parking lot—crutches forward, swing onto my left foot, repeat. My arms are burning from the out-of-the-ordinary exertion by the time I get inside.

"Maggie!"

I pause, barely catching my balance. Rayna's trotting toward me. She extends her hands. "Can I carry something for you?"

"I think I've got it for now. No thanks to Adam."

She hums in a noncommittal manner, sweeping stray curls away from her forehead. "What do you have first again? Algebra Two/Trig? I'll walk with you."

We have zero classes together, since Rayna is a major over-achiever and in all advanced classes. I'm not a total slacker, but school has never been my main focus. My grades are solid enough to get me into a strong drama program, which is all that matters.

"No, I start with World History. Super exciting." I start moving again.

"Right." She nods, slowing her pace to mine. "That's why I never see you. You're on a completely different side of campus."

"Yeah, you'll be late if you walk with me. It's going to take me forever."

"Maggie! You're back!" Carson appears out of a side hallway, coming up on my left side. "How's the foot?"

I look at Rayna, whose twisted lips imply she doesn't understand Carson's attitude change either. I answer without looking at him. "Broken. I'm having surgery Friday."

He groans. "That sucks. I'm sorry."

Now I do look at him, and my astonishment must show because he stumbles a bit. "What?"

I don't have the energy to figure out Carson today. "Nothing."

"Can I help you with anything?" He sounds so eager.

"Stop confusing me," I mutter, which causes Rayna to stifle a giggle with her hand.

Carson leans closer, his pale brows furrowed. His hair sticks up in tufts, like he took his hat off at the last possible moment before entering the building. "I didn't catch that."

Actually, there is something he can do for me: put an end to this agony over Theo. I pause in the hallway and fix him with my most intense stare. "Did you tell Theo about my foot?"

Carson runs a finger under the collar of his T-shirt, a fitted red V-neck. Almost all of his clothes are Under Armour, which is at least a consistent wardrobe statement. "I . . . we . . . don't really talk about you."

Ouch. "Thanks for that." I turn away from him and start moving again. "As for your question, I don't need any help from *you*," I call back.

It feels sort of mean after he was checking up on me, but what was that? He helped me outside Starbucks, seemed to care enough to keep me from driving, but then *didn't* care to tell Theo about it?

"Well," Rayna says, reminding me Carson and I weren't the only two people stopping up the hallway. "That was interesting."

"Ugh. He's the worst."

"He always has been . . ."

She looks entirely too thoughtful. "Whatever's in that overly analytical brain of yours, please put a stop to it now."

"Hmm."

I hate it when she does that, and it's the second time this morning already. Apparently she has opinions about Adam *and* Carson. "There's your hallway to advanced biotechnology or whatever it is you're taking this semester."

She places her right hand over her heart. "You *do* listen to me."

I roll my eyes. "Ha. See you at lunch!"

She waves as we head in different directions.

·✦ ·✦ ·✦ ✦·

Clara, who has choir with me right before lunch, helps carry my food into the cafeteria. It's tricky weaving through the tables on crutches, with people pushing chairs in and out constantly.

Even trickier when Clara suddenly jumps in front of me. "Did I tell you what David's little sister did the other day?"

David is Clara's longtime boyfriend (they're so perfect together it's sickening), and he's the oldest of five. She often has funny stories about his siblings, but this seems like an odd time to start one.

She tosses her cap of chin-length, honey-blond hair so it swings against her ivory skin and smiles way too big, showing her crooked canine tooth. "She was walking around the house narrating everything she did. Like 'Belinda stood at the window, staring longingly at the puppy passing by on the street.' You can guess what she's trying to do."

Yes, and I also understand that Clara's trying to distract me. But since I want to know from what, I return her fake smile and say, "Adorable."

Continuing the story about David's sister, she turns left, even though our usual table is straight ahead. I don't follow, scanning the tables ahead. I gasp. I don't know how she thought she could have hidden this. It's like there's a bright neon arrow overhead blinking down on the scene.

Theo. Facing me. His arm around Katelyn freaking Saverin, the girl I despise most in the world. And not around her in a casual way but tucked close, with his hand curved over her shoulder and his nose nuzzled near her ear. Her silky dark brown hair is swept into a perfect topknot, leaving her neck exposed so that I can see exactly what Theo is doing to it.

What. Is even. Happening?

I can't move. My hands are frozen around the grips of the crutches, my broken foot hanging above the floor.

"He said there was no one else."

"Maggie, this way." Clara appears in front of me, attempting to block my view of Theo and Katelyn. Normally it would work pretty well. Clara's the same height as me, but with the crutches, I can just tip my chin up so I can still see.

But she's persistent. "Rayna and the others are waiting for us," Clara says firmly.

Why does the world hate me? What did I do to deserve this? I can't imagine what I could have done to lose so much within a few days—and to Katelyn. She already has a different part in *A Midsummer Night's Dream*, but she'll try out for *Footloose* and possibly get the role I wanted. That would just be the icing on the Maggie-choking cake.

"Maggie," Clara says pleadingly.

I snap out of it and follow her to the table, where Rayna, as well as our friends Jada Dewan and Zoey Hartford, are waiting. Jada attempts a smile, but her light brown cheeks flush pink and it's clear she doesn't know what to say. She tucks a strand of wavy, nearly black hair behind her studded ear and looks down at the table.

Zoey, on the other hand, glares toward Theo and Katelyn and then meets my gaze head-on, her gray eyes full of righteous anger. "This sucks."

I couldn't have put it better myself.

As soon as I get situated, Rayna leans over and squeezes me. "I'm sorry."

I jerk away. "Why didn't you tell me?"

Because this must be what she was hinting at yesterday. I didn't want to ask, but it would've been better if I had. Because it isn't just someone; it's *Katelyn Saverin*.

Her shoulders droop. "I didn't know how."

"I can take any truth; just don't lie to me," I say.

"I'm sorry," she says again, her eyes darting to the side. She completely misses that I'm quoting Barbra Streisand. She usually picks up on that stuff.

I cast a look toward Theo's table, and they're still over there cuddling, oblivious to us. He knows how much Katelyn and I dislike each other. Why her?

The only person who looks back at me is Carson, and as soon as I glimpse his expression of pity, I turn back to my friends. "This is the worst week of my life."

They grimace in sympathy, but no one tries to reassure me it isn't so bad.

My phone buzzes in my pocket, and when I check it, I have another text from an unknown number.

Bad day? Bad week? Would you like to revisit your BEST day?

These marketers are *good*. But honestly? I don't even need a best day. I just want my life back the way it was three days ago. There has to be a way to reclaim it. I delete the text and focus on my friends.

8

It's so early in the morning when we go to the surgery center, I'm only half-awake when they take me back. They make me change into an ugly gown and put a cap over my hair. Thank God no one can see me in here. The nurse explains what she's giving me so I'll sleep through everything. That sounds excellent.

"Can you make that retroactive? So I can forget the past week?"

The nurse laughs.

Um, I was serious.

"Now I want you to count to one hundred while I put this over your mouth and nose," she says.

Mom is holding my hand, rhythmically stroking the back of it. Dad is on my other side.

"One, two, three, four, five . . ."

Seconds later, the nurse is poking my shoulder. "Maggie, we're all finished."

"Finished with what?"

It's really bright in here. Why do they have all the lights on like that?

"The surgery. Everything went well. Dr. Rowland will be here in just a moment."

I already had surgery? But I was just counting.

"How do you feel, sweetheart?"

Mom is beside me, Dad peering anxiously over her shoulder.

"Um . . ." I don't feel anything really. Where is my foot? Is it still there? Maybe Dr. Rowboat cut the whole thing off. "Where's my leg?"

Mom glances over at Dad like she's about to laugh before smiling reassuringly. "It's right there. Don't worry. Here's Dr. Rowland. She'll explain."

Rowland, not Rowboat.

"Hi, Maggie." Dr. Rowland stands at the foot of the bed. "I was able to put the screw in the bone just right. I don't expect any complications. We've also applied a nerve block for the pain. It will wear off in about twelve to fifteen hours."

"Why?" I should just keep that nerve block thingy.

She smiles. "Because that's how it works."

She says more about the surgery, but I don't really care about it right now. I like this feeling, the not caring. It's so much better than what I've been through the past week. Pain. A broken heart. Broken *dreams*. Life was so much better before. Like on that day I met Theo.

You know what? Maybe that *was* the best day of my life. It's the only one I can specifically remember being so great all around. If I recaptured the magic of that day, maybe I'd figure out how to get my life back on track. Because when I was with Theo that day, I felt as deliriously carefree as I do right now, and I'm sure he did too. Where did we lose that spark?

Surely Katelyn has tricked him somehow. My mouth curls just thinking about her, and Mom leans over, asking if I'm in pain.

"Nope!" I say. "I don't feel a thing. Except you're the best, Mom. I really love you!" I brandish my hand grandly. "And Dad too!"

I must doze off because the next thing I know, Mom's helping me get dressed and they're putting me into a wheelchair to leave the surgery center. Good thing, because all my muscles are liquid. Crutches would be impossible.

Once I'm in the car, I lie across the back seat and ask for my phone.

"You left it at home," Dad says.

"Why would I do that?" Now what am I supposed to do on the way home? "I need to talk to Rayna. I love her too."

Mom looks back at me with her lips twisted to the side. I don't understand why she finds everything so funny. "Rayna's at school."

"Oh. Yeah." Glad I'm not there. "Can I do school remotely?"

Mom laughs as she backs out of the parking space. "No way."

I lay my head on my arm. "Worth a try."

In no time, we're home. Just when I get settled on the couch, the doorbell rings. Mom goes to answer and calls back, "Looks like you have a delivery."

Like in *The Music Man*!

"The Wells Fargo Wagon is coming, Mom!" I say, then sing through the chorus like I'm a 1910 River City resident, hoping the package is for me.

Mom shakes her head as she opens the door. "If it were anyone but you, I'd blame that on the anesthesia."

I have no idea what she means by that, so I continue singing that I wish I knew what it could be.

Hmm. I'm not sure I'm totally on pitch. I'll have to work on that if I want to use this for my next audition. Except I wouldn't use this song for an audition.

Would I?

Have I?

"Here you go," Mom says, thrusting a bouquet of balloons in my face. There are probably half a dozen, all brightly colored, with messages like "Get Well Soon" and "You Got This" mixed with stars and smiley faces.

"Whoa!" They're kind of overwhelming. "I love them!"

"Of course you do." I haven't seen Mom smile this much in a while, but I like it.

"Who are they from?"

They'd better be from Theo, apologizing for dumping me and rebounding with that boyfriend stealer, Katelyn.

Mom studies the card. "Carson?"

"What?" I bat at the balloons. "I hate them! Take them away! I don't want them!"

She holds the balloons out to the side. "Why not? Who's Carson?"

A cartoonish picture of his smirking face fills my mind. "The last boy I would ever consider accepting a gift from. Ever. Ever ever ever."

Mom raises an eyebrow. "Well then. I guess I'll just . . . remove them."

"Thank you." I never want to see the Carson balloons again. Not when they should have been Theo balloons. "Where's my phone?"

Mom has already left the room with the abhorrent balloons,

so she doesn't answer right away. "I'm not sure you should be operating a phone right now. Maybe after you're fully alert."

"But I promised Rayna I'd let her know how the surgery went." I remember Dad saying something in the car about Rayna being at school. "She can check her phone at lunch." That sounds coherent, right? I have got to tell her about those balloons.

Mom stands with her hand on the back of the couch, studying me.

I press my palms together in a praying position. "Pleeeease."

Mom points at me threateningly. "Only if you promise not to post anything until I give you the all clear."

The all clear for what? I'm perfectly fine.

Well, except for my *foot*. But I don't feel that at all right now, so I'm better than fine as far as that's concerned.

"Maggie?"

I really want to roll my eyes, but even with who knows what drugs coursing through my veins, I understand that will not get Mom to hand over my phone. "I promise."

She hesitates, and I want to scream, because it's not like I can hop up and get it myself.

"All right," she finally says. She disappears down the hall and returns a minute later with my beautiful, wonderful connection to the outside world. She holds it just out of my reach. "No social media. Got it?"

I stretch as far as I can and grab it. "I already promised, Mom."

You'd think we were making some super-important life pact. What does she think I'm going to post on there? A picture of the balloons with a caption about how much I hate Carson Lockwood?

Hmm.

But I did promise.

So I stick to what I told her I would do and text Rayna.

Maybe it's more than one text.

Surgery's over and there's a screw in my foot. I'm screwed!

I totally wanted to say that to someone else. It makes me giggle uncontrollably for a minute, until the truth of it sobers me and the tears leaking from my eyes turn real.

But really. I am. This is the worst week of my life.

I don't care if I'm repeating myself. It's true.

How am I supposed to go back? Why is he with HER?

😫😫😫😫😠😠😠😠😤😤😤😤

She's just as dramatic as me.

I need to figure out what went wrong.

Or just remember how we got together in the first place.

So I can make him choose me again.

I won't be able to dance or walk across a stage for weeks.

I miss him!

Do you think he told Carson to send the balloons?

Maybe so Katelyn doesn't know they're actually from him?

Because why would CARSON send me balloons? It doesn't make sense.

I wish I could go back to the day I met Theo and recapture our magic.

Do you remember it? Bridgeport Days last year?

So many good things happened.

Remember how much fun we had before you had to leave?

If I could go back and see why Theo wanted to be with me in

the first place I bet I could fix us. Then I'd at least have Theo again.

I don't want to be alone.

A tear drops onto my phone screen. I wipe it away and wait for Rayna to respond and reassure me I'm not alone, but according to the time at the top of the screen, lunch is still forty-five minutes away. Why'd they have to schedule my stupid surgery so early in the morning?

I drop my phone into my lap and lean my head against the back of the couch. The sun is streaming in through the window behind me, mocking me with its cheeriness. I clench my eyes tight to block it out.

My phone buzzes in my lap; I reluctantly open my eyes and lift it. My brow furrows. Another text from an unfamiliar number.

Do you want to go back to your Best Day?

Yes! I do want to go back! A second text comes through.

Click below to relive your Best Day:

A generic short link follows. A warning bell sounds in the back of my mind—something to do with links and clicking—but it's more of a chime than a gong, and this text is exactly what I'm looking for.

So I click.

9

Instead of the link opening up a new window on my phone, everything around me distorts, like I'm walking through a hallway in a funhouse with crazy mirrors. I blink, trying to clear my vision. Maybe Mom's right about the anesthesia messing with me. It might be better to put down the phone. But when I blink again, I'm no longer sitting on my couch with my foot propped up on pillows.

It's there, stretched out in front of me, but there's no bandage! No ugly bruises. Admittedly my toes could use a new coat of polish, but I'm completely healed! I wiggle my toes and lift my foot off my bed.

Wait! My bed. I was just on the couch.

Um.

Did I dream that whole thing about breaking my foot? About Theo dumping me? That would be amazing, and yet . . . something about that doesn't feel right. Also, my room seems different. I'm not sure exactly what it is.

I sit up and swing my legs over the side of my bed, taking a careful look around.

Fuzzy teal comforter. Check. *Wicked*, *Hamilton*, and *Into the Woods* posters on the walls. Triple check. But where's my *Playbill* signed by the cast of *Hadestown*? Theo got it for me when his family visited New York. It was my favorite gift last Christmas. So thoughtful of him. It's been framed over my desk ever since. If Adam came in and took it as some sort of prank, I will spray his boxer drawer with that musty violet perfume from Great-Aunt Pauline so when he changes in the locker room, he smells like he's been hooking up with an old lady.

But that's not the only thing that feels off in here. I press my knuckles against my lips, trying to figure out what else is bugging me about my room. My fist drops to my side, and I stand on my two healthy feet, spinning a slow circle as it hits me. The walls. They're cream—a dingy cream from years of me tacking things up and taking them down again. But I painted them light gray over fall break last year. Rayna and Clara came to help, and we blasted music and flung paint at each other. Even with my furniture in the center of the room, my dresser ended up splattered.

There's no evidence of paint on my dresser now, and I don't think I imagined all of that either.

I need a calendar. I rush for my desk, where every night I tear off the day in preparation for the next.

I brace my hands on the edge of the desk and gape at what is supposedly today's date.

August 6.

That's seven months ago.

It's the page I saved—"genesis: the origin or mode of formation of something"—except it only has a big star on it in red pen. The heart I added for meeting Theo is missing.

I move items around on my desk to be sure, searching for the calendar Grandma gave me this year—*Life's Little Inspiration*

51

Calendar. I think today's was something like "You can't fake grit." Whatever that means.

Nope. Only this calendar.

Either I'm losing my mind or . . . I really get to relive the day I met Theo?

Even if it's both, I don't care! I pirouette in the middle of my floor, and just the fact I can do that makes me feel even better.

I have to tell someone about this. Rayna will know what to do.

I search for my phone and spy it on my bed. I start to open my text messages, but right beside it, my calendar app has been replaced with a yellow square. Centered within it are the words "BEST DAY" in a bold font, enclosed in a rectangle. It reminds me of a *Playbill.*

This app must be connected to the message that zapped me into this pain-free day. I was super woozy when I clicked on the text, but it definitely had to do with returning to my "best day."

I tap it open. I don't have time to register any details about it other than my name at the top before a notification pops up, covering most of the screen. It says, Act One is about to begin. Please take a seat.

10

Act one? Of what?

Another notification pops up, a bit more emphatic. Please be seated.

Um, that's a little creepy. But I decide to go with it. I twirl toward my desk and plop into my chair.

"Welcome to your Best Day," says a super-prim female voice—RIGHT INSIDE MY HEAD! I almost fall out of the chair. Guess that's why I was instructed to sit.

"You will play the part of Maggie in this simulation," she continues. She sounds a lot like the woman who played Grace Farrell in the old movie version of *Annie*.

"Simulation? So this isn't real?" I knock on the desk. "Sure feels real."

Except for the whole *voice inside my head* thing. That's definitely not normal.

"It's meant to. Your role is to re-create the original day as closely as possible. I'll serve as your guide."

An invisible guide? This keeps getting weirder, in the most spectacular way. "So it's like . . . I'm playing myself in a show?"

"Yes," the voice says. "The Best Day app has been customized to you, with details and reminders about the day.

Since you're involved in theater, the app follows a theater theme."

I check my phone. The notifications have disappeared. At the top, it says, **MAGGIE SCOTT ACT ONE.**

"A whole app centered around my best day with my interests in mind? Seems impossible." And fantastic.

"A few minutes ago it would have seemed impossible for you to be standing here with two working feet," the voice says.

"Right." I nod as I absorb that. Part of me thinks I'm out cold on the couch, but this is feeling very real. "All part of the simulation, I guess. Cool."

I wonder what type of theme it would give Rayna if she wanted to relive a day. The scientific method or something? If this happened to her, she'd definitely have a bazillion more questions, but I just want to escape the misery my life has been the past week. This opportunity, no matter how unbelievable, is a priceless gift.

I start tapping through the menu, but most everything has a little lock symbol. "Why can't I open anything?"

"Most areas of the app will unlock as you reach that part of the day. Don't worry, you'll receive a notification."

I open **SCENE ONE: GETTING READY.** At first I'm confused by the lines listed for me, but then I realize they're song lyrics. I must have been singing while getting dressed. Sounds about right.

With a decisive nod, I head for the closet and slide open the door. I run my hand along the hangers until I find a red, light-weight top with a sweetheart neckline that buttons down the front. I start carrying it toward my dresser, where I keep my shorts.

"Perhaps you should check COSTUMES," the voice says.

I look left and right. It's weird to have a disembodied voice in my head. "Why?"

"Because that's not the right top," the voice replies.

"What?" I hold my top out. "You must have some faulty information, because I'm positive this is what I was wearing the day I met Theo. He's told me, multiple times, it's his favorite for that very reason."

The voice chuckles. "That's *not* why it's his favorite."

My brows furrow, and I really wish there were an actual *person* for me to scowl at. "What does *that* mean?" I glance back down at the top; it's definitely one of the more clingy things I own. "Oh."

I'm glad my boyfriend notices my assets, but I also thought it was sweet he remembered what I was wearing the first time we met. It's disappointing to know he made that up.

I shake it off. That's not important. So many other times Theo did remember important details—like my favorite drink or flower. I'm not going to let such a minor detail push me off course.

I get back on my phone and navigate to **COSTUMES**. Unlike the other areas of the app, this one is completely unlocked. Clicking on **SCENE ONE** pulls up a sketch, like something a costume designer would draw, but it's hideous! I'm in the sleep shirt I'm wearing right now, with my hair sticking out in five different directions. "Yikes!"

I quickly close that nightmare and choose **SCENE TWO**. In this sketch, I'm wearing a green-and-white-striped boatneck shirt and black shorts. My hair is in a French braid, and I've accessorized with my thespian mask necklace and gladiator sandals.

"Huh. Now that I see it, I do remember wearing that to Bridgeport Days."

Curious, I click on the other scenes. My costume doesn't change the rest of the day.

"Okay, then." I return the red top to the closet and retrieve the other items, then braid my hair. All set.

"Do you have a name?" I assume the voice can hear me—and that she's a real person behind whatever wicked advanced tech this is. The idea that she might be some sort of AI is even freakier.

"You may call me whatever you'd like."

Cryptic much? But I don't really care as long as I get to relive the magic with Theo today. She's sort of making my dreams come true, just like Grace Farrell does for Annie, so she can keep her secrets. "How about Grace?"

"That's fine," she says, "but you're getting behind schedule, so you should go to the kitchen."

"You're awfully bossy, Grace."

"If you truly want the simulation to work, you need to follow it as closely as possible."

I'm not sure we have the same priorities about this day, but I'll go along with her instructions for now. Because I do want to experience everything with Theo to the fullest. "Fine."

When I open my door, I'm greeted by the delicious scent of crêpe batter. This is already an amazing day.

As I'm rounding the corner into the main living area—never before so grateful for two working feet—Grace says, "SCENE TWO: BREAKFAST unlocked."

I'm so startled I turn into the wall and stub my toe on the baseboard. My heart pounds, visions of the steps outside Starbucks and my dented foot flashing through my brain.

"Geez. Do you want me to break my foot on this date too?" I wiggle my toes, but they seem okay.

"Would you prefer the scene script notifications be silenced?"

"Please."

"All right," Grace says, "but I will interject if you stray too far off course."

"Noted." Satisfied Grace will leave me alone for the moment, I flex my foot one last time and continue toward the kitchen.

Mom's at the stove, flipping crêpes in a large skillet. "Morning, sweetheart."

"Morning, Mom. Smells fantastic." I look around the kitchen for Adam, who'd usually be sniffing around the stove like a bloodhound, his plate at the ready.

"Adam's at a soccer tournament today," Mom says. "And he barred us from attending."

"Yes!" I say a little too loudly, and Mom frowns just as Grace scolds, "You're straying."

"Sorry," I mutter to both of them. But this is confusing. Also, I'm kind of surprised my joy at Adam's absence would be that off character. "Where's Dad?"

"He'll be down in a minute. Why don't you get out the Nutella and strawberries. We're almost ready for them."

For the next few minutes, we work in a comfortable pattern, and Grace remains silent. I guess there isn't anything for me to mess up. By the time Dad comes down, Mom and I have everything set out on the table in the adjacent breakfast room.

"What can I do?" Dad asks.

Mom purses her lips at him, but it's obvious she's not really upset. "At this point? Eat."

"My favorite part."

He reaches for the Nutella, but I flutter my eyelashes at him. "You wouldn't take that from your most precious daughter, would you?"

"Maybe not, but these"—he snatches the bowl of strawberries—"are all mine."

"You'll share eventually." I smother my crêpe in Nutella and hold my hand out for the bowl of strawberries.

Dad sighs heavily. "Fine. You can have some."

I smirk. "Knew you'd cave."

"You two." Mom shakes her head.

"What are you up to today?" Dad asks.

"I'm meeting Rayna at Bridgeport Days." And then Theo! I lick a dollop of stray Nutella off my finger. So delicious.

I forgot I was going to text Rayna about this whole replay thing. I wonder if that's against the rules. I should probably check first.

"What time?" Mom asks.

"Um . . ." What were we talking about? Oh, meeting Rayna at Bridgeport Days. Honestly, I'm not sure. This was seven months ago.

"Noon," Grace says in my ear, "after she's finished marching in the parade."

I repeat the words, trying really hard not to sound robotic.

Mom leans forward with her elbow on the table and her chin on her palm. "You're not going to watch her?"

"No," I say slowly, the memory coming back to me without Grace's assistance. "She told me not to. That they'd only practiced the songs a few times and they really weren't ready yet."

Which, now that I think about it, is kind of weird. Rayna usually wants me to come watch her play. She's an amazing clarinetist.

"Sounds like you have a few hours free," Mom says.

I glance at the time glowing on the oven. It's only nine. "I do."

"How about we get mani-pedis?"

That's right! Another detail I forgot. I'm really anxious to get to the carnival, but it's not like I can speed up time.

Unless the app has some feature that does that?

"No," Grace says.

Bummer.

"I don't know." Dad holds out his hands and studies his nails. "Do you think I'd look better with a bright crimson or a soft pink?"

"Hmm." I take his left hand and turn it both ways. "More like a glittery periwinkle."

He nods. "Then I'm in."

"You're not invited," Mom says with an affectionate smile.

"I'm so hurt." Dad pushes away from the table and walks away, affronted.

"Don't forget your dishes!" Mom calls.

He turns back, his chin in the air, grabs the dishes, marches into the kitchen—and bangs his hip into the counter. We burst out laughing.

Even though I don't remember all of this, it really is the perfect start to my day.

"I'll be ready to go in five minutes." I clean away my own dishes and dash up the steps.

It's really happening, all over again. I'm not wasting it. I will collect every bit of intel I can and use it to win Theo back.

11

On the way to the nail salon, I try to explore the app, but it's still mostly locked, so I can't study up in advance like I would for a play or musical. The only semi-cool thing is that my "costume" is slightly different in **SCENE FOUR** and following—my nails are sparkly purple—so at least I know what color to choose.

SCENE THREE unlocks right when we walk inside. I only get a quick glance before the technicians settle Mom and me at adjacent stations and I have to set my phone aside.

"So"—Mom twists her head toward me—"are you ready for sophomore year?"

I start to shrug, but June (my technician) is using the file on my right hand, so it ends up being an awkward jerk of my left shoulder. "I guess."

"What are you looking forward to most?"

So it's going to be this sort of mani-pedi—where Mom wants to have an in-depth chat about my life. I'm beginning to think I must have blocked this part of the day out. This is when reading ahead would have been helpful.

"I don't know."

Then Grace prompts me, and I echo, "Driver's Ed?"

That does make sense. I turned sixteen in December, right as I completed Driver's Ed.

"Your dad and I will have to discuss what you'll drive," she says.

"A Corvette would be nice," I suggest, knowing full well I'll be driving a dependable, ten-year-old Toyota they'll buy from a friend. It's slightly nicer than Adam's Hyundai, which was a hand-me-down when Dad got a newer model.

Mom and Dad say these cars aren't technically ours, but since getting my license, I've never gotten in trouble for taking "my" car out without asking first.

Mom chuckles. "Are you excited about the cast announcement today?"

"I feel pretty good about it." I wait for Grace to step in. Nothing. Must have been the way I really felt. As part of the Future Stars Troupe, I'm guaranteed a spot in the show, but outsiders have come in before and stolen the leading roles.

"I'm sure you'll get a great part." Mom smiles, although there's a sad tinge to it. I wonder what that's about. She's always been super supportive, driving me to acting, singing, and dance classes, then auditions. I can't imagine what would get her down about it now.

My phone buzzes, and when I glance down, it says, Backstage Pass unlocked. That's new. I haven't been able to access anything in that feature yet. I'm dying to know what *that* is, but June would probably be annoyed if I yank my hand away to touch my phone in the middle of my manicure.

Grace chimes in. "Would you like to activate Backstage Pass audio mode?"

I clear my throat, trying to inject an *uh-huh*, hoping that will suffice as an answer.

"I hope I get to see the show," I hear Mom say. *"That the doctor doesn't come back saying this cyst is cancer."*

I twist toward Mom, about to ask what she means when Grace interjects. "You can't say anything to her about what you just heard or you'll end the Best Day simulation immediately."

But I don't understand what just happened. Those words were so clear that I was sure Mom said them out loud. But she's just sitting there, looking at me with that slightly sad smile.

Did I just hear her thoughts?

And are they true? Does she have cancer she's been hiding from me for seven months? My heart thuds in my chest.

Grace doesn't answer any of these silent questions. Instead she says, "Your next line is 'I think they'll cast me as the queen.'"

What?

"Maggie, your next line is—"

"I think they'll cast me as the queen," I blurt out.

Mom's smile quirks to one side. "I can see it now. You'll be demanding Adam call you 'Your Majesty' for the next three months."

I grimace-smile. "Totally."

I don't know what just happened, but I think my day just took a turn for the worse.

12

The whole drive to Bridgeport Days, I'm dying to pull out my phone and look closer at this backstage pass thing. It *seemed* like I heard Mom's thoughts, but how is that possible? Though, how is any of this possible?

"Have fun and let me know if you need me to pick you up after." Mom brushes her fingers across my temple in a farewell gesture.

I look at her closely, searching for hidden signs. *Are you sick?* I want to ask. *Does Dad know? Does Adam?*

"Smirk and say, 'Sure, Mom,'" Grace instructs.

Now she decides to start talking to me again? Also, smirking at Mom seems especially insensitive if she *did* take me out because she's sick, but I do what Grace says and wave as she drives away, taking with her any chance of answers.

"What was that about?" I ask.

A guy standing at the curb looks up from his phone. "Are you talking to me?"

I edge away. "No." I need to be a little more careful about talking to the voice in my head.

Grace remains suspiciously silent. I move toward a set of

benches beside the playground and sit. I remember waiting for Rayna here, although not how long, so I take the chance to whip out my phone and quickly navigate to **BACKSTAGE PASS**.

The only option is **SCENE THREE: NAIL SALON**, and when I select it, I read, **MOM THINKS: I HOPE I GET TO SEE THE SHOW. THAT THE DOCTOR DOESN'T COME BACK SAYING THIS CYST IS CANCER**. There's no mistaking the words now. I deflate against the bench, trying to wrap my mind around it.

What am I supposed to do with that information? Grace clearly didn't want me to ask Mom about it. I scroll around the app again, but there's not much new to click on. I do now have access to **SCENE FOUR: MEETING UP WITH RAYNA**, so that's sort of helpful. At least I know what I'm supposed to say for the next few minutes without asking Grace.

I'm still concerned about my mom, but at the same time, this was seven months ago. If she was sick, wouldn't we know by now? It was probably a false alarm.

Putting that out of my mind, I close the app and swing my foot around. The sun glints off the sparkles in my pedicure. It's nice out today, the perfect blend of heat and minimal humidity. If I'd known I'd be meeting my future boyfriend the first time, I would have left my hair down, but right now I'm grateful for the French braid keeping it off my neck.

Still no sign of Rayna, so I start scrolling through my friends' latest posts, and it's kind of a trip, seeing what everyone else was doing on this day seven months ago. Alexis posted a poll asking what role we think we'll get in *Frozen*. It's fun seeing the answers when I already know several of them are wrong—some in a good way. I wonder what would happen if I threw out the correct casting? Then a message pops up from Rayna saying she'll be here in a minute. I shoot back a thumbs-up and pocket my phone, resisting temptation.

My foot swings double time as I consider the day ahead. When I first see Theo, will my heart shuffle step hop like before? Or will that part be different since it won't really be the first time we meet?

"Grace, how—" I stop because I spot Rayna coming up the path. She's running her fingers through her dark hair, which is straight today. Actually, I remember, it was straight all last summer and fall, before she started letting it return to its natural curl. I don't recall why she changed it.

"Hey," she says when she gets close. "I changed in a public bathroom and stuffed my uniform in one of the flute players' cars. But this"—she gestures at her head—"I can't do anything about. Those hats are an abomination."

"You sound like a Southern preacher." I stand and puff out my chest, then point my finger at her. "These abominations will not be tolerated. We must abolish the abominations we so abhor and aim for absolute . . ."

I pause as if I don't know how to finish the sentence, like the first time around.

"Abstinence!" Rayna shouts gleefully, causing the playground moms to turn toward us with surprised, slightly disapproving expressions. "Nice alliteration."

I start walking toward the carnival. "Hey, I aced that poetry unit last year."

"And you can project too," Rayna says. "Maybe you should consider debate."

"Eh." I flick my fingers in dismissal. "How was the parade?"

My phone vibrates in my pocket, just as two girls pass us on the path, chatting loudly.

"No idea," I hear, and it *sounds* like Rayna, but it can't be. I studied the script pretty closely, and that wasn't in it.

"Pretty sucky actually," she continues. *That* was there. "I'm glad you didn't come. It'll be better in a few weeks when we play at the first football game." She nudges me. "That's when you can make your move with Peter."

My brow furrows. Did I just hear Rayna's thoughts like I heard Mom's earlier? Did she *lie* to me?

"Peter Wilkinson," Grace says. "Member of the drumline and your crush as of noon on August sixth."

I know who Peter is. I'd rather have answers about Rayna. But maybe it wasn't her. I bet it was one of those girls who passed us. Because Rayna would never skip a band commitment or lie to me.

Refocusing on what she actually did say about Peter, I reply, "Can't wait," but Rayna gives me a funny look, so I must still appear confused by it all. "You ready to go hit some rides?"

She hooks her arm through mine. "Bring it on. Except that one where you go really fast in a circle like fifteen times. The last time I rode that I threw up on the operator's shoes as soon as I got off."

I crinkle my nose. "Let's skip that one. You'll ruin my new pedicure."

We follow the path toward the ticket booths. The carnival's in full swing, with rides running in both directions, hawkers calling out to come play their games, and customers lining up for food. My stomach grumbles. "I might have to start out with a corn dog or something."

Rayna scans the concourse. "Oh, we can do way better than a corn dog."

She drags me toward a booth selling barbecue, and I have to agree that's a superior choice.

As we're waiting for our food, I have just enough time to glance and see that **SCENE FIVE: LUNCH AT THE CARNIVAL** is now unlocked, but not to read through my lines or check anything else.

We sit down to eat, and just when I've stuffed my mouth full of tangy pulled pork, I hear Theo say, *"Where is she?"*

13

Theo?

I try to swallow and almost choke.

"Are you okay?" Rayna leans across the table, concerned.

My eyes are watering. I take a big swallow of my strawberry lemonade, then a second. My throat still burns, but I feel like I'll be able to eat again. "Just tried to inhale my food."

Did that happen originally? Grace didn't lay into me, but I guess she's not going to be all, "STOP CHOKING! THAT'S NOT IN THE SCRIPT!"

But it's too early for Theo to appear. I twist my head back and forth, searching for Theo, but I don't see him anywhere.

"Who are you looking for?" Rayna asks, her fork halfway to her mouth.

"My future boyfriend?"

"Maggie . . . ," Grace says warningly.

So she is still listening.

Rayna grins. "I don't think Peter's here. I heard him say something about a family wedding today." She sticks the forkful of meat in her mouth.

Maybe I imagined it. This whole experience has made me jumpy. Theo hasn't met me yet, so he can't be looking for me.

We finish eating, and Rayna leans back and rubs her hand over her stomach. "I think we'd better hold off on the rides for a bit."

I lead the way to throw out our trash, and we stand for a moment, surveying the crowd. Grace doesn't give me any lines, so I wait for Rayna to speak. It'd be nice if this simulation allowed a pause between scenes for me to study up.

"Want to play games or see who's on the main stage?"

I pull her against my side. "We could do the Ferris wheel. It's nice and slow, and it's so rom*an*tic." I flutter my lashes at her.

She laughs and pushes me away. "You're not my type."

I sigh. "Alas."

She shakes her head. "You watch too many of those Shakespeare remakes."

I was supposed to *be* one of Shakespeare's heroines next week. Stupid broken foot. "No such thing."

"So what next? For real?"

I pause for an awkward amount of time, and finally Grace tells me we should walk toward the main stage.

My phone vibrates again, which I take to mean we're entering another new scene as we leave the food area.

It's gotten even more crowded since we arrived. My eyes are peeled for Theo, but I know it isn't actually time for us to meet up. I hung out with Rayna for a while first.

But I can't help looking, so it's not a huge surprise when I ram my shoulder straight into another person on the path.

"Oof!" we both say.

I stumble backward and catch my balance, looking up to find an unexpectedly familiar face before me. Wide sky blue eyes under surprisingly long pale blond eyelashes. I've only ever been this close

70

to him when he helped me to my car. I'm about to say his name when Grace stops me. "You don't know Carson yet."

Right. Although now that I've seen him, it comes back to me that he was at Bridgeport Days with Theo, later in the afternoon. I'd totally forgotten—or blocked him out of my perfect day.

"*I should say something,*" Carson says—except he doesn't.

Not him too! Carson is the last person I want inside my head.

"Sorry," Carson mumbles aloud.

"You need to keep moving," Grace says.

Which is unnecessary because I have no desire to stand here blocking the pathway talking to Carson anyway.

"No problem," I mutter. I start walking again but pause when "On Top of the World" by Imagine Dragons starts playing in my head. I glance back, trying to figure out where it's coming from. Probably one of the tents, except it's strangely fading while I'm standing still.

"That guy was kind of cute." Rayna bumps my shoulder, prompting me to move.

Carson? Cute? I guess if you don't know his personality, you might think so. "He's too pale."

"O-kay," Rayna drags out, and I remember that Peter Wilkinson is also a pretty pale guy. I guess this is what happens when I don't follow the original lines for the day.

When we reach the main stage, a group of young girls is up there tap-dancing. "Oh, that's adorable."

Wait. That's right. We're almost to where I met Theo. Because he came here to watch his little sister dance. There she is, the second one from the right, her dark hair up in a tight bun and a glittery red bow on top. Therese is so cute, and she *loved* coming to my shows. She's definitely a little performer in the making.

The girls finish their dance to "All That Jazz," and the audience erupts in applause. About halfway back along the aisle, Theo jumps to his feet and whistles.

Target spotted.

Now what? I realize that my memories of the moment we met are not as clear as I thought. I remember rosy moments of us talking for the first time and playing cheesy games and riding the Ferris wheel. But I don't remember what happened right now.

Rayna groans beside me, dragging my attention away from Theo, who is moving toward the front of the stage to greet his sister. She's glancing at her phone and looks totally crestfallen.

"What's wrong?"

"It's Mrs. Ling. She just texted me that she needs to take her sister to the emergency room and asked if I could come watch Sophie."

As soon as she finishes saying this aloud, I hear her voice in my head, saying something totally different. *"Adam's team lost early in the tournament; I knew that last game wasn't going well. He's really bummed and needs me."*

"WHAT?" I explode. My *best friend* wants to ditch me to go comfort my stupid *brother*?

14

I have entered an alternate universe where everything I believed to be amazing is actually a nightmare. Unless Rayna's talking about a different Adam who had a tournament today.

Rayna recoils. "If you care that much about it, I'll tell Mrs. Ling to find someone else."

Is she really lying to me? And wait. If I heard her correctly that she had no idea about the parade earlier . . . Was she *at* Adam's soccer tournament instead of the parade this morning? My body feels like a rubber band, ready to snap.

"Calm down, Maggie," Grace commands. "What Rayna actually *said* was that she needs to go babysit. That's what you should react to, not her thoughts about Adam."

Grace is expecting way too much of me. Throwing contrasting words and thoughts at me—how am I supposed to keep that straight? Especially when the thoughts include such disturbing, stomach-turning revelations. Like the fact that my best friend is lying to me.

"Maggie?" Rayna waves a hand in front of my face, and I'm oh so tempted to ignore all the warnings from Grace and blast Rayna with a dozen questions.

Why is my brother calling you for comfort?

Are you dating?

If you are, WHY? He is the biggest A-hole in the world, and I'm not sure I can forgive you for it.

"Um, what?" I finally reply.

Rayna huffs. "Do you want me to tell Mrs. Ling to find someone else?"

I want you to tell my brother *to find someone else. For today and anything else that's going on between you.*

Except . . . if Rayna stays here, it will change my first meeting with Theo. And that's the most important thing. I can't let Rayna and my *brother* distract me.

Rayna's still waiting for an answer.

I paste on a sympathetic smile. "No, sorry. I was just looking forward to hanging out with you today."

The tension drops from her shoulders, and she grimaces. "I know. I feel awful leaving you here, but I don't want to let Mrs. Ling down."

It takes a monumental effort not to snort as I say, "Of course not."

She gestures at the easel positioned behind the rows of chairs. "Looks like there's a hypnotist up next. That could be fun."

"Maybe." *If you went under hypnosis and admitted your lies to me and everyone in the audience.*

"Oh! And isn't Clara here somewhere with David?"

As if that makes ditching me all right. I force a smile. "Go take care of Sophie."

"Okay." She hesitates, then gives me a quick hug. "I'll text you later."

"Yep. Later." I wave her off, trying not to think about her with Adam. Ew.

There are too many people around here for me to talk out loud to Grace (if she'd even give me the information I want anyway), so I open up the app, hoping I'm wrong about what's going on. But when I click through to **BACKSTAGE PASS**, I find a more comprehensive list of scenes than before:

SCENE THREE: NAIL SALON

SCENE FOUR: MEETING UP WITH RAYNA

SCENE FIVE: LUNCH AT THE CARNIVAL

SCENE SIX: BUMPING INTO CARSON

SCENE SEVEN: RAYNA'S DEPARTURE

I'm curious about hearing Theo's voice at lunch and why there's something when I bumped into Carson, but mostly I want to know about Rayna. When I click, my heart thuds into my stomach.

RAYNA THINKS: ADAM'S TEAM LOST EARLY IN THE TOUR-NAMENT; I KNEW THAT LAST GAME WASN'T GOING WELL. HE'S REALLY BUMMED AND NEEDS ME.

She really did lie to me. How could she?

I push it far, far back into a corner of my mind. This day is not about Rayna.

I have to turn this Backstage Pass feature off before my meet-cute with Theo. I came here to find out why he fell for me in the first place, not to hear a bunch of thoughts about—

Wait. It would actually be helpful to have access to Theo's thoughts the day we met, to experience his side of our first day too. Maybe this isn't such a bad thing.

But I still need to keep it from happening in real time. Because it's super disorienting to hear other people's thoughts while we're talking. I'll just go back and read through Theo's thoughts later, to get the full scoop on how enchanted he was with me.

Unfortunately I can't find any sort of settings like a normal app would have. I open up **DIRECTOR'S NOTES** and type in a message to Grace.

How do I turn off audio mode for backstage passes?

"Are you sure you would like to turn off audio mode?" The words also appear in the message thread.

Yes.

"Audio mode has now been silenced," Grace replies.

Clearly that doesn't work on *her*.

Thanks.

I switch back to the scenes and locate **SCENE EIGHT: MEETING THEO.** I dance in place with a small squeal as I prep myself for our first encounter.

I follow the instructions, reading through the script as I walk away from the main stage. Kind of creepy how it narrates my thoughts: **MAGGIE IS PONDERING WHETHER TO TEXT HER MOM TO COME PICK HER UP OR GO FIND OTHER FRIENDS AT THE FAIR WHEN—**

A small force hits me from the side, sending my phone flying. I look down, and there's Therese, still in her dance costume, her brown eyes wide in a *please don't scream at me* expression.

"Ther—erm, hi," I say.

She continues to stare at me, shell-shocked.

"Shrug and walk away," Grace instructs.

I frown, because my phone's still on the ground. Oh! That's right. I suppress a grin as I lift my shoulders and resist the urge to reassure Therese. Poor kid.

I start walking, anticipation zipping through my veins. Here it comes. My first moment with Theo!

"Hey!" he calls from behind me, but I don't stop walking. A small smile slips through, which a guy walking the opposite way returns. When he starts to slow like he's going to say something to me, I quickly send a *not now* look.

"Hey, did you drop this?" A tap on my shoulder.

This is it. I can't wait to read his side of this encounter. His first glimpse of me. How he felt, what he thought. But for now—my first look at him.

With a quick inhale, I turn around, and my heart tip-taps, just like it did the first time I saw Theo standing behind me, holding my phone. I don't know if it's part of the simulation or just my natural reaction to him. He's so handsome.

My phone lights up in Theo's hand, probably to signify it's unlocking another backstage pass—eep!—and Grace says, "Would you like to reactivate audio mode?"

No way! I'm not spoiling this moment. I shake my head minutely.

Theo scrunches his eyebrows adorably. "It's not your phone? I could've sworn—"

"Yes, it is." I reach for it and quickly stow it in my pocket. I flash my most winning smile. "Thank you. That was so sweet of you to chase after me."

In my memory, Theo looked down humbly and shuffled his feet, but in actuality he flashes a distracted grin as he turns back the way he came. "No problem. Have fun!"

He doesn't just walk; he jogs back along the path. I tilt my head, confused. I was sure he talked to me more than those few seconds. And seemed more interested than that. It's really tempting to pull my phone out and read what he was thinking in those moments, but I don't want to spend this day staring at the app. I want to spend it with Theo, enjoying our time together, remembering how we connected. That initial spark. And then, later, I can read through his side of it and get an even fuller picture.

A young couple pushing a stroller gives me a weird look. Guess I am blocking the path, staring at nothing. I turn toward the game alley. That's where our real story begins.

15

So . . . my plan might be flawed. Yes, good to avoid Theo's thoughts for now—especially because it didn't seem like Theo really *noticed* me. Which is not how I remember things at all, and if his fluttery feelings happened later, I'd rather not be disillusioned right now and screw up the day.

But also, since I'm in a totally different frame of mind than the first time around, I don't know where I'm supposed to be. I generally remember the day but not the exact order of things. The app has already unlocked the next scene—maybe because I left where I met Theo?—so I skim through the lines and movements for **SCENE NINE: THE DUNK TANK**.

Rayna was right about Clara being here. In fact, she should be popping up right about . . .

"Maggie!"

And there she is, a key player in the next scene. Her hair's a bit longer, and the tips are pink. I hug her. "Hi! You're here!"

"The Bridgeport Fire Department has a booth. With a dunk tank. Guess who got called in to serve."

"David?"

"Yep! His dad tricked him into taking his spot."

I snort a bit at the idea of David taking his dad's place.

"What?" Clara says. "He might decide to follow in his dad's footsteps someday."

I can't help my smirk. "He has a bit of growing to do."

David is adorable, and I love him. He and Clara have been dating since the summer after eighth grade, when they met at a summer camp. He's over six feet like his dad, the first Black fire chief in Bridgeport. But his dad was a weight lifter in college (which comes in handy as a firefighter) and has bulging muscles that would look frankly hilarious on David's wiry form.

"Who's up now?"

Clara wiggles her eyebrows. "Fireman Curl-My-Toes."

A recent graduate of the academy, Brent Curmitoz earned his nickname thanks to his effect on half the student population when the fire department came to do a safety demonstration at the high school.

Clara grabs my wrist and tugs me off the path back a few yards. The Bridgeport Fire Department has one of the community booths, separate from the carnival itself. I must have walked right past her when I was lost in my thoughts. The booth is set up with flyers about how to create a fire escape plan for your home, stickers and coloring books for kids, and a sheet you can fold into a fire truck. Several firefighters and EMTs stand behind the table in navy pants and T-shirts with the department logo. One firefighter is giving tours of a fire truck, while an EMT shows off an ambulance to a young family. Beside that is the dunk tank, with Fireman Curmitoz inside.

"Oh my." I lean into her ear. "He's shirtless."

"I know, right? Isn't this the best day ever?"

I blink. "Yeah." Her words throw me off enough Grace has to

prompt me on my next line, and I cringe even as I say it. "How creepy would it be for me to take a picture?"

"Super creepy." David sticks his head in between ours. "But I give you permission to take as many pics as your phone can handle of this amazingness."

He steps back and poses like he's Superman. He's no Fireman Curmitoz, but David's no slouch either.

I snap a quick photo, noticing the Best Day app shows several notifications now. "I think that's all my phone can take."

He nods solemnly, his green eyes glinting with mischief. "I'm not surprised."

Clara wraps her arms around his waist. "How cold do you think that water is?"

A loud yelp makes us all turn back to the dunk tank. Fireman Curmitoz rises from the water, rivulets sliding down the crevices between his muscles. Someone should put that man on the cover of a romance novel. Or an underwear ad.

He shivers, somewhat diminishing the effect.

"Pretty cold," David says with a healthy dose of dread.

"David, you're up!" the firefighter calls as he climbs out. He towels off and slips on a dark T-shirt.

As David reluctantly approaches the dunk tank, Fireman Curmitoz strides toward the pathway. "Step right up, folks! Now's your chance to dunk Chief West's pride and joy!"

"A dunk tank?" says a voice I'd tried to block out of this memory. "I'm in!"

Of course Carson's up for a game of humiliation.

16

Carson and Theo move toward the dunk tank line. It's a one-dollar donation for three throws.

"That guy"—I nod toward Theo—"I ran into him earlier. What do you think?"

Clara gives him an appraising look. "I'd give seven-eighths of a David."

No guy is ever equal to David in Clara's opinion, but seven-eighths is pretty high.

She shifts her gaze to the left. "His friend's about the same."

I skimmed through the scene, but I must have missed that line, and it makes me stumble. "Car—that guy? Not even close."

Clara grins. "I never figured you for the preppy type."

It's a fair comment. My (forgotten) marching band crush tended toward quirky T-shirts and jeans year-round, while Theo pretty much always looks like he'd fit right in at a country club—although not in a snobby way.

"There's something about him."

"Hmm. An 'it' factor." Clara shrugs. "Sometimes you don't know where 'it' will strike."

She casts a fond smile toward the dunk tank, where David

is trying to get comfortable on the tiny seat. As if he senses her gaze, he straightens and puffs out his chest. "All right, who's gonna dunk me?"

"Me!" a woman at the front of the line says. "Your dad made me run four middle school fire drills last week. I had to break up several hot and heavy make-out sessions in stairwells between kids that didn't look like they'd gone through puberty yet." She shudders.

David makes a *bring it* gesture. "Show me what you got, Captain."

Clara and I edge closer to the line—and Theo. He and Carson both look back at me, and my phone buzzes again. Another backstage pass! Theo must be thinking about me. How sweet.

We watch as the woman misses twice, then finally dunks David. He stands up and shakes it off. "I will definitely be reporting this behavior."

"You do that," she says before striding toward the tent.

I scan the laughing crowd and find Theo is much closer than he was a minute before.

"Hi again," he says, his voice open and friendly.

I smile. "Thanks again."

"I'm Theo." His return grin makes my knees weak.

I wish he would hold out his hand for me to shake, just so we could touch, but he doesn't.

"Maggie," I reply.

"And I'm Clara." She inserts herself with a mischievous grin. "That's my boyfriend your friend's about to dunk." She tips her head. "Or is he?"

Theo presses his lips together, considering. "He used to play baseball. Plays golf too. So I'd say yes."

It's an understatement to say Carson plays golf. He's obsessed—probably why he smelled like grass the other day. Theo plays, too, but he's not quite as intense about it.

"Hey, Lockwood," Theo calls, "pressure's on. All eyes on you!"

Carson flashes a grin in our direction, and I feel a punch to the gut. It's just so unusual to see him relaxed and . . . I don't know . . . charming? That can't be the right word. He turns back to face the dunk tank and lines up like a bona fide pitcher.

David does a full-body wiggle. "I'm not worried. I bet you're all show."

"Sorry, man," Carson calls. "You're in for another soak."

He winds up and lets the ball fly so fast it hits the tank release almost before I realize he's thrown it.

"That's my boy!" Theo pumps his fist. "Impressive, huh?"

Maybe a little. "I guess."

"That was an amazing throw." Theo looks down at me, a crease between his brows that I really want to reach up and smooth.

I wonder why he's pushing it so much. "It's just a dunk tank."

I'm starting to get confused myself.

"Line?" Grace says, startling me. I'd almost forgotten about her and the app, losing myself in the moment. When I don't answer, she must take it as a yes because she continues, "Ask him where he ran off to before."

I lean toward Theo and twirl the end of my braid around my finger. "So where'd you run off to so quickly earlier?"

Theo casts a quick glance toward Carson, who's chatting with

David while he climbs back onto the dunk seat. "My sister had just finished performing. She's the one who bumped into you behind the main stage."

"Ohh." The pieces click into place. "So you had to get back to your family."

"Yeah. Before my parents took her home to change. She wasn't happy to leave the carnival." He smiles ruefully, relaxed again for the first time since he introduced himself. Because he's talking about Therese.

"I bet. You didn't want to take her around?"

"I . . ." He glances over at Carson again, then focuses entirely on me. "Not today. What about you? I'm guessing with the way you dismissed my guy's skills you aren't here to dunk anyone."

Maybe if Carson got in the tank . . . "No particular plans. The friend I met here got called away."

Though I'm trying to keep things light, I can't help the hint of bitterness in my voice. I'm still ticked at Rayna for leaving me to meet my brother.

A thought suddenly occurs to me, and I swivel toward Clara, so carefree with David and Carson. Does *she* know about Rayna and Adam?

Great. Now I'm going to suspect everyone. I glance at my phone. Maybe there's a whole section of Clara wondering if I've discovered Rayna's secret.

"What's wrong?" Theo asks, and Grace clears her throat in my ear. A warning that we're straying from the script. I wonder if I get a certain number of strikes before I'm zapped back to my anesthesia-induced state in the real world.

I turn back to Theo with a bright smile. "Nothing! I was just going to walk around for a while and see what else there is to do."

"Oh." Theo studies me, and I hold his gaze, willing him to take that next step. "Do you want to walk around with me?"

There it is. "I'd love to."

17

"Yo, Lockwood," Theo calls. "Maggie here is gonna go around with us."

Wait. Us? He definitely asked me to walk around with *him*, not *them*.

I want to reach for my phone to check the scene, but that would be weird. I relax my hand against my side.

Carson turns and jogs toward us, followed by Clara.

He stops and holds out his hand. "Hi, I'm Carson."

I reluctantly take it, even though IT'S THE WRONG BOY'S HAND. His shake is firm, and he maintains eye contact the whole time. He looks so *friendly*. I seriously don't remember him acting like this. I must have been too wrapped up in Theo to notice—or the way he acted afterward erased this strange *I'm a normal person* interaction from my mind.

"Maggie." I offer my name begrudgingly.

"Maggie." He still hasn't let go of my hand, so I tug it free and slip it into my back pocket.

"What are you guys gonna do?" Clara asks.

Theo turns his beautiful mouth down, ambivalent. "Games?"

"Sounds good to me." I remember playing games with Theo.

But how are we getting rid of Carson? I glance at Theo, but he looks questioningly at Carson.

"I'm good with games," Carson answers. "But you'll be sorry when I beat you."

There's the Carson we all know.

I give Clara a hug. "Text you later?"

"You'd better," she says in my ear. "I want to know what part you get!"

Right, that's happening today too. Not until later, though.

"I'll let you know," I promise.

"Ready?" Theo asks.

"Yep." I happily move up beside him but I'm dismayed when Carson steps up on my other side. We move into the main walkway.

"Do you go to Bridgeport High?" Carson asks.

I nod. "I'll be a sophomore this year. What about you guys?"

"We'll be juniors," Carson says. "Guess that's why we haven't seen you before."

One reason. Also, our school is huge. There are plenty of people in my own grade I've never met.

"My brother's a junior," I tell them. "Adam Scott."

"The soccer player!" Carson raises his eyebrows. "He carried the JV team last season. Is he playing varsity this year?"

Ugh, an Adam fan. Another reason I can't stand Carson. "Yep."

Theo tips his head to the side. "You don't seem excited."

"My brother and I aren't exactly close."

Theo hums in the back of his throat. "That's too bad."

He sounds so saddened by this I'm compelled to reassure him.

"It's okay. We're just too different. It sounds like you get along with your sister, though."

The lines smooth around his eyes. "Therese is my favorite person in the world."

"Hey." Carson stumbles back with his hand over his heart.

Theo shakes his head. "Sorry, Lockwood, but you gotta admit, the kid's adorable."

Carson nods. "It's true. Therese is pretty much the coolest nine-year-old ever."

My heart is melting right here, listening to Theo talk about his little sister.

Carson turns to me. "But Adam's pretty cool too. He was in my history class last year. Gave the most hilarious presentation on the Donner party and . . ." He trails off at my expression, coughs. "Uh, you had to be there."

"So are you an athlete too?" Theo asks, clearly trying to diffuse the moment.

"Not even close. I tried soccer in kindergarten and kicked more of my teammates than the ball. They understandably kicked *me* off the team."

His smile hasn't subsided since we started talking. "So what *do* you like?"

"Acting, singing, dancing. I'm part of the Future Stars Troupe at Metro Theater Arts."

Theo snaps his fingers. "That must be what Therese was talking about. She said she'd seen you in a play at her camp."

"Oh." I straighten. "Yeah, we just wrapped up a play. Tons of camps brought kids to see it. But I'm surprised she recognized me."

"She was pretty starstruck," he says. "She'd probably ask for an autograph if she were here."

"That's so sweet! Is she interested in acting?"

"I don't think so. At least she hasn't brought it up. She's really into dance right now. And making stop-motion videos on her iPad. She keeps begging my parents to let her start a YouTube channel."

Carson leans around me. "I'd subscribe. Her videos are killer."

"Yeah, but you never know who else might follow her." Theo scrunches his nose, but it only makes him more appealing since it comes from worry about his sister.

"Now I'm very curious about these videos," I say.

I smile up at Theo, and he grins back. "Maybe you'll get a chance to see them someday."

Oh, I would. I have spent many hours watching Therese's videos. They are impressive for a nine-year-old.

"So what was the play you were in?" Carson interjects, ruining my moment with Theo.

Which play? When?

"*Robin Hood*," Grace reminds me, and I parrot it to the guys.

"I'm guessing you were Maid Marian?" Carson grins at me. It's disconcerting.

"No, I was one of the outlaws."

"Oh." He nods like he has no answer to that.

"Did you get to shoot arrows?" Theo asks.

Now that's the right sort of question to ask. It's what I wanted to know when I got the part.

"Not as many as the guy playing Robin Hood, but a few. Unfortunately they were just those Velcro arrows, but I did have to practice my aim."

Theo nudges me, sending a tingle of sensation throughout my body. "Maybe you should've gotten a ticket for the dunk tank. Could've given Carson some competition."

I'm still off-kilter when I answer, "Totally different skill."

"I think I saw a bow-and-arrow game on the concourse," Theo teases. "Maybe you can win me a prize."

Carson inhales oddly, and Theo's grin flickers. "Hey, Carson," he says, "where do you think we should start?"

I know Grace would butt in if I was changing anything, but what's weird is that this *feels* completely different from how I remember my meeting with Theo. I'm supposed to feel like my feet are gliding along the path and we could burst into an impromptu dance number at any moment. I'm supposed to barely notice Carson's even here, but thanks to seven months of history with him, he's like a rock weighing my feet to the ground.

Carson looks between us. "You know, I think I'm gonna head out."

Yes! I quickly direct my gaze at the ground to mask my overreaction.

"What? Hold on a sec, man." Theo follows Carson off the path, and I step off too.

They walk several paces away, so I can't hear what they're saying, but I don't need an app in this case to know it's about me. It doesn't matter. The point is, Carson's about to leave, and Theo and I will finally be alone.

A couple of minutes later, Carson waves. "See ya, Maggie!"

Good riddance, Carson.

At last, we can get this day on the right track.

18

"So," Theo says.

"So." I rock up on my tiptoes, ready for things to get amazing. "Let's go then." His grin is contagious.

We head back onto the path, and finally my feet are skimming above the earth like they should be. Theo's hand is swinging beside mine, and my fingers itch to reach for it, but I know it's too soon. Later, I promise myself.

When we reach the midway games, he turns and levels a serious look at me. "I have an important question for you."

I stare into his gorgeous, teasing eyes. "Hit me."

His eyes widen like I've just said something especially funny. "With a gigantic, blow-up baseball bat or an enormous, stuffed unicorn?"

I raise an eyebrow. "That unicorn could do some damage, but I'm not a fan of jumbo prizes in general."

"I was gonna suggest the authentic"—he makes air quotes—"signed poster of the Jonas Brothers circa"—he furrows his brows as he peers into the nearest booth—"2009? But you left yourself wide open for that."

I love everything about this conversation. I want to hold every word he says in my memory forever. "Maybe so, but the poster would have been a direct hit to my heart." I place a hand over the organ in question. "Because three-year-old Maggie? Totally in love with the Jonas Brothers, especially Nick. Whew." I wave the hand in front of my face.

"So that's your type, huh?"

I glance over at the poster. Nick is wearing a red plaid shirt with the sleeves rolled up to his elbows. While it's a little more lumberjack than what Theo was wearing the day we broke up, it's the same look. My lips twist bittersweetly as I say, "Plaid all the way."

Theo's smile broadens. "I'm glad you like it."

I close my eyes briefly, a forehead-smacking emoji flashing on the back of my lids. Theo's wearing plaid shorts. Could I be more obviously into him?

"It's what you said the first time too," Grace reassures me.

Like that makes it less embarrassing. Actually . . . it does help. It clearly didn't put him off.

I give him a once-over. "I mean, your plaid's not going to get you as many groupies, but it's okay."

"Maybe I already have groupies. Maybe they're hiding behind the Skee-Ball, waiting to jump out and mob me."

"I'll have to fight them off with the inflatable baseball bat," I say coyly. "I'm willing to risk it if you are."

"Lead on, slugger." He motions for me to go ahead of him. There are a couple of young kids playing Skee-Ball with their mom, but two lanes at the end are open. I know he's going to pay, but I pull a few folded bills out of my pocket in a show so he can wave them away. It's the first real sign he's treating this like a date. I squeal internally. It's finally starting to feel like my best day.

If you can hear my thoughts, Grace, I got this. Could you just butt out from now on?

There's no answer, which I'll take for now.

Theo pays the hawker, who releases the balls down the chute. I nod toward the young girl two rows over. She's about five and is sporting pigtails with two neon green bows. "Is that your groupie?"

He picks up a ball and tosses it between his hands. "You know it." He swings back and releases the ball, sending it rolling down the lane. It pops over the hump, straight into the center circle.

The little girl rushes over. "You got the jackpot!" She turns to her mom. "Mommy, he got it right in the middle! He's gonna win the unicorn!"

"Yes, sweetie." She gently pulls the girl away while I smother my laughter at Theo's smug expression.

"Please don't hit her," he says.

"I'd never." He still looks way too happy with himself. That just won't do. "I'm thinking that was a fluke and you can't do it again."

"Oh, really?" He picks up another ball. "Challenge accepted."

Theo lobs the ball down the lane and hits the center ring again. "How about that?"

A grin tugs at the corner of my mouth. "Luck."

He grunts, picks up another, and does it again. He nails it eight times in a row.

I narrow my eyes. "Is there some sort of trick to this I haven't learned?"

He grins down at the ball return as he picks up the last one. "Grandparents who spoiled me with way too many hours at Chuck E. Cheese?"

"And you spent all your time on Skee-Ball?"

He sends the last ball down the lane. It catches on the edge of the cup and spirals a few times before dropping in, making his perfect score complete.

"Big winner! Big winner!" calls the game hawker. "What prize do you want?"

Theo's groupie is still standing there, watching us with wide eyes. The choice is obvious. I point at the jumbo stuffed prize. "The unicorn."

Theo sees where I'm looking and nods his agreement. When the guy pulls it down and hands it to Theo, he raises his eyebrows at me, and I signal we're on the same page. He holds the unicorn out to the little girl. "Here you go."

"Really?" She claps and jumps in place, then turns to her mom. "Can I?"

Her mom frowns. "Are you sure?"

She's asking me, not Theo. Does she not realize it's ten times more adorable for him to give the prize to her little girl? Maybe not. I squat in front of the girl. "It would be a huge favor to me if you could take care of this extra-special friend for me. I'm afraid I'd lose her."

She looks up at her mom for permission to take the unicorn. She nods.

The girl grabs the unicorn and hugs it tight. "Thank you, thank you, thank you!"

The family heads off with Theo's prize.

"You still gonna play your other game?" the hawker asks me.

"I couldn't possibly after that display."

"You want me to win you a unicorn too?" Theo teases.

"Tempting, but"—I pout—"it just wouldn't be the same now that you've already given the first one away."

"Then the only answer is crazy Skee."

Ooh, this is where things get interesting. I resist the urge to dance in place and paste a blank look on my face. "What's crazy Skee?"

Theo rubs his hands together. "Okay, first ball: between your legs."

I pretend a light bulb has gone off. "I see. It's like crazy *bowling*."

"Yep." He sweeps his arm to indicate I should go.

"All right." I pick up the ball and spread my legs, which doesn't feel like the most flattering position, but Theo's standing to the side rather than right behind me. I lean over, quickly swing the ball between my legs, and release it.

"Nice form," Theo says.

Is he talking about my Skee-Ball form or my body? A warm flush steals over me. "What's next?"

"Now you have to do it with your eyes closed."

"That sounds like cause for injury. Better make sure you're out of range."

"Oh, I'm not worried." His smile makes my pulse skip erratically.

I close my eyes, and I'm just about to swing the ball back when his hands land over the top half of my face, making everything so much darker.

"We can't have you cheating," he murmurs in my ear.

I catch a whiff of something fruity that must be his shampoo or hair gel and the faintest hint of sweat, but it doesn't put me off.

Not when it's eighty degrees outside and I'm feeling sticky myself. He's put himself off-center so that I can still swing my right arm. I roll the ball and listen to it plunk into a hole, but I don't care where it went. I'm too focused on Theo. His hands slide down to my shoulders.

"Nice one."

I hum an agreement, since I didn't see the end result. If he turned me around now and kissed me, I think I'd let him, even with all the people going by. It wouldn't be as romantic as our original first kiss on the Ferris wheel, but the thing is, I've been kissed by Theo countless times, and I know what it's like. How alive I feel when our lips touch.

He releases me. "Okay, stand on one foot."

"What?" I blink up at him, still dazed.

"The next task," he says with an innocent expression. "Stand on one foot while you roll the ball."

He looks completely unaffected by our touch, like he really just wanted to make sure I wasn't peeking down the lane. My phone buzzes in my pocket, as if Grace is reminding me she's still here.

But I just want to stay in this moment, where he's standing here, completely focused on me.

I follow his instructions for the next few balls, turning around and throwing through my legs backward, crouching on the ground and pushing it up the lane, swinging in slow motion.

"I don't know . . . if the . . . ball will . . . make . . . it," I say as we watch it glide slowly upward.

When it bumps over the hump and into the ten-point slot, Theo oh so slowly raises his hand for me to slap, and we both start laughing. It feels good to laugh with him. I can't remember the last time we did that, just felt so comfortable that we laughed until our sides hurt.

I press my lips together to stop. "One ball left."

He nods seriously. "The toughest challenge." He moves in front of the game and stands with his legs shoulder width apart. "Between *my* legs."

"Um." My skin heats.

"I trust you," he says.

I got through this the first time; I'll get through it now.

I cock my hip and hold out my hand. "Ball, please?"

The gleam in Theo's eyes makes it clear he's pleased I'm not backing down.

I'm no mathematician, but I put considerable thought into that triangle I'm aiming for. I let go at just the right moment, my fingers only inches from his shorts. I quickly stuff my hands in my pockets, watching as the ball soars up the lane and pops right into the five-hundred-point slot.

"Yes!" I jab my fist into the air.

Theo studies the lit scoreboard with a way-too-satisfied smile. "Looks like you just needed the right motivation."

I side-eye him. "That could've gone really wrong for you."

He puts his arm over my shoulder and squeezes. "I never doubted you for a second."

19

After the games, we check the performance schedule and see there's an improv show. We're early, which gives me a minute to run to the bathroom and then time for us to talk.

By ten minutes to showtime, I've "learned" all sorts of facts about Theo. He tells me his parents have been married for twenty-two years, and he's the oldest. He calls Therese a miracle baby, because his parents tried for years to have her. That's why they all adore her so much.

"How long have you been friends with Carson?" I ask. He's still fresh in my mind.

"Maggie . . . ," Grace says warningly.

Oh. Guess I didn't bring him up before. I should've checked the script when I ran to the bathroom, but everything's been flowing so well I didn't think I needed to.

"Carson?" Theo tenses.

Oh, no. Now Theo's acting like it's odd I mentioned him too. It's just strange. Even though I pretty much try to forget every Carson interaction immediately after he's out of sight, I really don't think he was with us that long. Plus, their vibe seemed so off.

"Wasn't that your friend who was here earlier?" I ask in an *I'm so clueless* voice, which I hate, but it seems to work as he relaxes.

"Yeah," he says in an easier voice. "Best friend. Since we met at junior golf league."

I seize on the topic change. "Golf!"

His eyes widen at my eagerness, but Grace doesn't say anything, so maybe this is where the conversation was supposed to go.

"What about it?"

"You said you play golf."

For the next few minutes, he tells me all about it. Since I've heard it all before, I paste on my interested face and reflect on what I've already learned today. From the beginning, talking to Theo was always easy. I realize that's one of the things we somewhat lost in the past few months. I'm not sure how much I've really asked him what's going on with his family lately. It's mostly about our schedules or school stuff or if we want pizza or burgers when we go out.

My heart lightens. This day is working. I'm starting to understand where we went wrong. Theo and I need to laugh together like we did at Skee-Ball. And we need to talk more. Because clearly *I* had no idea what was going on with him if he was at the point of breaking up with me.

A loud *thump* from the stage cuts him off. A red-headed college-age guy in a solid green T-shirt and khaki shorts is standing center stage with a microphone. "Good afternoon, Bridgeport!"

"Good afternoon!" we echo back.

"We are the Wing It Players." He turns around to show us the back of his T-shirt, which says "WIP" for short. "We have a fun show planned for you today. It's going to involve some audience participation."

A little boy near the front practically bounces on his seat, raising his hand.

"Not yet," WIP guy says. "But your enthusiasm is noted. So we're the *primary* WIPs," he continues, as another guy with a close-cut Afro in a solid red shirt and a blond girl in a solid blue shirt join him.

Theo groans beside me, but in a good-natured way.

Blue Shirt steps forward and takes the mic. "To begin, we're going to play a little game called Actor Switch. Anyone heard of it?"

Theo bumps my shoulder and raises his eyebrows at me. "Of course," I mouth at him, leaning forward in my seat. It's a great exercise for learning character. We've done it tons in my acting classes.

My phone buzzes. I shift, wondering what he's thinking while he gazes down at me so expectantly. But I don't wonder long, as the show begins.

"Who can give me a scenario involving three characters?" Blue asks.

The little boy raises his hand, practically standing in the front row. "A boy who's eight and loves monster trucks and gummy worms."

"Got it." Blue points to an older lady in the back.

She glances at the man beside her. "A cranky old man who complains about *everything.*"

A chorus of oohs spreads through the crowd. No one else is

raising their hand after that, so Blue scans the audience and lands on Theo. "You. Got a job?"

Theo starts. "Um, yeah, I work at a movie theater."

Red rubs his palms together. "We can work with that."

The WIPs assign an audience member to act as the moderator and yell "switch," then get into position, placing two chairs on the stage for Green and Red, who sit.

Green pulls his legs up onto the seat so he's crisscross applesauce and cups his hands like he's holding something. His whole face lights up in an innocent, childlike expression. Red slumps into his seat with a scowl, his hand extended to the side like he has a cane.

"When is this movie gonna start?" he grumbles. "I've seen two of these gall-darn preshow entertainment commercials already."

"Mister, mister!" Green says. "Did you know lots of monster trucks use tires like on tractors? I got to ride on a tractor once. I—"

"Young man!" Red sits up, leaning on his "cane." "Can't you see I'm watching something?"

"Ladies and gentleman . . ." Blue's posture shouts *please don't look at me.* She wrings her hands, staring at the floor. "Um. We're working hard to get *Swimming in It* started. If—"

"Switch!" the moderator calls.

I love this part, seeing how each of them completely evolve into a new character. I find myself pondering how I'd portray each one.

"Go!"

Green copies Blue's previous posture. "If you could just be patient—"

"Patient?" Blue shouts in a grumbly, low voice. I'm already chuckling, as are Theo and several other people around us. "I've already been sitting here four minutes!"

She reaches into an imaginary bucket of popcorn, mimics a handful, and throws it toward Green. Not what I would have done, but I like it!

Green wards it off with his hands, dodging invisible kernels of popcorn. "I'm sorry! I'm just the messenger! Don't shoot!"

"Shoot!" Red acts like he's rolling his monster truck toward Green. "We're gonna make you flat, Mr. Messenger!"

Classic. So little boyish and definitely what I *would* have done.

Green backs away. "Please! I'm deathly afraid of monster trucks. I was diagnosed with monsterjamaphobia years ago."

Theo grabs my hand and leans over to my ear. "This is hilarious."

I curl my fingers around his, holding on tight. "I know, right?"

I was so focused on the show that I almost forgot Theo for a moment. I guess it isn't *too* surprising. Theater has always been my first love.

"Switch!"

The actors scramble to their next role. By the end of the scene, when the kid throws his drink on the old man and the theater employee quits, Theo and I are both laughing so hard we have tears leaking out of our eyes. Thank goodness for waterproof mascara!

We break into applause as the actors move forward to take a bow.

Theo releases my hand to clap, but as soon as they settle into their next bit, he reaches for me again.

Buzz.

I can just imagine what he's thinking—how he wants to hold my hand as tightly as I want to hold him. And I think I just figured out another important point for my mission to win him back: I have to keep my focus on him.

20

I'm energized when we leave the improv show, now that I have specific action items for when I'm back in the normal world. It will be work, getting Theo to laugh and talk with me again, but I can do it. After all, we have seven months of history.

"You hungry?" Theo asks.

After that barbecue, I don't think I'll be hungry for the rest of the day. I shrug casually. "Not really."

He surveys the rides. "What are you up for?"

"Anything." I'm not just saying that to impress him. Rayna says I have an iron stomach. Even full, I won't have an issue on any of the rides. "What about you? Any limitations?"

Theo exhales gustily. "Sorry. I just can't do that one." He points at a kiddie ride that requires you to climb inside giant teddy bears. "I'm deathly afraid of bears. I was diagnosed with arkoudaphobia as a child."

Did he steal that idea from the skit? Having just watched the improv show again, the monster truck phobia is fresh, but I laugh anyway. "Arkoudaphobia? Is that a real term? It sounds like you're afraid of giant boats."

He tugs me close. "I love your laugh."

I curl my lips in, completely undone by such a simple statement. "Really?"

"Most girls don't laugh for real."

Maybe it's okay he stole from the show. "Do most girls fall for these types of made-up words?"

His eyes dance. "Oh, it's a real word. Therese just did a report on bears, and it got stuck in my head because it was so odd. You can look it up if you want."

"I guess I'll trust you." How could I not trust a guy who gets his information from his little sister and isn't afraid to say so? I totally forgive him for using secondhand material. "But I dare you to ride the bears."

"I'll only do it if you protect me," he says in a small, ridiculous voice.

"Come on." I drag him toward the teddy bears. I know he's playing me, but it's an adorable play.

Theo gives the appropriate number of tickets to the handler, and we climb inside a blue bear.

"This is unnatural," Theo says in an exaggeratedly quivery voice. "What if the bear closes its mouth and we never get out?"

We're not even in the bear's mouth. It's a kids' ride, so we're in the bear's belly. Wait.

I scoot over close to him. "Is that better?"

He wraps an arm around my waist. "I feel much safer."

I bet he does. I don't remember him having this much game.

The ride starts up with a jerk, throwing us even closer together. My pulse speeds up at his proximity (definitely not at the ride). Our bear slowly rotates around a center gear.

"You wanna spin?" Theo asks.

No, because that means he'll have to take his arm from around me.

"Yes," Grace prompts, so I tell Theo I do.

We both place our hands on the spinner in the center of the bear and turn to the right, making our bear spin slooooowly in the opposite direction. It's more work than it's worth, but Theo looks adorable, his brow all furrowed in concentration.

"You realize you're probably upsetting the bear's stomach, groping around in here like this," I say.

Theo throws his hands up in the air. "You're right! We need to be as still as possible so he doesn't detect us." He hunches over and scans the dark recesses of the ride. "Let's be completely motionless until we can escape."

I giggle.

"Quiet! You'll wake the bear!" Theo scoots around the circular seat until he's by the gate. "We're slowing down. We'll be able to get out soon. Hopefully before he comes out of hibernation."

He's so *funny*. Seriously, where has this guy been lately? I haven't seen him, but I knew there was a reason I was so sure this day was perfect. This Theo is so much more engaging. His smile, his warmth, his eyes so focused on me. I want *that* Theo back.

The ride stops, and Theo doesn't wait for the operator. He pulls the pin out and pushes the gate open, jumping down and motioning for me to follow quietly, like we're sneaking out of a heist. I trail him along the fence and out into the main walkway.

Theo stops. "We made it. No more bears, please."

He has some decent acting chops.

"I challenge you to . . . the Rock-O-Planes."

Theo gives me an impressed look. "Challenge accepted."

21

An hour later, we've ridden everything except the Ferris wheel, and there's a long line for it.

"Do you want to wait?" Theo asks, eyeing the line like he thinks it's not worth it.

Because *he* doesn't know that we'll be stuck at the top for five minutes, and he'll kiss me there for the first time.

"I *love* the Ferris wheel." I smile way too enthusiastically for a rickety carnival ride. "Reminds me of the final scene in *Grease*."

He frowns, and while it's disappointing my reference goes over his head, he follows it up by moving into the line.

"I hate to do this, but"—Theo smiles down at me apologetically—"my phone's been vibrating in my pocket nonstop, and I just wanna make sure there's not an emergency at home."

Wow. That's so considerate. Not that he kept it up forever, but I still appreciate the gesture. I'm not always as good about that myself.

"No problem." I turn toward the front of the line to give him some privacy while he's checking. Actually, this gives me a chance to read ahead really quick. Making sure he can't see, I click through to **SCENE FOURTEEN: FIRST KISS** (squeal!) and skim through my lines, noting that annoying Adam is going to show up and interrupt us.

It's *really* hard not to check **BACKSTAGE PASS**, but I've already gotten this far. Better to wait until after our first, on-top-of-the-world kiss and then go back and assess everything later.

Just as I'm pocketing my own phone, Theo steps up beside me. "Thanks."

I glance up at him. "Everything okay?"

He smiles warmly at me. "Everything's *great*."

I feel that smile spread all the way to my fingertips. By the time we get to the front of the line, Theo has gotten me to tell him all about the last two shows I was in. Plus, somehow I've given him my weekly schedule of evening classes. He was obviously figuring out when he'd be able to see me again.

Theo hands over our tickets and we climb into the gondola. It's shaped like the bottom half of a bowl, with an aisle through the middle and gates on each side. We sit together on one side, and it's cozy but not crowded. Theo's thigh rests beside mine. His shorts are too long for any skin-on-skin contact, but I remember how exciting it was that first time. It takes *forever* for the operator to load the two other gondolas on our rotation—there's a little kid who's afraid, and his parents keep insisting he has to try it.

"Just let the kid off," Theo says quietly in my ear.

"Amen," I breathe in response.

After three more minutes of screaming, the parents finally give up, and a quiet older couple takes the family's place.

Theo nods in their direction. "I bet they're making out as soon as the ride takes off."

I smirk. "You're awful."

He grins down at me. "Am I?"

No, you're perfect. "I think you're a little too sure of yourself."

"I've always heard confidence is an attractive trait."

The Ferris wheel comes to life, saving me from answering—or heaping more compliments onto his already gorgeously swelling head. He was a model boyfriend, which is why his behavior these past few days seemed so out of character. Dumping me so callously, ignoring me even after I broke my foot. That guy is not *this* guy.

We soar around the wheel two times, and Theo tugs me close, his arm secure around my shoulders.

Here it comes. My heart thumps erratically.

Lurch. The Ferris wheel stops, right at the top.

Theo leans over the side. "Looks like they're loading up another group." He swivels back toward me. "That took forever last time."

"It did," I agree, hoping my smile conveys my willingness for him to make his move. I know he's going to, but the anticipation is killing me.

Theo scoots back in beside me. "So, Maggie Scott, has this been an amazing day or what?"

"The best," I say, but my voice comes out super husky.

He leans in. "I have a great idea how to top it."

I almost laugh, even though I just read it in the script. It's sort of cheesy, since we're at the top of a Ferris wheel. But maybe he said it that way on purpose. I don't care. I meet him halfway, pressing my lips against his.

Grace clears her throat, interrupting for the first time in an hour, probably to remind me I let Theo do all the work the first

110

time around. I'm not sure how to be first-kiss Maggie when Theo and I have shared hundreds of kisses. It's not new and tingly and exciting. But it's familiar, a gentle hum that starts at my lips and extends to my fingertips and toes. I know this boy, and I want him back, so I wrap my arms around his shoulders and pull him closer.

"Ahem!" Grace says even louder. "This is not your opportunity to jump ahead in your relationship. It will invalidate the simulation."

Oh, I bet it will. But I got to the kiss, so what do I have to lose?

"You will lose access to the Pass feature."

Oh.

Lurch. The ride starts moving again, and Theo lets me go. No! It can't be over already.

Buzz.

A wisp of hair blows into my mouth, and I realize Theo must have undone my braid. Huh. I didn't think we'd gotten *that* hot and heavy. Actually, now I'm a little concerned about what he thinks. It might be seven months in to me, but it's still the first day to him. It was barely a peck on the lips the first time around.

Buzz.

"You should check your phone. You have a text message from your brother."

Right. The script warned me about that.

I grimace-smile at Theo. "My phone's going nuts. I'd better check it."

His eyes are a bit glazed, I note with satisfaction as I check my messages.

Theo rubs his thumb along my palm. "You ready to get something to eat?"

I sigh. "I have to go. My brother's on the way to pick me up."

Theo frowns. "Right now? Are you sure?"

I hold up the phone. "He'll be here in ten minutes. Unfortunately."

He asks for my number, and I happily type it into his phone. I'm tempted to put hearts after my last name and write "Your Girlfriend" in the company line. But I definitely didn't do *that* before. I might have considered it, though . . .

"Here you go."

The ride has stopped, and I don't want to leave Theo, but I know better than to make Adam wait. It seems anticlimactic to exit the gondola after that mind-blowing kiss, but this is where our story ended August 6.

He helps me out and keeps his hand on my back as we walk down the gangplank toward the crowd. I expect him to take my hand again once we're free of the gate, but he sticks his hands in his pockets and waits for me to lead the way. I stop when we reach the fork that leads toward the drive where Adam is waiting. I don't want him to spoil my goodbye with Theo.

"My brother's that way," I tell Theo, willing him to kiss me goodbye, even though I know he won't.

I wonder why.

Theo takes my hands and rubs his thumbs along the sensitive spot between my thumb and pointer finger. His warm smile makes me want to tug him in close again, but I don't.

"I'm so glad I met you today, Maggie," he says.

I root my feet to the pavement as I smile brightly up at him. "Me too. It's been an unbelievable day."

In more ways than he could ever imagine.

"We'll do it again soon." He squeezes my fingers one more time, then salutes as he strolls back toward the carnival.

I know we will, but how do we keep the magic every day?

22

I practically skip toward the exit. I don't even care that Adam is waiting at the other end. The day with Theo was everything I hoped it would be, and I still have the backstage pass scenes to look forward to. Once I read through those, I'll have the full picture, all the information I need to win him back.

This really is the best day ever!

Except for what happened with Mom and Rayna this morning . . .

I refuse to consider it. Neither of those fit into my perfect day.

Adam's waiting at the curb in his beige Sonata. When I open the door, I'm assaulted by the smell of stale chips. Crumpled Lays bags litter the floorboard, and there are two empty bottles of Gatorade in the cupholders. Was Rayna seriously in this car with him earlier?

No. No no no no.

"Have fun?"

I'm so shocked at this uncharacteristically normal question that I blink at him. "Um . . . yeah."

"Cool."

What is he thinking? He'd better not be in a good mood because he was fooling around with Rayna all afternoon. Gross!

I could find out. Check the app right now.

"Would you like me to reactivate audio mode?" Grace asks.

I make a strangled noise in my throat, and Adam casts me a weird look. "Are you sick or something?"

"No." I hope Grace also takes that as an answer.

What's weird, though, is that despite Grace's question, my phone didn't buzz to notify me a backstage pass had been unlocked for this scene. Does that mean Adam isn't thinking about anything?

Seems about right. I laugh-cough into my hand at my own joke.

Normally, being stuck in the car with my brother, I'd pull out my phone and scroll through my social media feeds, text Rayna, Clara, my theater friends, or find some other way to block him out, but I'm afraid the temptation to read Theo's thoughts will be too great. And I'm hesitant to do that while I'm with Adam.

"This day will not last forever," Grace says. "The backstage passes are waiting for you in the app, but you will no longer have access to them once you leave the simulation."

Good to know. Still not prepared to read Theo's thoughts with Adam beside me. What if it's something private? So I'm left with total awkwardness.

"How'd your tournament go?"

Adam narrows his eyes, suspicious that I asked. No one ever nominated me for best sister in the world either.

Adam's an amazing soccer player. Mom and Dad used to drag me to all his games when I was younger, before I got so busy with my own stuff. The games were boring overall, but I did feel a niggle of excitement when Adam would dribble the ball down the field and score a goal. I must possess a small measure of sibling pride.

"Sucked. Lost the second game."

"Sorry," I say.

His expression slackens. "Thanks."

Grace doesn't scold me. Is it possible Adam and I were actually nice to each other on this particular day in history? If so, it deserved special notice.

It's on the tip of my tongue to ask what he did the rest of the day, but I really don't want to know the answer.

Actually, he wouldn't tell me anyway, would he? Not if he was with Rayna.

Words are caught in the back of my throat—words that mention my best friend, accuse Adam of taking advantage of her. Rayna's never had a boyfriend before. That must be why she's taken in by Adam.

I mean, objectively, I can sort of understand an attraction to Adam. It gives me all sorts of cringey feelings inside, but I've heard other girls talking about how hot he is. We have the same wavy medium brown hair and blue eyes. He has the most disgustingly long lashes that of course he doesn't have to emphasize with mascara like I do. We also share freckles, which I usually mostly cover with a light foundation, but he obviously doesn't. And he's out in the sun all the time playing soccer, so they tend to stand out more and give him a boyish appeal. He's had a steady stream of girlfriends since he was fourteen. But he broke up with the last one earlier this summer. I hadn't really noticed there wasn't a girl hanging around our house until just now.

Except . . . there is a girl hanging around our house. I just thought she was there for *me*.

This is totally screwing up my magical day. I don't want to think about Rayna and Adam. I want to think about Theo.

Theo and how he laughed with me at the show. Theo and that incredible kiss on the Ferris wheel. Theo holding my hands and promising we'd meet up again soon. Theo thinking about me while—

"Are you going to sit there all day?"

Despite the nature of the words, Adam's tone actually isn't as rude as usual. He's already out of the car, leaning in from the street in front of our house.

I shake myself out of my Theo haze and exit into the steamy but much cleaner outside air, trying to remember what else is still in store for me today.

23

Mom practically pounces on me when I come through the door. "So?"

I draw back. "So, what?" clearly isn't the right response, but I'm unsure what is. She doesn't know about Theo. She can't. I just met him.

Dad comes up beside Mom, and since Adam walked in before me, I'm now faced with a wall of expectant faces.

"The cast announcement," Grace reminds me.

Ohhhhh. Of course. I should've looked at that already. I'm surprised Grace didn't prompt me to do it in the car.

"You forgot about the cast announcement the first time around as well," Grace explains. "You were too lost in a haze over Theo."

"Oh, right!" I wish I *had* been thinking about Theo the whole time instead of stewing about Rayna and Adam.

"Well?" Dad steps forward. "What part did you get?"

"I haven't checked yet," I hedge, and when Grace stays silent, I remember I confessed this sheepishly the first time too.

"What?" Adam bursts out. "I can't believe you weren't monitoring your email constantly for that announcement."

It's a fair statement. Without Theo, I would have been laser-focused on my email, waiting for the cast list to appear.

"I was busy." I try to shrug it off, but I can tell from their perplexed expressions I don't succeed.

"Doing *what*?" Mom asks, and then her eyebrows sweep up high. "You *met* someone."

"What?" Dad looks between me and Mom. "A boy? You didn't look at the cast list because of a *boy*?"

He works his mouth like he has more questions but is afraid to ask. The longer we stand here awkwardly adjusting to this reality, I realize I have mixed feelings about the fact that a boy overshadowed important casting news. A point Rayna made about not making Theo my main priority pushes itself to the forefront. But this is different. It was our first meeting. That has to be an exception.

To make it all stop, I pull out my phone. "I'll look now." Avoiding everyone's eyes, I skim past a bunch of store ads to the email from Metro Theater Arts. "Found it. *Frozen Jr.* Cast."

Out of the corner of my eye, I see Mom grab Dad's hand. Weird. They're not usually this anxious.

I open the email, but it's really a show for them since I already know what part I got. I try to remember how I felt when I first opened this email. I expected—or at least hoped—to be cast as the queen, so I probably frowned a bit when I first saw that Katelyn of all people had gotten that role. Her name does cause my nose to scrunch, more because of Theo than the role. I remember feeling surprised at being cast as Oaken. It took a moment to wrap my head around it.

I furrow my brows as I look down at the email, scanning the words, then bite my lip as if considering. Slowly, I let a grin overtake my mouth and nod. "Okay. I can work with that."

"What is it? Who are you?" Mom says.

"I'm Oaken, the guy who runs the shop in the movie, but it's different in the musical. He's a really fun character."

"You're playing a *man*?" Adam guffaws. Dad claps him on the back, and Adam chokes. "I mean, isn't that guy supposed to be big?"

Fair point. "It doesn't matter. I'll make it funny."

And I will. I'll get more laughs than any other character in the whole show. They'll see.

"So you're happy?" Dad asks.

"Ecstatic." I nod and put my phone away before I'm tempted to look at anything else.

"Fantastic!" Dad sweeps me into a hug, and Mom joins in. Adam doesn't, but I'd never expect him to.

Dad keeps his hands on my shoulders as he steps back. "Where should we go to celebrate? Did you already eat dinner at Bridgeport Days?"

"Nope." I actually am hungry, now that he mentions it. "Can we go to Kitaro?"

Mom smiles. "I'll go make a reservation."

Yum.

"Then you can tell us about this *boy* who must be remarkably fascinating," she adds.

Um, no thanks.

Although, I have a vague recollection of telling them about Theo. Not in a ton of detail, but some. I'll probably have a chance to check the script on the way to the restaurant.

My phone buzzes. More thoughts? Seems unlikely in this case. Probably my friends chatting about the cast list. I should be too. I just don't have the energy for it at the moment, faking excitement over something that happened months ago.

I'm about to enjoy a delicious meal with my family and celebrate yet another win in my dramatic career. Bonus: I already know what a big deal this role will be for me. So that puts me in even more of a celebratory mood.

24

Dinner at Kitaro is fantastic. Cooking our meal tableside, our chef is both an amazing cook and showman. Once again, Dad defeats us all in the shrimp toss, catching fifteen in his mouth in a row.

But at the same time, it's also exhausting, because even as I'm stuffing fried rice and chicken down my throat, I'm studying Mom for signs of illness and Adam for stray Rayna hairs or some other evidence he's been with her.

Dad's the only one I feel completely safe around. There hasn't been any shocking information about him. But then, I haven't been around him most of the day.

I've been with Theo.

I'm not so sure the backstage passes are a good thing. Or that I should trust them. Mom seems fine to me, and I've never seen any hint that Rayna is into Adam. So how can I trust anything I'd read in there about Theo?

And even if it were true, doesn't he have a right to his privacy? I wouldn't want him to hear *my* thoughts.

Once we're back home, I book it for my room, because I've made a decision: it's time to end this thing. "Grace, I don't want to read any more backstage passes. I appreciate the opportunity to relive this day, but I'd like to go home now."

"Are you sure, Maggie? If you leave now, all the data currently on the app will be deleted."

Am I?

I open the app and click on **BACKSTAGE PASS**. There are passes listed for almost every scene. It's so tempting. But it also feels like cheating. I want to win Theo back honestly. "I'm sure."

"All right. If that's your decision."

"It is. How do we end this thing? Do I click my heels three times and repeat 'There's no place like home'?"

Grace doesn't laugh. "You may if you'd like, but you are already home."

Trust Grace to be overly literal.

I click my heels together, just because I'm cheeky like that. "Goodbye, Grace. Thanks for everything!"

"So long for now, Maggie."

I don't have long to wonder about that hedgy farewell as everything goes warpy again. My seven-month-ago room swirls around me, and I'm back in the same funhouse from when this all started. It makes me dizzy, so I close my eyes.

But without being able to see, I feel completely off-balance. I sink onto the floor, grateful I keep everything in my room pushed to the side so I can practice choreography. There's nothing for me to bump into.

Once I'm sitting, I curl into a ball and rock. The dizziness passes, but I still wait a minute to make sure it's finished.

"Grace?" I ask. "You still there?"

No answer.

I feel a change even before I open my eyes, a general heaviness in my brain and body from the anesthesia. But still, I look. Sure enough, I'm back on the living room couch, my foot propped up on a pillow, wrapped in an ACE bandage, my purple toes sticking out. I don't feel any pain, so I guess the nerve block hasn't worn off yet. I blink several times, just to make sure I'm not losing my mind.

Again.

The Best Day app!

I grab my phone and unlock it, but the app isn't there. My calendar app is back in its normal spot, next to Messages. But the app started with a text, so I check there.

I sift through the new messages from friends checking in on me earlier. The next one should be from Grace (or whoever she really is), but it's gone. My messages skip straight from Clara, Alexis, and Yvonne (my Future Stars director) to Rayna, assuring me I'm not alone and she'll be here after school. I cringe at the long stream of texts I sent her. According to the time on my phone, school will be out in about an hour. I somehow missed these other texts coming through.

Does that mean . . . I was asleep? Did I dream that whole scenario, reliving August 6 of last year?

But it was so clear! Crêpes with Mom and Dad, the nail salon, Rayna meeting me but then leaving, running into Carson, the dunk tank with Clara, and every single moment with Theo. While I remembered that day before, none of the memories were so distinct I could see Carson's light blue eyes staring into mine on the pathway or hear Theo's rumbling laughter during the improv show. I've never had a dream that vivid.

Or remembered every moment of it afterward like it had actually happened. Usually as soon as I wake up, I can only access snippets of a dream. This one involved all five senses, and I recall every single one of them, including what everyone said.

It seemed so *real*.

But there's no trace of the app on my phone now.

And it didn't change anything with Theo either. No message asking how my surgery went. No apology for dumping me and dating my worst enemy. Nothing.

Voices in my head? Rayna dating *Adam*? More like a nightmare!

But just to be sure . . . "Grace?" I ask again, from my living room.

"Do you need something, Maggie?" Mom calls from the kitchen, startling me into dropping the phone.

I twist around until I can see her there, set up with her laptop at the table. "No, I'm fine. Have you been there since we got home from my surgery?"

"Mostly," Mom says. "You haven't been much company," she jokes. "I might have even heard a few snores."

I crinkle my nose. "Sorry."

Mom confirmed I was asleep. The app doesn't exist on my phone. There's no other proof any of that happened, so the only other conclusion is that I just had the most real dream of my life, probably brought on by the drugs they gave me during surgery. Those are some crazy side effects!

"I'm just glad you're not in pain," Mom says.

"Me too." A yawn takes me by surprise.

I can't believe I'm tired again. I just woke up! Maybe it's the stress of believing, even briefly, that stuff about Rayna and Mom might have been true.

On the other hand, the Theo part was great. I wouldn't mind returning to first-date Theo. I close my eyes, letting the whir of the overhead fan lull me back to sleep.

25

Loud whispers awaken me. Where am I? No longer on the couch, clearly, as I'm lying down and have a pillow under my head. Dad must have carried me to my bed.

It's still light, but shadows creep across my floor. I blink over at the clock—five thirty. So school's been out a few hours. Rayna was supposed to come see me, wasn't she? My foot's still numb, thankfully.

The whispers are coming from the hallway outside my door. They increase in volume, to the point I can distinguish the words.

"We can't go on like this forever." That's Adam.

"I know. I'm sorry. I really am. But you know how she feels about you."

I'm groggy, so it takes a moment to process. That's Rayna. Are they talking about me?

Adam laughs humorlessly, no longer whispering. "The feeling's mutual."

"Hey," Rayna protests. "You really could try harder. Like what you said to her the day she broke her foot? That was way harsh."

Thank you, Rayna. She's always got my back.

"How was I supposed to resist that? She was trying out for *Footloose*." He chuckles like he still thinks it's funny.

It's not.

But I'm surprised—and hurt—to hear Rayna muffle a laugh.

"If you want this to work, you have to resist from now on."

Want what to work?

It sounds a little too familiar. Like a continuation of that dream.

"Is that an ultimatum?" Adam asks.

"Maggie's in serious pain right now. She needs a lot of support to get through this."

I do. I need Rayna. Adam not so much. He'll just make everything worse.

"If I'm nicer to Maggie, will you go to prom with me?"

My gasp fills the room. Rayna and Adam both stick their heads in, their faces twin expressions of shock. Rayna sways slightly, her features frozen.

I find my voice before they do. "Please tell me this is a joke. That Adam did *not* just ask you to the prom."

"I—I—I—" Rayna continues to stutter and sway, until Adam reaches out to steady her.

He straightens, keeping his hand against the small of her back. It's such a proprietary gesture. Like she belongs with him.

"Yes. You heard right. Rayna and I are together."

I'm at a total disadvantage lying here in the bed. The best I can do is push myself up to sitting so I can at least face them better. I lean against my headboard as I fire my next question.

"Since when?"

My heart pounds as I wait for the answer, haunted by a hazy memory of being at Bridgeport Days and hearing Rayna *think* something about Adam. *Please* don't let her say last summer.

Rayna and Adam are no longer staring at me. Instead they're gazing at each other, at silent war over what to tell me. It's the sort of wordless communication I often witness between my parents, and it confirms what I fear before Rayna turns back toward me with an expression full of regret.

"Since last July."

The date drags the air from my lungs. July. That's even longer ago than I suspected. I turn accusing eyes on Adam.

He doesn't look sorry. He looks bitter.

"July. Are you, like, an actual couple or is this a . . ." I hesitate to use the word in reference to my brother and best friend, but I need to confirm what's actually going on here. ". . . hookup thing?"

"We're a couple." Rayna moves into the room until she's standing beside my bed. She twists her hands together. "I didn't know how to tell you. I wanted to—"

Adam grunts, making it clear she hasn't been pushing too hard for that.

She glares back at him and continues. "I did. I wanted to tell you, but your history with Adam is so complicated. The longer things went on, the harder it was to come clean."

I have to know how much of that dream actually happened, so that's what I fixate on first instead of what would probably be the next logical question when discovering your best friend has been secretly dating your brother for eight months.

"Did you lie to me at Bridgeport Days? When you said you had to go to an emergency babysitting job?"

With wide eyes, Rayna retreats a step.

I press on. "Were you actually meeting up with Adam because his team lost at the tournament?"

She looks back at Adam again, like he can save her from answering. He shrugs, either because he's equally bewildered why I'd ask about an event seven months ago or in a *just give up already* motion.

"I . . . I've lied to you a lot," Rayna confesses.

Of course she has. She'd have to in order to keep up a secret relationship for so long. Two-thirds of a *year*.

"Why? Why *him*?" Because we wouldn't have this issue if it were any other guy. She'd have been gushing to me the same way I've spilled to her about every crush since middle school.

Her *regret meets cornered animal* expression softens into a smile as she gazes at my brother of all people. "He cares about me. He *loves* me."

Whoa. Whoa whoa whoa. "He loves you? He actually *said* that?"

Not sure I've heard Adam use that word in years. Definitely not to me. Maybe to Mom when she says it first?

"Yes," Rayna says firmly. "And I love him."

Ew. That's just wrong. "You can't be in love. If you're in love, you don't hide it from everyone. If you're keeping it secret, there must be a core issue with the relationship."

Even as I say this, my brain starts arguing my point, throwing out names of star-crossed lovers who probably would have been fine if the world had just let them be. Romeo and Juliet. Catherine and Heathcliff. Jack and Rose.

Well, maybe the *Titanic* was too much of an obstacle for that last one.

"Our core issue is *you*," Adam says bitterly. "Nobody else cares if we're going out, but you do, so Rayna does."

"You think that makes a difference—that she cares? It doesn't change the fact she's been lying to me!" I'm nearly shouting now. I'm surprised my parents haven't appeared outside the door to watch the show. Maybe I'm all alone in the house with Adam and Rayna.

The liars.

The traitors.

I can't even escape them, trapped here in this bed. I don't see my crutches anywhere, but even if I did, what kind of lame—oh dear God—getaway would that be?

"I didn't want to," Rayna pleads. "But now that you know, can I just explain—"

"NO!"

Rayna flinches like I slapped her. I'm not sure I've ever shouted at her before. Maybe when we were younger and got in a stupid argument over what game to play.

"Get out!" In case the words aren't clear, I point at the door.

Rayna inhales like she's going to protest again, so I repeat it. "Out!"

Adam leans down and whispers in her ear. She deflates and walks with him toward the door. Once she's out, Adam turns back to me with narrowed eyes. "If you weren't injured and drugged up, I'd—"

"What, Adam? Because this is low, even for you."

It's not like he'd physically attack me. He might think the worst I'm dealing with is my foot, but the emotional bruising is so much deeper than what you'd see under my bandages.

26

What has me reeling more than anything isn't that Rayna and Adam are in a secret relationship.

It's that I already knew about it.

What if it wasn't a dream?

No. Too impossible.

There are other explanations. Like maybe the anesthesia and painkillers somehow helped me pick up signs I'd subconsciously seen but ignored (I wouldn't have wanted to see a relationship), and I then had a very vivid dream manifesting those signs.

I could have made connections that aren't really there. I have no reason to assume Mom's cyst or Theo's initial indifference are true based on this one thing.

This one *horrible* thing.

I still can't wrap my mind around it. Adam and Rayna. Rayna and Adam. Together. For eight months. Longer than me and Theo.

I have so many questions. Like when they were meeting up. And how he convinced her he was any sort of decent human being. Because Rayna's not the sort to be taken in by appearance alone. At least I didn't think she was.

What a hot mess.

I'm a hot mess. To miss this so completely for so long. There had to be clues. I grab my phone and pull up Rayna's social media posts. They're almost as familiar to me as my own, but I'm not looking at them as a best friend now. I'm studying them for clues.

For every post, I click on the likes to check for Adam, and sure enough, he stamps his approval on nearly everything Rayna puts out there. He rarely comments. When he does, it's a comment about her looking hot, which never stood out to me before because he did that in person too. I just thought he was being obnoxious. I always believed Rayna felt the same way, but her viewpoint obviously changed.

I go through Adam's feed next, and the fact she's been returning the like-fest does surprise me. I follow him since he's my brother, but I don't pay attention to what he's posting. Rayna hasn't actually commented on anything. Probably too afraid I'd happen to see it.

"See this, Rayna."

I take a picture of myself with pursed lips and narrowed eyes, pick the most flattering filter, and start drafting a caption.

Picture of a girl who just discovered the person she trusted most doesn't deserve it. #betrayed #bfnf

I'm about to add another hashtag when a voice urges me to consider whether I want to make that statement public. It sounds suspiciously like the voice from my dream. Is it the voice of my conscience?

If so, my conscience is a total downer. I'd get a ton of likes and responses from that post. But it would also make things worse for Rayna. Most people know she's the person I trust most and would start digging for the juicy gossip. It didn't turn out great when I posted prematurely about breaking my foot. My *A Midsummer Night's Dream* understudy, Riley, saw it immediately, and within a couple of hours I had an email from our school drama teacher, Mrs. Pintado.

I delete the caption and consider whether the photo could still work for an update about my surgery. I don't look happy, which I'm not. Good enough.

> Surgery went well! But I'm stuck in bed for today ☹. No weight on it for two weeks. Not sure when I'll be back at school or theater, so don't have too much fun without me, kids! xoxoxo
> #brokenfootfixed #noweight #stuckathome #noschool #notheater #nodancing

Almost immediately I receive a notification that Rayna likes it. What is she doing, spying on me from another room? She's probably relieved I posted this instead of something about her. A part of me is still tempted to.

To keep my resistance up, I open a new message to Clara.

Did you know Rayna was secretly dating my brother???

Clara's response comes back almost immediately.

What?? 😯 So she didn't tell you?

I chew on my nail while I wait for her to answer. I don't think I can handle it if Clara's been lying to me too.

No way. I wouldn't have kept that kind of secret from you.

I believe her. Clara's a big believer in honesty. Also in confronting people directly if you have an issue with them. If she'd known about Rayna and Adam, she might not have broken Rayna's confidence, but she would've been on her case to come clean.

I know.

I just can't believe she did. Or WHY.

Clara replies, I'm so sorry she did. I know how much that must hurt you.

Well, yes. But also, Adam's such a jerk!

The dots stay on my screen forever. Then disappear. Then reappear. She's going to give me a lecture. This is why Clara's a good friend but not my best friend—because she feels the need to correct me.

Her answer finally appears, and it's so long I roll my eyes, but Clara's my next closest friend, so I can't just ignore her.

I know you don't get along with your brother, but I bet he has some redeeming qualities. He must if Rayna likes him.

You could give him a chance. I'm sure Rayna didn't tell you because more than anyone she understands the tension between you and she didn't want to upset you. But she loves you. Don't forget that.

That could've been worse. The problem is, Rayna apparently loves Adam too. And at the moment, I'm not so sure which one of us she loves more. If I gave her an ultimatum, would she pick me? When I was lying there in the bed and Adam tried to make her choose out in the hall, she wouldn't commit. Maybe that means she would choose me. I guess in a way she has by keeping their relationship secret.

No. That's Clara getting inside my head with her *unicorns and rainbows are everywhere* mentality. Rayna's been choosing *him* by lying to me.

Lies!

Realizing that might come across as an accusation directed at Clara, I quickly add . . .

She's been lying to me for 8 months!

You can't make excuses for that.

Okay, that's sort of a dig at Clara, but I'm just so angry.

Sorry. I add a kiss emoji to show I still love her.

It's okay, she replies. I understand you're upset. Can I bring you anything?

It's Friday night. She probably has plans with David. Since he goes to a different school, the weekends are when they get the most time together, and yet she's offering to come over here. She's so sweet she'd probably cancel their plans to hang out with me. But I don't want that. Actually, I think it would be better for me to be alone and try to figure things out.

Thanks but I'm just going to sleep.

If you change your mind, let me know. You'll be dancing again in no time!

She signs off with a string of hearts.

Oh, Clara, I wish I had your optimism.

27

Discovering Rayna and Adam really are together has shaken me. The dream isn't as clear after my nap and the argument, but I remember every feature of the Best Day app within it.

I glance over at my wall, and there it is, the August 6 "genesis" entry with the red star and heart. I haven't taken it down (although I did remove my prom countdown). It makes total sense my subconscious would pick that day. Even now, I can't think of any other day that stands out as better.

Most of the day was as amazing as I remembered. But if Rayna and Adam being a couple is true, what else do I need to watch out for? Are other things from the dream also real?

"Maggie?" Mom knocks on the doorframe. "Oh, good, you're awake." She steps inside holding a bowl. "I brought dinner. How are you feeling?"

Confused. Betrayed. Exhausted.

Suddenly wondering if you're sick, even though you look perfectly fine. The words are on the tip of my tongue: "Mom, did you have a cancer scare seven months ago?"

But I hold them in. I got away with asking Rayna about an event that long ago because we were in the middle of an argument. Mom would probably question it. Unless she believed I'd found evidence of it somewhere . . .

Yeah, right. What sort of evidence would I find lying around?

"Maggie?" Mom moves inside and sets an aromatic bowl of soup on my nightstand.

"Okay," I quickly reply. "Still don't feel my leg from the knee down."

She wrinkles her nose. "Unfortunately that won't last forever. But you seem much more alert." She brushes the hair off my forehead. "You were pretty amusing there right after the surgery."

"Aren't I always amusing?"

She chuckles. "Absolutely." She glances at the doorway. "Were you awake when Rayna came by?"

Surely Mom doesn't know about Rayna and Adam.

Unless they told her today, after the blowup? Hard to tell from her expression.

I decide to avoid that discussion for now. "Nope."

Mom nods as if confirming something to herself. "Well, I'm sure she'll stop by again tomorrow."

She'd better not.

28

Pain. Sharp, stabbing pain, radiating from the place where I expect the screw must be.

I groan and look at the clock beside my bed. Four thirty in the morning. I'm dying.

"Help," I croak.

Of course no one hears me.

I can't stand this. It's excruciating. So much worse than the pain when I first broke it.

"Help!" I call louder. I know Dr. Rowland prescribed something. Mom might have been hesitant to give me drugs initially— and honestly I didn't really need them after that first day anyway—but this is totally different.

"Help!" I raise my volume to a scream. Is everyone else in the house dead? Maybe I should try calling them on the phone instead. I'm about to when Adam appears in my doorway in boxers and nothing else. Ew.

He rubs his eyes. "What's wrong?" he slurs.

"It hurts," I whimper. "I need drugs."

"Just say no," he shoots back.

I might actually find that funny if it didn't feel like my foot was about to explode.

"Please," I say, which gets his attention. I never beg him for anything.

"Where are they?" he asks, suddenly alert.

"I don't know. Mom has them."

"Okay." He nods. "I'll go find them."

"Hurry!"

In an uncharacteristic show of kindness, Adam doesn't say anything sarcastic in return and books it out of the room. Pain continues to stab at my foot. I can't believe that much agony can be contained in such a small area.

A few moments later, Dad rushes in with a glass of water and a bottle. "So the nerve block wore off, huh?"

I reward his attempt at humor with my most wrathful glare of all time, then promptly burst into tears.

"Okay, okay." He squints at the bottle. "It says you can have two for extreme pain or one for moderate."

"Give me two," I growl.

Dad blinks. "Wow, you sound like that creature Sigourney Weaver turns into at the end of *Ghostbusters*."

"I feel like that creature is chomping down on my foot right now."

Dad shakes his head sympathetically. "You'll need to sit up."

I'm dizzy when I do, but I manage to swallow the two pills and half the glass of water. I expect them to work immediately, dulling the pain the way the general anesthesia for the surgery instantly put me to sleep. But the pain doesn't stop.

"Daddy," I moan.

"Oh, sweetheart." He sets the pills aside and urges me to scoot over until he's next to me on the bed. I haven't curled up to sleep

140

with my dad for many, many years, but I hold on to him tight, digging my nails into his side while I will the pain to subside. He doesn't complain.

I finally drift off, only to wake up again at five thirty. This time my foot aches on the top and side. It's not stabbing like before, but it's still uncomfortable. I know I can't take anything else for hours. Dad's still beside me, lying on his back with his mouth hanging open. I shift toward my wall to give him more space. It's cool that he stayed with me, even when there's nothing he could do about the pain. But maybe he did do something, just by his presence.

Even Adam helped me tonight. The thought makes me uncomfortable, recognizing anything good in Adam. I don't want to consider there might be a reason Rayna would want to be with him.

I'll just chalk it up to a momentary lapse.

29

When I wake up, Dad's gone. My phone tells me it's eight thirty, which is later than I usually get up, even on a Saturday, but I'm super groggy. My foot still really hurts, but it's not quite as stabby as it was in the middle of the night. I don't really want to move from the bed, but I need to use the bathroom, so I have to. The crutches are propped against my nightstand. Oh joy.

I reaffix my surgical shoe and swing into the bathroom I share with Adam. He left the seat up again. Ugh!

As I'm heading back through my room, the calendar Grandma gave me catches my attention. It's still on yesterday's "grit" saying, so I rip it off to reveal today's entry, hoping for some wisdom to get me through. "Today is the day," it says.

That's it. Thanks for nothing, *Life's Little Inspiration Calendar*.

By the time I reach the deserted kitchen, I'm completely exhausted. I make it through to the breakfast room and collapse into a chair. I hate to just yell into the house, but the pain is returning, and the crutches are so much effort. I prop my foot up on the chair beside me and call out, "Mom? Dad? Anybody home?"

A moment later, Mom emerges from the laundry room.

"Hey, sweetheart, want some breakfast?"

Even though I came into the kitchen, I don't feel that hungry. "My stomach is kind of unsettled."

Mom nods. "Probably the anesthesia still wearing off."

"Oh, that definitely wore off, and so have my pain meds," I say as stinging needles radiate through my foot.

Mom crinkles her nose apologetically. "Well, since you took two, you have to wait a bit before you can take any more."

That sucks. But I know better than to say so aloud.

"How about some eggs?" she says brightly.

The thought makes my stomach revolt. It must show on my face because she says, "Or dry Cheerios?"

"That might be okay."

I try to get comfortable while she bustles around, pouring the Cheerios into a bowl and getting me a glass of ice water. She sets everything out and sits across from me, propping her elbows on the table.

"Dad said you had a hard night."

"Yeah," I grumble around a mouthful of Cheerios. "It was nice of him to stay with me."

"He was worried about his baby."

I scrunch my nose, but I get it. I'm the youngest.

Mom looks healthy. It's hard to believe she could be hiding cancer. I've watched lots of movies and TV shows about people with cancer. They're always pale and tired, often losing their hair. Mom's highlighted blond hair is full and shiny. Her energy seems boundless—definitely more than mine the past week. Her color is good. It *has* to have been a dream.

But if it isn't, I want to know. I don't want to be broadsided with the news my mom is dying.

I swallow and set down my spoon. "So, Mom, how are you feeling?"

"Fine," she says, a *where is this coming from* question in her voice.

A dozen silent answers run through my brain.

I'm afraid you're hiding something from me.

Are you sure you're really okay?

And the big one: *Do you have cancer?*

But she's sitting there so expectantly, not showing any signs of illness, and it would be absurd for me to ask that out of nowhere.

So instead I say, "I just wanted to check, since you're focused on taking care of me."

Smiling, Mom reaches across the table, and I meet her hand halfway. "That's what moms do."

I've also watched enough movies and TV shows to know that's not always true, but I'm glad mine takes care of me.

"Thanks, Mom."

Since I'm too chicken to ask her about this hopefully imaginary cancer, I'll have to find another way to investigate.

30

As I'm sitting on the couch that afternoon, bored out of my mind, the date clicks in my head, and a different kind of pain hits me. Today is audition day for *Footloose*.

Oh, well met, *Life's Little Inspiration Calendar*. "Today is the day" indeed.

I know I shouldn't, that it will only make me more miserable about what I'm missing, but I pull up my feed and start clicking on the profiles of all my theater friends.

Unlike *Frozen*, *Footloose* isn't being produced by my theater company, so there's no guarantee of getting in, but a lot of my friends are still trying out. Our summer production isn't until August, while this one is at the end of June, allowing us to do both. Between school, Future Stars, and other productions, I hardly ever have any downtime from shows, and I love it. Being forced to sit out both my school play and the first summer production is torture. I only hope my foot heals in time for the August show.

My friend Elana posted a photo of everyone from Future Stars who's at the auditions. At first glance, Elana Benowitz is one of those people you wouldn't expect to be in musical theater. A quiet girl, she wears makeup only on stage, plaits her chestnut hair into a simple braid most days, and dresses mainly in loose T-shirts and knit shorts. While she's a powerhouse when performing, she tends to hide slightly behind others in photos. Like now, where she's positioned herself behind Alexis, who's gone all out with false eyelashes, a smoky shadow, and crimson lipstick. She's further made sure the audition panel will remember her with a silvery tank and leggings. Beside her is Hailey Runyon, the preppy one of our group, with a black tennis skirt and violet dance halter that make her tan skin glow. She's tamed her long, meticulously highlighted blond hair into Dutch braids and pinned them around the crown of her head. Like Alexis, she exudes confidence. And then there's Tyrone Kang, effortlessly gorgeous in a fitted white tee and black dance pants. His shoulder-length ash brown hair is pulled back with an elastic at the base of his skull, and he smolders more than smiles at the camera, like he's everyone's favorite member of a boy band. He's joked more than once that his Korean grandparents have suggested he go for it.

There's quite a crowd in the background. It's a fun show, so they were expecting a big turnout.

Break a leg! I comment. Just not a foot because that totally sucks.

No surprise: Katelyn's missing from the photo, but I know she's there because she posted about it separately earlier. Even though she's part of our troupe, she's not really a part of the *group*. She comes to rehearsals and performs her roles, but she's never become friends with anyone. I don't think that attitude's going to get her very far in the industry. As the great Julie Andrews once said, "How dare one act like a diva when you have a lot of work to do and you need to find your disciplines and so on?"

Although, admittedly, Katelyn's not the sort of diva who

sloughs off the work. Just the kind who thinks she's too good for the rest of us.

I may not be able to audition, but I can still be a good friend. I learned early on being friendly to everyone else in a cast ensures they'll also help you shine as brightly as possible. But it's also easy to do, since everyone's such a blast to be around.

I set up a video feed, happy now that Mom convinced me to shower. The shower bag they gave me to protect my foot is pretty cool actually. I sit on the shower seat (like I have been ever since Dr. Rowland told me I couldn't put weight on my foot) and pull it over my bandage. It has stretchy material that clings to the skin under my knee to keep the bottom half of my leg dry. I was exhausted when I finished, but I still put on some mascara. I'm not as made-up as usual, but I *am* playing the role of invalid at the moment.

I hit Record. "Hey, guys! I just wanted to wish you all luck at the *Footloose* auditions today. I'm so bummed I can't be there with you, but I know you'll all be awesome. Just so I can feel like I'm there, answer a question for me, 'kay? Tell me what character you most want to play."

I add an open-ended question and post, sinking back onto the cushions. That was more draining than I expected, pretending to be perky and excited for the people doing what I want to be doing.

My phone chirps, announcing the first response. Hailey, who played Elsa in our production of *Frozen*, is shooting for the lead, Ariel. She definitely has the voice, but she's not the strongest dancer. If Metro Theater Arts were putting it on, she'd have a pretty good shot at the role, but there's a bigger pool here. It will

147

probably go to someone else, but I still send her a fingers crossed emoji.

Alexis is going for Rusty, Ariel's best friend and the perfect character for me. In the original movie back in the eighties, she was played by Sarah Jessica Parker, who I adore. She's fun and bubbly and the perfect foil for Ariel. Plus she has a cute love interest without it being the main focus. If it can't be me, I'm all for Alexis.

Anyone but Katelyn.

The replies keep coming in. Tyrone is going for Reverend Moore. I would've pegged him for Ren, the lead, but I can totally see him in that part, lording it over Ariel and the town.

After an hour, I've cast all my friends in the show, happily ignoring the other hopefuls trying out. Of course, Katelyn doesn't get a part in my version either. In all honesty, I know they wouldn't just cut her entirely, so I put her in the chorus and pat myself on the back for being magnanimous.

Alexis starts up a conversation with me afterward, telling me more than one hundred kids showed up to tryouts. That's pretty stiff competition. I might have to revise my casting. She also asks when I'll be back. I *want* to be with them, but I can barely get from one room to another right now. So I just say, As soon as I can!

I sign off feeling like I put on a good show for my troupe, but when a single tear drips down my cheek, I realize it wasn't a good enough show to fool myself.

31

The sun is bright in my room when I awake the next morning, and my phone is lit with messages from Rayna.

I gave you a day to cool off, but that's it.

We're having this out today.

Um, no. We're not.

Except if she shows up, I can't exactly run away from her. Which means I'll have to explain the situation to Mom and Dad.

That's gonna go over well.

Mom sticks her head in my room. "Oh, good, you're up. How'd you sleep?"

Barely at all. I took my meds about eleven thirty, but they never kicked in. Pain kept shooting up my foot in different spots, sometimes from my big toe down, or from the middle of my foot shooting up. Whenever I picked up my phone to check the time, not enough had passed for me to take more medicine. I was tempted to call Dad back in to hold me like he did the night before, but I didn't want to act like a total baby. When my phone showed two o'clock, I just groaned and stared at the ceiling. I finally dozed off because the next time I checked my phone, it said three twenty-eight. I took two of the strong pills, and they finally worked.

I'm about to blurt all of this out, but Mom looks so hopeful I just tell her I slept fine.

"I'm so glad. Dad and Adam went to church, but I don't think you're ready to go out, so we'll just watch the livestream."

I'm so out of it I completely forgot it's Sunday. At least Rayna won't show up for a few hours. Even if she assumes I stayed home, she'll probably wait for Adam to return for the extra moral support.

Ugh. I hate even thinking he could provide someone with moral support.

"Mom, I have to tell you something."

Mom blinks; she pulls my desk chair closer to the bed and sits. "This sounds serious."

I draw in a deep breath and exhale loudly. "It is."

Her brow furrows. "Is it something about Theo? I know it's not that you're pregnant, because you already had to answer that before the surgery and—"

"Mom!" I feel heat creeping up my neck. "No! Theo and I never—no."

Mom nods to herself. "I didn't really think you had, but you said it was serious. It's been a while since we had that talk, and your breakup was so dramatic I wondered if there might have been a reason you were so distracted you fell down the stairs afterward."

I can't believe that's where she went. "I really just wasn't looking where I was going."

I wait for her to expand on the question about me and Theo. We've been so focused on taking care of my foot that she's avoided the Theo conversation. Maybe this is why. I brace for her to finally broach the subject, but she just twists her lips to the side. "Maybe you should come up with a better story."

I laugh. "You want me to lie about it?"

"It doesn't look so great on your resume." Her smirk widens into a full smile. "A dancer who can't even manage stairs."

"Ha ha." I don't appreciate the reminder about my resume, though. It'll have a huge gap thanks to this incident.

"So what *is* the serious thing you wanted to talk about?" Mom leans forward with her elbows on her knees.

"It's about Adam." I twist my blanket around my fingers. "And Rayna."

"Oh," Mom says cautiously.

I swivel toward her. "You know?"

She throws up a defensive palm. "Only since last night. Adam told us after I brought in your dinner."

Mom is way too calm about this. "Did he tell you how long they've been seeing each other? That they've been hiding it since LAST SUMMER?"

"Sweetheart—"

Oh, no. I'm not letting her downplay it. "She's been lying to me! For months and months! My best friend. How could she do that?"

Mom bites her lip, taking a moment before she answers. "Is that what you care about most? That she lied to you? Or that she's with Adam?"

Don't they go together? "I don't . . . both!"

She appears to consider her words carefully again. "You might think we don't notice the tension between you and Adam, but we do. It's something your dad and I haven't been sure how to address." She waves a hand helplessly. "Maybe we were hoping you'd both grow out of it and become friends someday."

I scoff. He's just made the chances of that even slimmer. "This is another example of what a jerk Adam is. He's trying to take away my best friend!"

"Maggie," Mom says sternly, "I don't think this has anything to do with *you*."

Didn't we just establish it has everything to do with me? Or maybe that was just in my head.

"How could it not? It's my best friend and my brother. Of course I'm in the middle of it."

"I think the reason they didn't tell you is so you *wouldn't* be in the middle of it," she says wryly.

It's clear she's never going to take my side in this.

Is anyone? At least Clara understood how much it hurt for Rayna to lie to me. Mom is too biased in Adam's favor.

"Never mind. The point is, when Rayna comes here today, I don't want to see her."

Mom shakes her head. "You can't avoid Rayna."

I lift my chin. "I can."

"Maggie, I understand you're upset. But you should at least talk to her."

"Why does everyone keep saying that? Like she can explain away months of lies? That's some sort of fast-talking."

"Maybe she can't. Maybe you won't resolve anything today. But ten years of friendship should hold enough weight for you to hear her out."

I hate that reasoning. "Fine. You can let her in the door. But no guarantees after that."

As Mom starts to go, I call out after her. "Mom, did you have any idea?"

She grips the doorframe and looks off to the side for a moment before facing me again. "I really didn't." She sighs like she doesn't know what else to say. "I'll have the livestream ready to go in the living room at ten thirty."

Mom leaves, and I'm more unsettled than before our conversation. On Friday I convinced myself I'd somehow seen the signs Rayna and Adam were sneaking around together, but Mom didn't notice either.

What if . . . ?

No. It's too impossible. It couldn't have been real.

But what if it was?

And I gave up the opportunity to learn everything I absolutely could from it?

This whole thing with Rayna and Adam sucks, but maybe I missed out on *good* information with Theo.

I know it's a long shot, but if there's the slightest chance at all, I have to try.

I open the App Store and do a quick search for "Best Day App," but that's a wash. An internet search brings up two sites, and neither of them have anything to do with what happened to me. A search for "best day of my life" returns the song by American Authors, and now that's totally in my head.

A text! That's how it all started—even before the day of the surgery. I got those texts that made me start thinking about my best day. Then the one asking if I wanted to go back. I deleted the first two, and the third was gone from my phone when I returned, lending proof to my dream theory. But if a text started this whole thing, perhaps it could lead to new answers.

There's no number for me to send to, so I open a message to myself.

Grace, are you still there? Was it all real? If so, can I go back again? I would really like more answers.

32

By midafternoon, I've checked my phone about a hundred times to see if there's a reply to my text. Or a text from a random number about best days. Or if an app has magically appeared on my phone.

Nothing.

So, yeah, I'm really losing it, texting messages to the voice of my subconscious.

And then Rayna shows up. My morning meds have worn off, so I'm not in the best frame of mind to listen. From my position on the living room couch, I hear Adam greet her in the entryway, probably murmuring words of encouragement before she confronts his fearsome, resentful sister.

Whatever.

She enters the living room holding a Starbucks cup.

I narrow my eyes. "Is that a mocha cookie crumble Frappuccino?"

She approaches me cautiously with the drink, obviously confused by my *back off* expression. "Yes."

I look toward the kitchen. "Thanks for the reminder. That's the drink Theo ordered for me as a consolation for dumping me."

"Um. So you don't want it?"

I totally do. It's my favorite drink, but she can't buy my forgiveness. I fix a pointed stare on her. "No."

"Okay. I guess I'll just . . ." She looks around for a solution. "Put it in the fridge!" she says as if I haven't cruelly shot her down. She strides into the kitchen and deposits the drink, returning empty-handed.

Without waiting for an invitation, she sits on the couch beside me, leaving almost a whole cushion between us. I don't look at her.

"I know you're angry, Maggie, but you have to believe I didn't mean for this to go on so long."

That gets my attention. "You didn't mean to stay with Adam so long?" I ask curiously.

She shakes her head slowly. "No, Adam's . . . no. What I meant was that I never intended to lie about it for so long."

Oh. "See, the fact you have to add 'so long' is an issue. You shouldn't have lied *at all*."

"You're right." She wrings her hands together, then suddenly smacks her palms on her thighs and stares up at me with a determined gleam. "But it's your fault I did."

"Excuse me?" I slap my chest. "You're blaming *me* for your choice to lie?"

"Yes." Her voice quivers on the word, but it's firmer when she continues. "I knew how you'd react, and I needed to find out if I could have something real with Adam without dealing with you freaking out about the fact I was even trying."

"Your logic is astounding." Usually Rayna's the smart one between us. "Is that how you've been justifying it this whole time? By putting it back on me? Because yeah, I wouldn't have been happy about it last summer, but we would only have been talking about you liking my stupid brother"—I hold up a hand so she won't protest his stupidity—"not however many lies you've told to hide it from me. I'm guessing thousands of tiny ones and quite a few larger ones."

Rayna winces, guilt written all over her face.

"You think you know how I would have responded if you'd told me you liked Adam, but you can never know that for sure."

It's really not fair of her to put me in that sort of box.

She gulps. "I guess not. But—"

My phone dings loudly, covering whatever else she was about to say. I don't really want to hear it anyway, so I pick up the phone to check the message.

"It's Riley. I'd better see what she needs."

"Riley? Your understudy? You have to deal with that *now*?"

The hurt and disbelief in her voice cause an answering twinge in my own heart, but I'm nowhere near ready to forgive her. I raise my eyebrows. "It's show week. Besides, we're done here, right?"

Rayna chokes, like I've jabbed her windpipe. "I guess we are. I'll just go find Adam then."

Ouch. She knows how to stab back.

Oh, wait. I already knew that. Because she's been stabbing me in the back for months.

33

The text from Riley isn't urgent. She's just checking up on me, but it was a good excuse to end that agonizing conversation with Rayna.

They gave me good meds, I reply, even though they're not really working right now. How's play prep going? You ready to become Helena?

I'm torn. I both want her to do an excellent job and wouldn't mind if the audience thought, "She's great, but she's no Maggie." As Bernadette Peters once said, "You've gotta be original, because if you're like someone else, what do they need you for?"

I want them to still need me, even while I hope Riley shines.

If my youth pastor could hear me, he'd totally give me a sermon about pride. Humility definitely isn't one of my virtues.

Riley's response finally comes through.

I'm freaking out! I can't seem to nail down my lines. What do I do?

It's gratifying to know she can't just skip into the role with no problems. But I really do want her to succeed, so I ask if she wants to come over and run them.

OMG, are you serious? That would be so fab!!!

She adds a string of emojis afterward that's so enthusiastic and *long* I blink in surprise.

No biggie! I'm not going anywhere. Bring snacks!

Bonus: Riley will provide an extra buffer if Rayna and Adam decide to come back into the living room. I can't handle any more excuses today. I send Riley our address and ask Mom for my next dose of meds to prepare for the incoming whirlwind of enthusiasm.

·✦ ·✦ ·✦ ✦·

When Riley arrives, the first thing I do is ask her to pour my Frappuccino into another cup so I can drink it without Rayna knowing if she comes back down. Riley doesn't question my instructions; she hands me the drink and then sits beside me, twisting her long, brown-black hair into a knot on top of her head.

She gestures at the bag she brought in with her. "Snacks. On hand, I found mixed nuts, chocolate-covered raisins, and shrimp chips."

"Ooh, I want to try those! But first, tell me what I've missed."

She jumps right in. Our school theater program isn't as intense as Metro Theater Arts, but our teacher still puts on top-notch productions. I'm proud of every show I've been in, and Riley's stories about missed cues, line flubs, and costume fittings—including a couple of guys protesting about tights since Mrs. Pintado decided to go with a faithful representation—make me miss it even more than I already was. But I'm still glad she's here.

When she winds down, I ask, "What part are you having the most trouble remembering?"

Her face crumples. "Everything!"

She tends toward exaggeration, so I doubt that. "Really?"

She tilts her head from side to side. "The hardest is act three, scene two. There's just so much going on there."

I mentally pull up the script. "Ah, yes. After both Demetrius and Lysander have declared their love for Helena and she and Hermia get into the fight. It's crazy—but fun."

Especially since I had a legitimate excuse to pull Katelyn's hair.

"For sure! I loved watching you in that scene."

I place a hand over my heart. "Thank you. Now let's get you ready."

For the next hour, we run through the scene, with Riley doing her best to recreate the staging in the middle of my living room. I play all the characters except Helena, which takes Riley a few minutes to get used to.

After about the twentieth time, I've gotten into the different characters, finding a rhythm with each one, and Riley's really started to nail Helena. She's not quite there yet, but she will be by the performance.

Mom peeks into the room, smiling fondly at us. Adam and Rayna also come into the kitchen once. Rayna looks like she wants to come in and say something or perhaps watch, but he pulls her away. It's the one time I falter in the lines, but I resolutely refocus on Riley and our task.

When it seems like there's nothing else we can do for the day, Riley pulls out the chips and offers the bag to me. As I take one, she plops onto the couch beside me. "How do you *do* that? Jump between characters so well?"

The improv show comes immediately to mind. It's actually an exercise we've gone through in my acting classes, along with other similar games. "It's about thinking quickly on your feet." Why are there so many sayings that involve feet? "Anyway, thinking quickly about who each character is and what they want. It might sound silly, but it's good practice and you could do it on your own. Just pick a scene from anything and take turns as all the characters."

"You seriously could be any character in this play." Riley gives me a sly grin. "You'd be better at Hermia than Katelyn."

Taking a moment to swallow, I don't let her see how the mention of Katelyn's name raises my blood pressure. It's been fun helping Riley, but we're not actually *friends*. She's fishing for something with that comment, and I don't intend to provide fodder for the gossip mill.

"I wasn't interested in playing Hermia," I say, completely avoiding the mention of Katelyn. "Helena was perfect for me." I lean forward to pat her knee. "And you're going to be great."

"Thanks." Riley screws her lips to the side, clearly trying to decide whether she should say whatever it is she really wanted to say when she brought up Katelyn. When a determined look crosses her face, it's clear she's not going to let me be, and I brace myself.

"Katelyn's been bragging to everyone how she stole Theo from you," she says in a rush. "She sits with him at lunch every day and is all over him!"

How *could* he move on so quickly? I just don't get it. Not after being reminded of how great we were together.

"And that with you out of the way, she'll for sure get the part of Rusty in *Footloose*," Riley gushes.

Ohh. If I could get my hands on her jazz shoes, I would so fill them with honey!

The thought of Katelyn landing the part of Rusty seriously burns, like flames licking under my skin, threatening to ignite me.

"That—that—" There's a word for Katelyn that I really want to use, but I can't bring myself to say it.

Riley has no such reservations, completing my sentence. I nod, looking around self-consciously to see if my mom's in the vicinity.

"She's so not a Rusty," I say. "If anything, she should be, like, one of the uptight moms."

Riley's mouth pops open for a moment, but she quickly recovers. "Totally an uptight mom."

Crap. I shouldn't have said any of that to Riley. She doesn't seem to care for Katelyn—honestly Katelyn doesn't make many friends with her attitude—but she'll probably still tell *someone* what I said.

I smile conspiratorially. "But who knows? She might get lucky."

Riley nods uncertainly. I'm tempted to ask her not to share what I said, but that's probably just putting extra temptation out there.

I pat the script between us. "So you work those lines the next few days, and you'll be all set."

"I will." Riley gathers her things. "Are you coming to the show?"

I want to, but I'm not sure what state I'll be in later this week. Mom and Dad and I haven't even really discussed when I'm returning to school. "I hope so."

She reaches forward to squeeze my hand. "I hope so too. Thank you so much for your help!"

"You're welcome. You're going to crush it!"

I find I really mean it. I want her to be (almost) as fantastic as I would have been.

34

After hobbling with Riley to the door, I head for my room, just in case Adam and Rayna reemerge. I get settled on my bed and pull out my phone to see what everyone's up to.

When I see a new message from an unfamiliar number, an excited chill races down my spine.

Click here to activate Act Two:

There's a new link. I blink at the phone, re-reading the message several times.

Act two.

Then it sinks in.

It's real. It really happened. It wasn't a dream.

NOT A DREAM.

I start to click, then hesitate. When I clicked before, I was under the influence of some extremely heavy painkillers. Going into the simulation led to uncomfortable revelations about Rayna and Adam and maybe about my mom.

But I didn't finish it, and it was supposed to be about my perfect day with Theo. I left before I gathered all the information I came for. I might have skipped out on vital intel that will help me win Theo back. It made sense at the time; I didn't trust what I'd seen in the app, and it also felt a bit like cheating, but I so need a win right now!

I click and close my eyes to stave off the warped dizziness from the last time. But after a few moments of nothing, I peek with my right eye, and I'm still exactly where I was a moment ago, sitting on my bed. I scan my room—light gray walls, signed *Hadestown Playbill*. I didn't go anywhere.

"Um, Grace?" I ask, feeling like an idiot.

Especially when no voice answers in my head.

My phone dings.

Oh, right.

I look down, and my pulse kicks. The Best Day app is back, except now it says, **MAGGIE SCOTT ACT TWO**.

It doesn't look the same, though. There are only two features— **DIRECTOR'S NOTES** and **BACKSTAGE PASS**. It must have something to do with what Grace told me about all the data being deleted once I left. No more scene scripts or costumes.

Well, the backstage passes are what I came for, so I go straight to those. There's a list of all the scenes from the day:

SCENE ONE: GETTING READY

SCENE TWO: BREAKFAST

SCENE THREE: NAIL SALON

SCENE FOUR: MEETING UP WITH RAYNA

SCENE FIVE: LUNCH AT THE CARNIVAL

SCENE SIX: BUMPING INTO CARSON

SCENE SEVEN: RAYNA'S DEPARTURE

SCENE EIGHT: MEETING THEO

SCENE NINE: THE DUNK TANK

SCENE TEN: CARSON'S DEPARTURE

I start at the beginning and move through them one by one. The first four scenes are blank. They don't even include the thoughts I already heard from Mom and Rayna. Did Grace return the app to me with no information at all? That would be the worst practical joke ever! But I'm not giving up yet.

When I click on **SCENE FIVE: LUNCH AT THE CARNIVAL**, it pulls up a video.

"Whoa, what's this?"

I try to pause it so I can ask through **DIRECTOR'S NOTES**, but no matter where I touch my phone screen, it keeps going. I closed my door when I came in my room, to keep out Rayna and Adam, but just to be safe I grab some earbuds from my nightstand.

I can't tell whose perspective I'm seeing things from, but the "camera" is at the edge of the food court. To my surprise, Rayna and I are sitting at a table eating barbecue.

"Where is she?" I hear Theo say, just like I did in the simulation.

The view moves again, and Carson's face fills the screen, really close up, like he's standing right in front of me.

Am I inside Theo's head? That's incredible! That's exactly what I need. And also kind of intrusive, but I'll take it.

"You're going to miss Therese's show if you keep waiting here," Carson says.

"I know. But I can't believe she'd stand me up," Theo says. "Maybe she got confused about where we were meeting? There are a few more food stands at the far end of the carnival. Would you mind . . . ?"

Carson first moves toward Theo, then out of view (to bump his shoulder or something?). "Sure, man. I'll go see if she's there and tell her where to meet you."

He heads in one direction, while Theo moves in another. The video ends.

I tap to watch it again, but nothing happens. I wish I'd known what was happening *before* I started watching.

Then it sinks in what I just witnessed.

Theo was supposed to meet some other girl at the carnival. She stood him up. A girl he cared enough about to send Carson running all over to find.

This is the information I missed by leaving the simulation early?

"It doesn't matter," I say aloud. "He chose me."

Plus, I apparently showed up to Bridgeport Days with a crush on someone else too.

So no big deal. But I can't help the sinking feeling it causes in my stomach.

On to the next scene—**BUMPING INTO CARSON**. Hmm. I don't think that happened the day I met Theo, but it's here, so I might as well watch it.

The camera (Carson?) moves along a crowded pathway—and then Carson's voice comes on, but since no one is with him, it must be his thoughts. *I'll give the food court another try, just in case Isabel got here late and is still waiting. Theo is completely crazy about this* girl, so whatever I can do to help. But I'm starting to think she isn't coming, whether she actually stood Theo up on purpose or has a legitimate excuse. Ew!"

The camera focuses on Carson's foot, about to step on an ice cream cone in the path. He dodges to the left.

"Watch out!" I say instinctively.

But it's too late. Carson smacks into me.

"Oof!" we both say on the replay.

I watch myself stumble backward.

What just happened? Carson thinks, since I know he didn't *say* that. *Whoa! Where did she come from? Those eyes. I could stare at them all day. How do I make her stay? I should say something.*

"Sorry," he mumbles, and it sounds different from the thoughts. Unsure.

Not enough! his thoughts shout. *Say more!*

But it's too late. I say, "No problem," and walk away.

Why don't I ever know what to say? Carson thinks. *But I'm still glad I bumped into her.*

Carson begins humming "On Top of the World" as he walks away. The video ends.

I'm floored. "No. Nope. Not even."

I click over to **DIRECTOR'S NOTES** and type a message. I did not bump into Carson that day.

"You did. You just don't remember."

I startle, but at least Grace is speaking through the earbuds this time instead of as a disembodied voice in my head. "How is that possible? That I would totally forget that?"

"Your memories of that day are wrapped up in Theo."

That's true. But still. "This can't be real, though. That Carson . . ."

I can't say the words aloud, even to Grace. According to this video, Carson reacted to *me* the way *I* acted toward Theo at our first meeting. Which makes no sense, considering how he's treated me ever since. In addition to the golf tournament incident, there was Theo's birthday at Dave & Buster's, when Carson glared at me the whole night from two games away. Or when he came along with Theo to *Frozen* and told me I was perfect as a man. I rack my brain, thinking back, and I really don't remember bumping into Carson. Either way, it's discomfiting to experience his side of the encounter. I don't know what to do with it.

Apparently I made Carson . . . hum. I squirm uncomfortably. "What about all the other things he was thinking? I only heard one thought from him in act one."

"Ah, yes. Imagine if we sent you *all* the thoughts everyone had while you were together. If, for example, you'd heard every thought Rayna had about her barbecue sandwich at lunch. It would be overwhelming."

"But why did you add those thoughts for Carson in now?" I *really* didn't need them.

"It seemed like relevant information."

Best to just change the subject. "Hey, why are these videos now?"

"Because it's act two," Grace says, like that explains it.

You know what? Nothing about act one made any sense, so why should I expect more from act two? I should probably be a bit more concerned about this. If they can see inside other people's heads, they could probably see inside mine. They're always warning us about privacy online, but this is something else entirely. Rayna would want a scientific explanation (and understand it if given), but I'm just along for the ride and to get my Theo back. And next up is a fresh look at our meet-cute.

I'm ready.

35

The video begins in the audience at the main stage, and this time I'm prepared to watch through Theo's eyes. Therese's group has just finished their performance; Theo jumps to his feet, clapping. He whistles, and Therese smiles directly at the screen.

"That's my girl," he thinks. A picture of Therese as a baby in the hospital flashes across the screen, blinking her big brown eyes.

Wow, now I'm getting his *memories* too. And isn't that adorable?

Theo moves to the stage, and when Therese leans over, he gives her a high five, but her teacher ushers her off with the rest of the group, so he joins his parents at the rear of the seating area. His phone moves into view, and he opens a thread to Carson: Did you find Isabel?

Isabel again?

The camera sways, like he's shifting from foot to foot, swings toward where Therese should come out, then back to the phone.

No. Sorry, Carson replies.

"Should I check on her again?" Theo's more uncertain than I'm used to. *"I was really looking forward to hanging out with her outside work. But I already texted once to see where she was, in a teasing 'are*

you okay' way. I don't want to text again and seem like a stalker or, worse, a pathetic loser."

Thanks, he replies to Carson. Guess she's a no-show.

I'll head back your way, Carson writes.

Theo starts to type a response, when he focuses on Therese barreling down the side of the chairs.

"Uh-oh," he thinks. "She's not paying attention. She's going to run into that girl!"

That girl being me—and she does. My phone flies from my hands, and Therese and I stare at each other for a moment.

"Poor Therese," Theo thinks. "She's terrified! If that girl chews her out, when she wasn't looking where she was going either, I will take her out."

Yikes! I guess he didn't notice anything about me then, but it makes sense. He was worried about Therese. I've always loved that about him.

After a moment, video me shrugs and walks away.

My phone's still sitting on the ground, and Therese hasn't moved. Theo jogs toward Therese, and his hand swoops across the camera view into the grass to pick up my phone.

"You okay, T?" he asks.

Therese blinks at the screen. "That girl. I recognized her. She did a play at my camp. She's famous!"

Theo chucks her under the chin. "So that's why you looked like you were playing freeze tag after you ran into her."

"What's that?" She points to something out of view.

"Her phone. I'd better go return it, so you go to Mom and Dad, and I'll be right back."

"'Kay." Therese runs off.

171

The replay moves toward the path I followed. *"Hmm,"* he thinks. *"Where did she go? I think she had on a green-and-white-striped shirt? There it is!"*

He speeds up.

"Hey!" he calls. A couple of people turn around to see if he's talking to them, but not me. I'm walking like I'm on a mission to buy funnel cake before the carnival runs out. Theo increases his pace until he's right behind me and then speaks as he taps me on the shoulder. "Hey, did you drop this?"

He holds out the phone as I turn around.

"She's no Isabel," he thinks, *"but she's pretty cute."*

Um, excuse me?

Video me stares at him with wide eyes, completely starstruck. Kill me now.

Then I shake my head the tiniest bit.

"Did I get the wrong girl?" Theo thinks, then says aloud, "It's not your phone? I could've sworn—"

"Yes, it is." I grab the phone and stick it in my pocket.

"Weird," he thinks.

"Thank you," I say, smiling. "That was so sweet of you to chase after me."

"Why is she looking at me so strangely?" Theo thinks. *"I've got to get back to Therese and my parents. I've returned her phone. We're done here."*

The view turns away from me, and his hand swipes through the edge of the screen. "No problem. Have fun!"

As he jogs back to his family, he thinks, *"There's still a chance Isabel will show up. No point wasting my time there."*

The video ends.

I feel like he's stabbed me straight through the heart.

WASTING HIS TIME? Seriously? I knew he seemed standoffish, but while I was completely entranced by him, his first impression was that I'd be a *waste* of *time*?

I don't know if I can handle watching any more of these. None of them have been good.

Well, I guess Carson had nice thoughts about me. But that's just—no.

I decide to give it one last try. **SCENE NINE** is **THE DUNK TANK**. Okay, that has to be a good one. It's when Theo *officially* met me and asked me to go around the carnival with him.

I'm not giving up on him or this app yet. Maybe I'm overly optimistic, but there has to be a reason for all of this, and *I* believe it's to help me win him back. So probably I just have to understand this Isabel stuff (ugh!) in order to get there.

Reminder to self: I got the guy at the end of the day. It means I already won against another girl before, and I'll do it again. I just need an inside look from Theo to figure out how.

On to the dunk tank.

36

The video begins on the path again. It jostles, and I'm looking at Carson.

"I'm sorry she ditched you, man, but I'll hang with you. I'm not the oh-so-hot-and-eternally-fascinating Isabel, but I'm still fun, right?"

He grins extra wide, then lets his tongue hang out. Theo laughs. "Sure. I'll stay."

Fireman Curmitoz steps out beside the Bridgeport Fire Department booth and calls out, "Step right up, folks! Now's your chance to dunk Chief West's pride and joy!"

"A dunk tank?" Carson drags Theo off the path. "I'm in!"

"You would be," Theo says in a resigned voice. He follows Carson to the booth, and I watch as Carson pays for a ticket.

"You want a try?" Carson asks.

"Nah," Theo says and then thinks, *I'm not in the mood right now.*

"You gotta snap out of it, man." Carson puts his dunk tank ticket in one pocket and his wallet in another. "No girl's worth that much angst. You never have any trouble finding girls. There'll be another one who—"

Carson stops.

"What?" Theo asks as he follows Carson's view to me.

Suddenly, the perspective switches from Theo to Carson. I can tell because I can see Theo now.

"It's the girl from earlier," Carson thinks. *"I need to talk to her!"* He means *me.*

"I know," Theo says. "Isabel's just really cool. Or I thought she was. I—"

"Theo." The view tips forward a moment, as if Carson has nodded. "That girl over there. With the braid."

Theo blinks. "What about her?"

Why am I inside Carson's head right now? I want to know what Theo's thinking!

"Go over there while I'm doing my thing at the dunk tank," Carson says. "Talk me up."

Nooo! This is all wrong!

"Ohh," Theo says, an interested gleam in his eyes. "Do you know her from somewhere?"

"This is so embarrassing, asking you for help," Carson thinks.

"No," he says. "I just bumped into her."

"Huh." Theo glances toward me. "She seems to make a habit of that."

He tells Carson about Therese's encounter with me earlier.

"So you met her too?" Carson asks.

"I wouldn't call it meeting her," Theo replies.

"Okay," Carson says. "Looks like the person ahead of me's finished, so I'm gonna go show everyone how it's done."

"You could just go talk to the girl," Theo suggests.

"Gotta build up my courage," Carson says.

Theo shrugs. "Your call."

The video cuts again, and I'm back with Theo, moving toward me.

Good. I don't want any more from Carson. This is about Theo and learning why he chose me. Not whatever was going on with Carson, which I can't process at all.

"Been a while since Carson was interested in someone," Theo thinks as he walks toward me and Clara. *"She is cute. I don't know why he's always so nervous."*

"Hi again," he says when he reaches us.

"Thanks again," I say.

"Wow, she has a really great smile," he thinks. *"I need to key it back so she stays focused on Carson."*

"I'm Theo," he says.

"Maggie."

"Ugh, like my great-aunt," he thinks. *"She always smells like stale cigarette smoke. I hope I didn't just grimace at her."*

"And I'm Clara."

"You're gorgeous!" Theo thinks. *"You know, maybe I could forget about Isabel. I'll get Carson all set up with Maggie here, and I'll hook up with you and—"*

"That's my boyfriend your friend's about to dunk," Clara says.

"Oh. Too bad," he thinks.

So not only was there Isabel, but he also was more interested in Clara than me? It's a double blow, and it takes a huge effort for me not to let it completely ruin the happy memories I have of the day. I miss some of what happens next in the video. Theo talking about Carson.

Then he calls out, "Hey, Lockwood, pressure's on. All eyes on you!"

Like he's trying to redirect me toward Carson. By now, I understand that's what's happening, but it's still hard to believe.

"*Carson dunks the guy on the first try,*" Theo thinks, "*and Maggie's completely unimpressed. I don't know what else to do. I suck as a wingman.*"

I see myself lean toward Theo and twirl the end of my braid around my finger, making a total fool of myself.

"*Wait,*" Theo thinks. "*She's flirting with me. Carson needs to get over here now!*"

The view swerves between me and Carson, like Theo's eyes are darting back and forth. My dialogue murmurs in the background all jumbled, like he's only half listening. Super flattering.

"*Okay, new plan,*" he thinks. "*If he joins us, this will all work itself out.*"

"Do you want to walk around with us?" Theo asks me.

Wait, no. I sit up straight on my bed. That's not what happened the last time. "He did not say 'us.' He definitely said 'me,'" I say aloud.

"You heard what you wanted to hear," Grace says unemotionally.

The video has ended, and once again I can't rewind or replay any of it to check.

"Why can't I go back?"

"Because this is act two."

That again.

"Would you like to exit act two?"

"No!" I'm not finished yet. I haven't gotten what I came for. Maybe it's here, in this next scene about **CARSON'S DEPARTURE**.

That must be where Theo tells him after talking to me he's really interested in me now.

It's not the magical start we had on my end of the relationship, but there are always two sides to everything. No two people fall at the same time, right?

As soon as I click on the scene, though, it's clear I'm in Carson's view.

"She's obviously not into me, so I'll leave you to it," he says.

"What?" Theo replies. "Don't give up yet! Once she gets to know you, she'll totally like you."

"She doesn't even see me with you here," Carson thinks.

I cringe internally. He's right. I didn't see him that day.

"No. I can tell she likes you. Go have a good time!" Carson says and then thinks, *"You deserve it after the way Isabel ditched you. Cold. And I wouldn't know what to say anyway. Maggie seems really cool, but I'd just keep acting like an idiot and scare her away. You have a much better shot."*

"If you're sure. She is really nice."

"I'm sure," Carson says, thinking, *"Even though it sucks she never gave me a chance."*

The video ends.

Yikes. Now I feel bad for Carson. But I also don't appreciate being handed off like a consolation prize to Theo.

"If Carson liked me, what made him turn so awful after that?"

I don't expect an answer from Grace, but I get one anyway.

"Perhaps that's something you should ask him."

Not likely.

At least the Skee-Ball scene is bound to redeem Theo. That's where we laughed together and had such a great time. But when I click on it, the video is locked. The rest of them are too.

"Why can't I watch the rest of these?"

"They're not ready yet."

I toss my phone aside. "Of course they aren't."

No matter. I'll just have to work with the information I have so far.

37

I keep checking the app on Monday, but the rest of the scenes are still locked. It really sucks, because my conclusions from the scenes I *did* see are so upsetting. Like how my first impressions of Theo and Carson were so backward.

I saved that calendar entry because I was sure the day at the carnival was magical, not only for me but for Theo too. That I'd hear from him soon and it would be the "genesis" of something wonderful, just like the word of the day predicted.

And I was right. He texted to ask me out the next day.

I'm positive the reasons he fell for me are in the scenes I can't access yet. I just have to be patient.

I am not a patient person.

It doesn't help that I'm stuck at home, relying on my parents for everything, separated from my best friend by lies, and mad at Adam (which I guess isn't unusual). It's making me grouchy, and I'm sorry for putting that on Mom and Dad.

Adam can deal.

On Tuesday, Mom urges me to try to do some of the homework piling up in my OnCampus account, but I can't get my brain to focus. Since I can't tell her about the app, I blame it on the pain pills, which doesn't go over well.

"Maybe we need to start weaning you off them then," she says.

Not wanting to encourage that line of thought, I pretend to do more work. It's a long, boring day. She does let me watch a movie in the afternoon, so at least that interrupts the boredom.

I check in with Riley. She replies during lunch and tells me rehearsals are going well, although she's nervous. I remind her that Idina Menzel says, "Nerves are good. They keep you alive."

I spend about an hour practicing our end-of-year concert music (it feels great to sing), then send encouraging messages to Alexis, Hailey, and the rest of the Future Stars who tried out for *Footloose*. They had callbacks yesterday, but apparently the director was super stoic and didn't give any hints how he was leaning on casting. The only person who responds is Tyrone, who's homeschooled. We chat until my doorbell rings twenty minutes after school lets out.

I'm afraid Rayna's come to plead her case again, but it's Clara. She sweeps into the room in a cloud of citrus. She always smells like she's just squeezed a bowl full of lemons to make fresh lemonade. Wouldn't surprise me if she had.

"You look great," she says with a hint of surprise.

"Gee, thanks," I say wryly. I actually put on something other than an old T-shirt this morning, plus applied mascara. I felt like I'd been a total slob the past few days. I wonder what Riley said at school when people asked how I looked. Like I belonged in bed with a bowl of chicken soup? I was so focused on avoiding Rayna I didn't even consider what I was wearing when Riley showed up.

Clara rolls her eyes. "You know what I mean." She peers at my arms. "Although, why do you have bruises there?"

"Oh." I hardly notice those, but I guess they do look pretty bad. I point to the one on my right forearm. "This one's from when I fell. And this other one"—I hold up my left wrist—"is from when they inserted the IV to put me under for surgery. I just bruise easily."

"Yikes." She points at my still-purple toes. "Those look weird too."

"Thanks," I say sardonically. "You haven't come to give me details about how Katelyn's all over Theo, have you?"

Clara looks genuinely surprised. "Why would I do that?"

Sometimes I don't understand how Clara survives in our high school.

"Never mind." Except . . . I might not be able to access additional scenes on the app, so maybe Clara can help me get more intel from the real world.

"Can I borrow your phone?"

"Why?" she asks with a pointed look at mine.

"There's something I want to check."

"You're going to cyberstalk Theo," she says disapprovingly.

"Come on, Clara. There's just something I need to know. I'm not planning to click on anything, but it's still safer to use your phone, just in case my thumb slips."

She stares at me for a long moment before handing it over. "I do not condone this behavior. It's unhealthy."

"Got it."

She scoots in closer as I pull up his feed. The first thing I see is a picture of him with Katelyn, a selfie outside school. She has one arm wrapped around his neck, and she's making a duck face at the camera with her cheek pressed against his.

"He doesn't look very happy with her, does he?"

"Not really," Clara agrees reluctantly.

My thumb hovers over his profile photo, and Clara grabs my wrist. "Do *not* click on his story. What if Katelyn gets a hold of his phone? No matter what, she'll suspect I'm spying for you."

I shudder. "That would be so humiliating."

I scroll through more pics of him with Katelyn, mixed with his usual photos of golf, goofing off at the movie theater, and Therese. I pause at one of him with five tall, empty, cream-coated glasses in front of him. "Looks like he did another disgusting food challenge."

He watched some show when he was little where this guy went around eating the biggest hamburgers or troughs of ice cream or whatever, and he decided to find all of those he could within a fifty-mile radius and post about them. I only went along once. It is *not* attractive watching your boyfriend down a softball-size meatball and a pound of pasta in one sitting.

"Are those milkshakes?" Clara asks with her lip curled.

"They *were*." I notice Katelyn isn't cheering him on. I bet Carson was there. He probably took the pictures.

"Gross." She considers me. "What are you looking for anyway?"

I don't answer, because I've reached the photos of us. Does he look happier with me than Katelyn? I *think* so, but it's hard to tell. I don't really want to take a trip down memory lane, strolling past each moment together, so I scroll quickly through the past seven months until I get to the date we met. It's marked with a picture of him posing with Therese after her performance, and I suddenly realize I already did this research. The day after I met Theo, after we followed each other (both our accounts are private), I did a deep dive on his social media and didn't see pictures of him with a girl other than Therese for several months back.

"Nothing I'll find in his pictures."

I click on his profile and then his followers list.

"Maggie . . ."

I ignore Clara's warning. Theo has more than four hundred followers, so it takes a while to scan through them. Of course a lot of them don't use their actual names, but I don't find anyone named Isabel.

I switch to the list of who he's following. About halfway through, I gasp.

"What?" Clara leans closer.

Isabel Velez. Her profile photo is from a distance, of her standing on the beach with her arms spread wide, so I can't really tell what she looks like. I click on her name, but it's a no-go. She has her profile set to private.

"Who's Isabel?"

"A figment of my imagination." I close out of the app and return the phone to Clara. "Or so I hoped."

Even with the Best Day app sitting on my phone, I was holding on to the possibility Isabel didn't exist. That not everything I'd seen was true.

I turn to Clara. "Can I ask you something?"

She sits cross-legged on the couch beside me. In her checkered romper, she looks like a five-year-old. "Ask away."

"Do you remember Bridgeport Days last year? When David was in the dunk tank?"

She doesn't even blink at my abrupt subject change. "Wasn't that the day you met Theo?"

I nod. "This is gonna sound weird, but . . . do you remember what Theo was like that day?"

She frowns. "What do you mean?"

"Like . . . I was in a total daze because I was so into him, but did he seem the same way about me?"

"Welll . . ." She pulls her upper lip behind her bottom teeth. "It kinda seemed more like . . . Well, I'm not sure you really want to hear this. Why are you asking about that day?"

I can't tell her about the app. It's just too unbelievable. Grace didn't expressly tell me I had to keep it a secret. But when I was in the simulation the first time, she said telling Mom would invalidate it. I don't want to lose the chance to unlock the rest of the backstage passes. So I scramble for a believable explanation. "Something Theo said during the breakup that didn't make sense to me but has been sticking in the back of my mind ever since. I just can't let it go."

"Okay, then." She nods, like she's psyching herself up. "That day, my first impression of watching you interact with Theo"—oh my goodness, she always stalls with too many words to put off bad news—"was that he kept trying to redirect your attention to Carson."

An uncomfortable buzz that has nothing to do with foot pain or the meds spreads through my body, humming under my skin.

I got the whole day wrong!

Clara reaches out to squeeze my fingers. "Are you okay? You went all pale."

"Pain," I choke out. Just not in my foot.

"I'm so sorry. Can I get you anything?" She stands. "An ice pack? Some water?"

"Water would be great. It's kind of hard for me to carry anything with these crutches." It'll also give me a minute to compose myself.

Clara's been in my house enough that she doesn't need instructions on where to find anything. By the time she returns, I'm steadier.

"So you thought that Carson liked me and Theo was acting as his wingman."

"Yes," she says cautiously. "But after that day, I never saw any sign of that again—on either guy's part. Carson was so standoffish, and Theo *was* into you."

Exactly. They switched roles after that day.

"But . . . didn't you say Carson helped you when you broke your foot? And sent you balloons?"

I *did* say that. But not to Clara. I tilt my head. "Did Rayna tell you that?"

Clara blushes. "She might have. Speaking of—"

I don't want to talk about Rayna. "What's your point about Carson?"

She twists her lips at how I avoid discussing Rayna but doesn't press me—for now. "Maybe he still cares."

"I hope not." I love Theo. I want him back. Carson is not the hero in my story.

"He's not all bad, Maggie."

I grin. "So says the girl who finds the good in everyone."

"But he actually has done some good," she says earnestly. "Just like—"

"Please don't." My smile drops. "I know where you're going with this, and I'm not ready."

She sighs. "What happens when you come back to school? You and Rayna are both my friends. I don't agree with what she did, but I'm not taking sides."

"I don't expect you to." That would be impossible for Clara. She's way too forgiving. "You can be like Switzerland."

She narrows her eyes. "Then you'd better supply me with some good chocolate."

"Noted."

·✦ .✦ .✦ ✦.

I may not agree with Clara about Rayna, but maybe she has a point about Carson. He made a nice gesture, sending me balloons, and I banished them to another room. Not that *he* knows that. All he knows is I didn't respond. For four days now.

I guess it would only be polite to thank him for the balloons, as much as it galls me. I locate his profile—I never followed him—and open a private message. What to say . . . Best to keep it simple.

Thank you for the balloons.

My thumb hovers over the Send icon. I feel like I'm opening a whole can of worms here, voluntarily engaging in conversation with Carson. Should I also thank him for helping me the day I broke my foot? Or even—I squirm—apologize for being so rude when he did?

I can't bring myself to take it that far. This is enough for now.

At least I can be sure act two won't show me anything else about Carson since he left Bridgeport Days. But I hate how confused this has left me.

He liked me when we first met. And he's been nice since Theo dumped me.

What is that?

I just need to unlock the rest of those scenes so things will go back to normal, with Carson acting like his typical jerky self and Theo by my side.

I open the app and send Grace a message. When can I get access to those final backstage passes? Can you put a rush on them or something?

I wait for a response, but there's nothing.

Of course.

38

At breakfast the next morning, I wait until my parents are both seated, then present my proposal. "I finally slept six hours straight last night, so I think we should discuss returning to school."

Mom and Dad share a look that doesn't bode well for me. "How much medicine did you take?"

"Um." I didn't realize that was a factor. "One before bed."

Dad raises an eyebrow. "And then?"

"Two at one a.m."

He nods as if I've confirmed his suspicions. "We're not sending you back to school until you're off the pain medication."

Yesterday I would have cried at the thought of reducing the meds. But today I'm itching to go back.

"It's so boring here!" I moan. Plus, I can't implement my plan to win Theo back from here.

Adam waves his toast at me. "I'd switch places with you if I could. Remember when we got to do school from home?" He looks across the table dreamily.

Yes, I remember. How could anyone forget COVID-19 sweeping across the globe and confining us to our houses for months? We had to cancel basically everything. Of course Adam kept up his soccer training in the backyard, even when it was forty degrees outside.

"I'd do that all the time," he adds.

"Oh, you would?" I pick up a crutch. "Let me help you with that."

Dad takes the crutch from me. "We don't need two of you injured at the same time."

True. I wouldn't want to be stuck with Adam on the couch beside me.

"Fine. But I need that torture device back or I'll be stuck at this table all day."

I wait for Adam to say I could crawl to the couch. I left him the perfect opening, but when I glance his way, he's stuffed in a mouthful of toast. Weird. It's not like him to pass up insulting me. He couldn't have been trying to make me feel better about staying home?

Nah.

I catch another pointed look between Mom and Dad. I have no idea what it's about, but Dad gives the crutch back to me. For what it's worth.

.⁺ .⁺ .⁺ ⁺.

My pain has been a lot less today, not so low that I feel like I can go without the meds, but I did take a lower dose at lunchtime and it's been manageable. So maybe I'll be able to go back to school by the end of the week.

All's been quiet on the Rayna front, which is suspicious. I don't trust the fact that Adam's being nice—or at least not being obnoxious—and that she's not pestering me to forgive her. It leaves me with way too much to think about.

Like whether I should take some of the blame for them hiding from me. Which is just plain wrong.

When the end of the school day comes, my thoughts switch to *A Midsummer Night's Dream*. It's the final dress rehearsal, and I wish I were there with everyone else, getting into costume and makeup, waiting in the wings for my first cue. I look for posts about the rehearsal, but everyone seems to be obeying the no-phone rule. Which is good for the show but a total bummer for me.

Adam doesn't greet me when he gets home from soccer practice, heading straight to his room. Not that I want to talk to him. Mom's in the home office, working.

I run through my concert songs again, even though I have them memorized now. I'm so bored I pull up my homework and do that for a couple of hours, knocking out quite a bit. I never thought I'd actually enjoy math, but it's effective for passing the time.

I'm surprised to see it's already six o'clock. I wonder where Dad is. He's usually home by now.

Just as I have the thought, I see his SUV pulling into the driveway. Maybe he'll play a game with me or something.

I hear the door to the garage open, followed by a strange squeaking sound. A moment later, Dad turns the corner, but he's lower than usual, the top half of his body gliding instead of loping in his usual gait. He bobs up and down over the kitchen counters as he approaches.

"What are you—" I stop as he wheels—yes, wheels—out of the kitchen onto the carpet.

"Ta-da!" He stands, raising his arms like he's just completed a complicated dismount at the Olympics.

"You got me a scooter." I don't mean to say that like an accusation, but that's how it sounds even to me.

"I borrowed it," Dad says. "From a lady at work."

I shake my head. "You can take it back. I don't want a scooter."

"You're going to try it," Mom says with steel in her voice. I was so focused on that . . . thing . . . I didn't notice her entering the room. "For two reasons: we're tired of hearing you complain about the crutches, and it will be safer and easier for school."

"Sounds like three reasons."

"Maggie . . ." Mom's tone warns I'm in for serious consequences if I don't shut up.

I really don't think it will be safer for school. My foot's going to hang off the back of that thing. People will bump it. But it's clear I've used up all my sympathy points.

"Fine, I'll try it."

"Good," Mom says.

Dad wheels it closer. It's black, with a rectangular pad atop four wheels and a basket in the front. Dad parks it backward in front of the couch.

"You lock it like this." He demonstrates on the handlebars. "And you'll be able to carry your books in this basket!"

Like I'm an eight-year-old riding around on a bike. "Maybe we can add streamers," I say under my breath.

"What was that?" Mom asks sharply.

I scoot to the edge of the couch. "Just figuring out how to get on."

I swing my right leg over the scooter and place my left foot on the floor for leverage, then stand. I gingerly lift my right foot behind me and place my knee on the cushion. "I'm lopsided."

"I can fix that," Dad says eagerly. It's actually pretty sweet how excited he is.

I sit back on the couch while Dad adjusts the height of the cushion. Out of the corner of my eye, I see Adam leaning against the wall, smirking. I ignore him.

"All better," Dad says. "Give it a go."

I get back up on there and follow Dad's instructions to release the brake. I push forward. The scooter doesn't move very fast on the carpet, and it's a bit awkward figuring out how to turn, but it's actually . . . sort of nice.

"What do you think?" Dad asks.

I glance back at the crutches. Pretty sure my armpits are permanently bruised from those things.

I hate admitting I was wrong, especially when I made such a big deal about it.

"I need to try it on the tile." I push myself toward the kitchen, and when I pass onto the smoother surface, the scooter takes off. I haven't moved this fast since before I broke my foot! I engage the brake a moment before I crash into the opposite wall. I'm surprised to find I'm smiling, and then a laugh bubbles out.

It might be completely dorky, but it's sooo much better than those crutches. I maneuver around until I'm facing my parents.

"This is . . . pretty great. Sorry I was a baby about it."

Dad strides forward. "I'm just glad it makes things easier on you. And it's fun too, huh?"

I'm not taking it that far. "Am I going to find you riding this around the house when I need it?"

Dad casts his eyes around the kitchen. "Who, me?"

"I'll take that as a yes."

But also, this scooter is another step toward returning to school.

39

At lunch the following day, I launch Operation Escape the House.

"I really appreciate everything you've done for me, Mom. Working from home so you can take care of me. Making my favorite foods. Knowing I'd love the scooter even though I was sure I wouldn't." I lean across the table to squeeze her wrist, miscalculating and almost causing her to catapult a bite of salad at me. I recover, adding, "I'm just so grateful. You're amazing."

She sets down her fork. "What do you want?"

"Want?" I cover my heart with my hand. "Just to express my love and gratitude."

"Uh-huh." She stares at me until I can't stand it anymore.

"Okay, fine. I *am* grateful. But I'd really love it if you'd take me to opening night of *A Midsummer Night's Dream* so I can see my friends perform."

And see how Riley handles my role. I actually enjoyed helping her prepare. I'd like to see the results.

"Tonight?" Mom's tone already sounds like a denial.

"It's not like going to school, Mom." I clasp my hands together. "Please, I just want to get out of here for a while. And to see the play. They have handicap seats."

Unfortunately they're way in the back, but at least it will be something different than the couch or my bed.

She studies me for what seems like a full minute. "I'll talk to your dad. I have a meeting tonight."

I wiggle in my seat. "But if he can take me, you're okay with it?"

She finally cracks a smile. "Yes."

"Thank you thank you thank you!"

"Now that thanks I believe," she says.

⋅✦ ⋅✦ ⋅✦ ✦⋅

It's really hard getting dressed for the play. None of my skinny jeans fit over my bandage, a challenge I didn't anticipate since I've basically been wearing pajama pants for the past week. A skirt's not the best idea since I need to keep my foot propped up. Leggings will stretch over the bandage, so I pair them with a tank I bought from a vendor at last year's Shakespeare festival and a knee-length cardigan. They did *Twelfth Night* last summer, so the quote says, "Be not afraid of greatness. Some are born great, some achieve greatness, and others have greatness thrust upon 'em."

The final touch are my Vans—well, one, anyway. I'm stuck with the super-trendy surgical shoe on my right foot. I go all out with my hair and makeup. I'll get enough sympathy comments tonight without giving anyone reason to add that I look sickly on top of it.

My "date," on the other hand, does not make so much of an effort.

"You ready to go?" Dad's wearing khakis with *pleats*. He

must have had those for twenty years, but there's no use trying to fix him.

"Please."

The most challenging part of leaving is maneuvering down the stairs into the garage. Our house is all one level, so I haven't had to worry about that while rolling from room to room. Dad ends up carrying the scooter down the three steps and holding my arm while I hop, but he forgets to put the brake on, so the scooter rolls away, and he has to chase it to the driveway. I'm left balancing on one foot with my hand braced awkwardly against the doorframe behind me, but it's so funny I don't care. I'm gasping by the time he returns with the scooter.

He smiles sheepishly. "Lesson learned."

"Good thing our driveway doesn't go downhill."

His eyes pop like he just got a fantastic idea. "Can you imagine if you took this thing to the Muny?"

"Oh my gosh, no!" The Muny is a massive outdoor theater we love to attend in the summer. But it would be awful with a scooter because it's on like a forty-five-degree incline. "Let's just stick with the school theater."

The drive to school is uneventful. I'm so happy to be out of the house I'm tempted to open the window and stick my head out like a puppy, but it's a bit cool for that.

Clara and David are waiting for us at the front door when we make our way up the handicap ramp.

"You're here!" Clara says as she wraps me in a citrus-scented hug.

"Looking good, Maggie," David says easily.

"Thanks for coming." I motion behind me. "You guys know my chauffeur?"

"At your service." Dad sweeps a bow, and I smirk, pleased he's playing along.

"Hi, Mr. Scott," Clara says. "Have you met David before?"

"I believe so." Dad shakes his hand anyway, and we're all a cozy group.

"Can I try your scooter?" David asks. "You know, when you're sitting down."

"I guess." I don't bother saying it's not a toy.

Clara breaks away from David to walk beside me. "Are you going backstage?"

Backstage! Why are those other passes still locked? But she means *literal* backstage.

We're here early enough for me to go visit, but it doesn't seem right. "I don't want to distract them. Or make Riley nervous."

"Did you tell her you were coming?"

"Not for sure. I didn't know I was until today. I've been under house arrest." I frown at Dad's back, but it's wasted. He's too busy chatting with David and now holding the door open for me.

"I noticed you didn't post anything about it, and usually you're all over social about shows," Clara observes.

Because I want people to come. Or show up where I am. And I do still want people to come see this one, but at the same time, I want to keep my presence low-key since it's my first time out. What if my foot starts aching unbearably in the middle and I have to leave? Or my presence throws the cast off? It *shouldn't*, but actors are awfully superstitious.

We chat with some other friends outside the theater until I'm tired of half standing, half kneeling and we make our way inside. As there's extra room in front of the handicap seat, Dad arranges the scooter so I can prop my foot on the cushion.

"If you're okay, I'm gonna run to the bathroom," Dad says.

"I'm fine." I wave him away.

Felix, the assistant student director, whips by me talking into his headset and does a double take. "Maggie?"

"Hi, Felix." So much for keeping a low profile. "Everything all set?"

"I—it's—we all miss you."

He has a million last-minute things to do before the show starts. I haven't been on his side of the production, but I've benefited from his reminders and great organization. He shouldn't be talking to me.

"Miss you guys, too, but don't you have a show to run?"

He gulps, running a hand over his messy mop of blue-streaked dark brown hair. His usually ruddy cheeks are kind of chalky. "Yeah."

I lean toward him. "Can't wait. Just do me a favor and keep it quiet I'm up here, 'kay?"

He nods convulsively, looking at me but not really, like he sees through me.

I laugh. "Go! I'll talk to you after."

It's actually pretty fun to be on the outside of the craziness. Other people come up to say hi but nobody else from the show. Felix is the only one out here, checking the theater. The sound guys are up in the booth over my head.

A few minutes later, Dad walks back in, chatting with Katelyn's parents. *Please don't come over here*, I transmit. He motions to me, and they all glance my way. I smile and wave, hoping that will suffice. I sigh internally as they return the smile-wave and move down the steps toward seats about five rows from the front.

Dad joins me in the back row. "Not used to sitting up here. The view's pretty good."

I give him a skeptical look. "It'll do."

He pats my knee. "Well, I do like having you all to myself for once. We should do this more often. You're always so busy."

I hear him, but I'm distracted by Theo entering the theater with a huge bouquet of pink roses. It hurts to see him looking so handsome, holding flowers for another girl when he used to bring *me* flowers. Why couldn't he date someone somewhere else?

I will him to look up, because he really hasn't acknowledged my existence since he dumped me. I want him to see me, to remember why he fell for me. Why he chose me instead of that Isabel girl. Our first date is fresh in my mind, but it's not the only good time we had together. We dated for seven months. It's worth so much more than the way he's treated me these past couple of weeks, and I miss that Theo.

It doesn't matter, because he spots Katelyn's parents and moves to sit with them.

Dad clears his throat. "Do you want to talk about it?"

With Dad? "Uh, no."

He acts all affronted. "I can do feelings."

"You do not want to go there. Believe me."

David and Clara come in, saving me from further probing. They file into the row ahead of us.

"See anyone interesting?" I ask.

Clara glances down at Theo. "Nah."

David peers at the program. "So what's this about anyway?"

"Mischievous fairies, a love quadrangle, a man who gets turned into an ass—you'll love it." I fill the rest of the time until curtain giving him a rundown of the story. When the lights finally dim, I settle into my chair more firmly, waiting to be transported.

.✦ .✦ .✦ ✦.

It's opening night, so there are a few minor issues, like Bottom missing a prop and Hippolyta's wig sliding sideways, but overall it's a great first show. It will get better each night, and I'm sad I won't be able to come to every one, but for the past forty-five minutes my foot has been throbbing. I've been dying for an ice pack. Really wish we'd thought to bring one.

The cast makes a final bow and heads backstage. I can imagine their exhilaration right now. They got through the first show successfully. Nobody fell off the stage or forgot what they were saying in the middle of a monologue—both things I've seen happen.

Clara leans over the seat ahead of me. "Are you okay?"

I bob my head back and forth. "Eh. I'll make it." I lower my foot to the floor and readjust so I can stand and get into proper position on the scooter. Blood rushes to my head, and Dad grabs my arm to steady me.

"Not too fast there," he cautions.

I take a few deep breaths and think about the most gracious character I can. Glinda is pretty good at faking her way through life, so I channel her, lifting my chest high and smiling.

"Wow," David says. "How'd you do that?"

"It's called acting," I tell him, still giving it my all. "And I need to keep this up until I get to the car so no one gets the idea I have sour grapes about not being in the show *or* that I'm judging their performances."

"Well, I'm impressed. Lead on," David says.

The theater has mostly cleared out by now. I head for the exit, ignoring my throbbing foot, signaling Dad to give me space. By the time we reach the lobby, the cast has spilled out from backstage. The first person to spot me is Riley. She breaks away from her parents to run over and hug me.

"You're here! How was it? Did I do all right? Not as good as you would have, but hopefully I didn't mess it up too bad."

I smile warmly. "You were great, Riley. I'm so proud of you."

I really mean it. She played the part differently than I would have, but I liked her unique take on it.

"That means so much to me!" She claps her hands together. "Could we take a pic together?"

"Of course. Dad, can you get one with mine too?"

Dad takes pictures, complete with the scooter in the background. It can't be helped.

For the next twenty minutes, other cast members commiserate with me, ask if I have any tips for the next performance, and just generally catch up. I don't let up on my smile, even when I see Katelyn watching me from across the room.

When there's a break in conversation, I make my way over to Mrs. Pintado to compliment her on the show.

"Thank you for helping Riley prepare," she says. "She told me what you did, and I could really see the improvement after her session with you."

"Oh, well, I just wanted the show to succeed." I didn't mean for Riley to tell everyone about it.

Mrs. Pintado is pensive. "You may have a knack for more than just acting. While you're sidelined, you might consider doing some coaching. Or even directing."

I prefer to be on the stage, but it was fun helping Riley and seeing the results. "It won't take *that* long for my foot to heal, but what would that look like?"

"I have a few ideas," she says. "We can discuss it later. There's someone else who wants to speak with you, I believe."

An odd note in her voice makes my stomach clench as I awkwardly turn the scooter.

Katelyn. Clutching her bouquet to her chest like a cuddly teddy bear. I hope she gets pricked by a thorn.

"Maggie, it's so good to see you," she says in a sickeningly sweet voice.

Because we never outright acknowledge our enmity.

I find my Glinda smile again. "Great job tonight, Katelyn."

Once again, a true statement. She made a fantastic Hermia. In fact, she was probably the best actor on the stage.

Since I wasn't there.

"Guess what?" Katelyn readjusts her bouquet so the plastic crinkles and I catch a whiff of the roses.

I refuse to say, "You're dating Theo?"

I can't imagine that's what she's going for anyway. It's not news anymore. She must have something else to share that she hopes will be especially tortuous.

When our overly polite staring contest reaches the point where my cheeks hurt, I give in. "What, Katelyn?"

She dances in place. "I got the part of Wendy Jo in *Footloose*!"

Zing! It's like one of those thorns ejected straight from the bouquet into my heart. She must've just found out, because I haven't heard from anyone else in the troupe yet. At least she didn't get Rusty.

I release my frozen smile to exclaim, "Wow, Katelyn, that's amazing! Congratulations!"

"Thanks!" She does another shimmy, and while it could be genuine excitement, there's a good chance she's emphasizing the fact I can't even shuffle my feet right now. "You'll come watch, won't you?"

Now that's just mean. "Wouldn't miss it."

Although if Alexis, Hailey, Tyrone, and the others are in it, I will.

Clara appears beside me. "There you are! Your dad says you need to get home." She turns to Katelyn. "Nice job tonight."

Clara ushers me away while Katelyn watches, beaming like we're all the best of friends. I can't get away from her fast enough.

40

I'm exhausted and my foot is throbbing when we get in the car, but I'm anxious to check in with my troupe friends about the *Footloose* cast list.

Dad starts talking about the show, how much he enjoyed it. I listen to him and murmur appropriate responses, pulling out my phone. He won't mind if I send a couple of texts.

Except when I unlock the screen, I notice a new notification on the Best Day app. Grace finally replied!

I quickly open it, but there isn't a message in **DIRECTOR'S NOTES**. I switch to **BACKSTAGE PASS**. Most of the scenes still have lock symbols over them, except the very last one—**SCENE SIXTEEN: THE CAST LIST**.

That's strange. Why would it skip to that one? What about all the ones in between? The important scenes with Theo?

I glance over at Dad. We still have ten minutes left of the drive. He's watching the road . . .

"Hey, Dad, Alexis just sent me something to watch real quick. I'm going to put in my earbuds so it doesn't distract you while you're driving."

He waves a hand. "Oh, that won't bother me."

"Still."

I put in the earbuds and angle myself against the door so he can't see the screen if he glances over.

The video begins with someone walking up to our front door and going inside, where our parents are waiting. So this must be Adam. Ugh. My brother's head is the last place I want a look inside!

"I wish I could go straight to my room and text Rayna, but Mom was very specific," Adam thinks. *"I have to support Maggie in whatever part she got in her next musical. I don't even remember which one she's doing now. Because they never. End.*

"I'm surprised she wasn't chattering about it the whole way home, but she had a dopey look on her face when she got in the car, and then she ignored me as usual. Except for that weird moment when she asked about my tournament. Like she cares. I'm forced to go watch all of her shows, but she hasn't been to one of my soccer games in two years."

Oh.

I haven't? That doesn't seem right. I feel like I went to a game earlier this year . . . Wait, I might be getting my timelines mixed up. Last summer, when he's thinking about, it's possible I hadn't been to a game in a long time. Do Mom and Dad really have a double standard about that?

I refocus to find Mom and Dad have already asked me about the cast list.

"Maggie's still in a weird daze," Adam thinks. *"Maybe she didn't get in! That's not supposed to be possible, but if she totally bombed her audition, they might have made an exception. What would that be like? A few months without Maggie endlessly practicing songs and lines around the house. So quiet. So peaceful. Mom and Dad might show up to more of my games, like they used to when I was younger."*

"I haven't checked yet," video me says.

"What?" Adam says aloud. "I can't believe you weren't monitoring your email constantly for that announcement."

"I was busy," I say with a shrug.

And then Mom guesses about Theo.

"Huh," Adam thinks. *"Kind of figured Maggie was only capable of imaginary relationships. She's never had a real one before."*

"What?" I splutter.

When Dad looks over at me, I realize I said that out loud. I shake my head to indicate it's nothing.

But Adam's so wrong. I had boyfriends before Theo. Several. Adam met them. How can he not remember?

There was Aiden Yarrish in sixth grade. We were together for six months. He was my first kiss, even before I had a stage kiss, since they always skip those parts in middle school productions.

Nobody in seventh grade, but I went out with Jack Lincoln for a while in eighth and Gabe Garcia in ninth.

Adam has no idea what's going on in my life.

While I'm fuming about that, the scene rewinds, until it gets to Adam and me standing by the door. Huh. It's changed viewpoints. That happened once before, with Theo and Carson, but it never did this rewind thing.

The video zeroes in on my face.

"Please let Maggie be okay with this part," Mom thinks. *"She has her heart set on being the queen, and instead she's playing the comic relief. She's good at comedy, but it's hard to tell if that's what she really wants. I gave Yvonne my blessing for the casting, but I'm not sure it was right."*

Wait, what? Yvonne asked Mom's opinion before casting me as Oaken? What kind of crap is that? I can take whatever part I'm given and roll with it. Something is majorly wrong with this scenario.

On the screen, I say, "Okay. I can work with that."

"What is it? Who are you?" Mom says.

I guess we know where I got my acting abilities.

As I'm answering about being Oaken, Mom thinks, *"Oh, thank God. She's happy. We won't be dealing with dramatics the next few weeks. Maybe it's thanks to this boy. Whatever the reason, it's a good outcome."*

"Seriously?" I say.

"What are you watching over there?" Dad asks.

Just like before, I can't stop the replay. I really wish I hadn't started this in the car, because it isn't finished. To my horror, it does the thing where it switches views again, and now I'm watching through Dad's eyes.

No, not Dad too!

He sweeps forward to hug me.

"She really is happy," he thinks.

That's not too bad.

"Where should we go to celebrate?" he asks. "Did you already eat dinner at Bridgeport Days?"

"Nope. Can we go to Kitaro?"

"She picked Kitaro," he thinks. *"Our special place. But it's fine. It'll be a fun outing."*

The video ends.

I look up at Dad, who is smiling slightly as he turns into our driveway. I don't get it.

Is it a money thing? I know Kitaro's not cheap, but I've never heard any hint from my parents that we're hurting for money.

I mean, they talk to us about being responsible. We have chores and an allowance and we're supposed to save some of it (sometimes I'm not so great at that). They both have solid jobs—at least I think their jobs are solid. They haven't mentioned concerns about losing them. But I guess I also don't *ask* them about their jobs. Dad works in IT at a big insurance company. Mom works in marketing for a law firm. My eyes tend to gloss over when either of them discuss work. They both seem boringly steady, so I don't know why they'd care about one dinner out.

It didn't really sound like a money issue, though. He said something about it being *our* place . . .

"We're home!" Dad says cheerfully.

So that ends that. Except once again, the Best Day app has completely belied its name.

41

The next morning, I message my troupe friends about *Footloose* while getting ready. Tyrone replies first. He's Reverend Moore, which he'll totally rock.

Then I hear from Alexis. I got Rusty!

I'd be lying if I didn't admit it causes me a twinge, but I'm glad she got it if I couldn't. Yesssss! Can't wait to see you kick off your Sunday shoes!

She sends back an eye roll emoji. When are you coming back? Miss you!

Not sure. Dr appt today. More news soon!

She leaves me with a kiss emoji. I hear back from Elana and Hailey as I'm going out the door; they're both in the ensemble. I know that's gotta hurt Hailey especially.

As soon as Dad gets me in the car to head for my post-surgery checkup (Mom has a mandatory meeting at work, so Dad's my chauffeur again), I pull my phone back out to continue a message to Hailey: So sorry! Are you going to do the show or try for Hairspray?

The auditions for *Hairspray* are at the end of April. The rehearsals overlap, so she couldn't do both. It's also nearly an hour drive, which is why we were all trying out for *Footloose* instead.

I'm waiting for her response when Dad says, "It's our second outing in less than twelve hours, Maggie. That must be some kind of record."

It takes a moment for Dad's words to register, but when they do, I also notice his tone, how he says it like a joke but not really.

I wonder if I actually have been ignoring Dad. We haven't spent much one-on-one time together lately. It reminds me of that strange comment he made in the video. Without waiting to see how Hailey replies, I put my phone away.

"Maybe we could go to Kitaro afterward," I say, just to see how he reacts.

He glances over in surprise. "I wish we could, but I *do* have to work today. You remember when we used to go there every year for our father-daughter Valentine's date?"

We haven't done that in *years*. I think the last time I was twelve. Score another point for Grace.

"Sorry I flaked on that."

"It's okay." But I can tell it isn't.

"How about we go for Father's Day? Just you and me? When you won't have to cart me around anymore."

He grins. "Deal."

I wish all of Grace's cryptic revelations were so easy to solve. I'm itching to see what Hailey says about the auditions, but I focus on Dad the rest of the ride.

When we arrive at Dr. Rowland's office, they take more X-rays, and then they begin unwrapping the bandages. I'm anxious to see it, since I haven't been allowed to take off the bandages myself. When the final piece comes free, I gasp.

"It's disgusting!"

Dad cringes. "You definitely shouldn't go out for any foot modeling jobs."

My foot is a kaleidoscope of purple, blue, and pink, with ugly yellow overlaying it all. It extends all along the right side and across the top, almost to my toenails. Stitches stick out of the side of my foot, about halfway up. And across the top . . .

"Why is there marker on my foot?"

It's like an arrow, written in purple marker.

The nurse turns from where she was disposing of the dirty bandages. "To mark where to put in the screw."

Before I can reply to that encouraging thought, a South Asian man about ten years older than my dad comes in.

"Hi, Maggie," he says. "I'm Dr. Umrani, the other surgeon here in the practice. I'll be doing your checkup today."

"Hi." I forgot about Dr. Rowland's vacation, but I'm okay with the substitution. With salt-and-pepper hair and a close-cut beard, Dr. Umrani looks trustworthy and like he stepped off the same Hollywood set as Dr. Rowland. Except who would watch a show about feet?

"Thank you for seeing us, Dr. Umrani," Dad says.

The doctor nods. "I took a peek at your records, and everything looks great!"

We obviously have very different definitions of that word. "Um, have you seen my foot?"

He chuckles, as if I'm an oh-so-amusing child. "That's completely normal. I've examined your X-rays. The screw is perfectly placed. The bone is already starting to heal, and as long as you keep off it for the next week, you *might* be able to put weight on it by next Friday."

"Are you serious?" I find that hard to believe considering how awful my foot looks, but he's the expert. Maybe *I* could still try out for *Hairspray*. If so, my dance recital's definitely a go! "Dad? You hear that?"

I turn toward him, and it's like there's a big caution sign stamped across his face. "Now, Maggie, hold on. He said you might be able to put weight on it. Not that you could hop back into dance class."

Oh. I guess there's a difference.

I swivel back toward Dr. Umrani. He's now sitting on the wheeled stool, his elbows propped on his knees, ready to examine my foot. While his expression isn't quite so *Slow down, Maggie!* as Dad's, it also isn't screaming *Grab your jazz shoes!*

"I'm afraid your dad's right, Maggie. But you can talk about that with Dr. Rowland next week. Let's just take it one step at a time."

Was that a foot joke? Dad gurgles a bit, so he caught it, but Dr. Umrani's focused on prodding around my stitches and doesn't notice.

He obviously isn't going to commit to any promises about walking—or dancing—but maybe he'll give me something else to work with. "Can I go back to school?"

"I don't see why not." He looks up at us. "From a medical standpoint, you certainly can be out and about, assuming you have the energy to get through a day at school."

"I think I could manage," I say with a pointed look at Dad.

To my surprise, he doesn't argue. "We'll discuss it."

I guess that's something. I want to ask about Future Stars rehearsal too, but I need the school win first. Dr. Umrani pokes a few more spots and wraps my foot more loosely than before. It's amazing how much more comfortable that feels.

"A pleasure meeting you. Dr. Rowland will be back with you next week," he says.

"Can't wait!" If there's even the slightest possibility I'll be walking after I'm next in here, I'll be counting down the minutes.

42

I'm so happy about school Monday morning I sing "Back to School Again" from *Grease 2* while I get ready. Mom returned to work today too, but not without telling me ten thousand times to call her if I get too tired. I'm sure I'll be fine.

What doesn't feel fine is that I'm not prepared to face Theo. I'm still confused about the day we met. I don't understand why the rest of the scenes are still locked. I've peppered the app with requests for Grace to unlock them, and I haven't heard *anything*. Scenes eleven through fifteen are still unavailable. I really wanted to return to school armed with all the knowledge I needed to win him back. Instead all I have is the uncomfortable surety I wasn't his first *or* second choice.

I was Carson's.

When we pull into the parking lot, instead of driving straight to his spot, Adam stops at the curb. Before I have time to react, he hops out and retrieves the scooter from the trunk. I haven't even gathered my backpack by the time he opens the door, so he reaches in and plops it into the basket, checking the brake. "Here you go."

He steps back, like he's waiting for me to get out before he moves. He's not even tapping his foot or anything. Who *is* this guy? Because he's not the brother I've been living with for the past sixteen years.

He's been acting way too nice for days, but it's not enough for me to forgive him and Rayna and accept them as a couple. If he really cared about my feelings in the matter, he would have started being nice to me months ago.

I probably should thank him for dropping me off at the door, but the words catch in my throat. So I climb out and nod at him instead.

He nods back, and as he's closing my door, I see his eyes flicker toward the school, just for a moment.

Rayna's waiting by the door.

Two weeks ago, when I was hoofing it on crutches, he didn't feel the need to impress her by dropping me off, but now he does?

I push with my left foot and almost go headfirst over the handlebars since I forgot to take off the brake. I glance around, but no one except possibly Rayna seems to notice, and I don't care what she thinks.

I release the brake and push toward the handicap door. Of course Rayna's standing right beside the button to activate it.

"It's good to see you, Maggie," she says as I punch the button with extra force. It takes *forever* for the door to swing open toward me. I keep my eyes resolutely forward and my jaw locked. As soon as the opening's big enough for me to glide through, I move forward.

"You can't ignore me forever," Rayna says, keeping pace with me.

I open my mouth to respond that I sure can, then realize that will be proving her point and snap it closed.

She sighs heavily. "Fine. But I'm not giving up. Because friends stick with you, even when you're being way too stubborn and only hurting yourself."

She's putting this on *me* again? I speed up, but it doesn't matter because she's stopped. Probably waiting for Adam.

She's misunderstood another key point about friends: they don't *lie*.

Actually, it's more than a rule of friendship. It's a basic guideline they teach you everywhere from preschool to politics. I don't know why Rayna thinks she should get a free pass, but I'm not handing one out.

.✦ .✦ ✦ ✦.

By lunchtime, I'm exhausted. I have to concede that as bored as I was at home, taking one shower per day and sitting the rest of the time with my foot propped up wasn't really the best judge of my energy levels. How am I ever going to dance again?

Clara walks with me into the cafeteria, but she still has to go buy a lunch, so I'm on my own trying to find a path through the tables. Halfway there I spot the same issue I had this morning and wish I'd waited for Clara.

It can't be avoided. *She* can't be avoided.

I proceed to the table and sit at the far end, leaving a spot for Clara between me and Rayna.

"Hi, Maggie."

I ignore her and focus on the other two girls at our table. "Hi, Jada. Zoey."

Zoey looks between me and Rayna before finally saying, "Hi," with a question in her voice, her strawberry blond eyebrows halfway up her freckled forehead. Jada looks similarly confused.

Rayna clearly hasn't talked about our rift with anyone else. For the first time ever, I'm sorry Adam doesn't share my lunch period. At least if he were here, she could go sit with him.

Clara finally arrives and sits between us. "Hey, girls. Check out this new pasta salad. It actually looks decent."

I glance at her tray. "I don't know. I've always thought it's weird to put dressing on pasta. Some things aren't meant to go together."

"Oh, really?" Rayna challenges, setting down her sandwich. "Maybe the issue is that Maggie hasn't given pasta and dressing a chance. Maybe they go together perfectly. Maybe they're way better together than, say, peanut butter and honey ever were."

She eyes my tortilla combatively, but we both know she isn't talking about my lunch. Even though the cafeteria around us continues with its usual din, it's dead silent at our table. Jada and Zoey watch us with wide eyes. Nobody takes a bite, waiting to see what we'll say next.

"Clara"—I hold up my wrap—"do you think I'm supposed to be the peanut butter or the honey in this scenario? Because Theo sure hasn't been sweet lately."

I look in his direction, and sure enough, there's Katelyn, her chair scooted right up next to his. Carson doesn't look any more thrilled with Katelyn than he was with me.

Rayna taps her fingers on the table. "At least he doesn't cause anyone to go into anaphylactic—"

"You're definitely the honey!" Clara chimes in.

"Sticky either way," Rayna mutters.

What is that supposed to mean? I suppose it has something to do with her comment this morning, about sticking with me, although it seems like she's getting her metaphors mixed up. It definitely doesn't feel like she's trying to support me right now.

"So." Clara clears her throat. "It's great to have Maggie—"

"That's nice of you, Clara, but I still don't see how you can eat that. Those two things are fine on their own. I mean, I'd eat an all-noodle diet if carbs didn't turn straight into sugar. But why would you put Italian dressing on noodles? It just doesn't make sense. The two are from different worlds: pasta"—I hold out one hand then the other as if weighing two options—"and salad."

Rayna glares at me. "She can eat it because she's willing to try new things. To see how they might go together and create something new that's really great. Maybe if you weren't so stubborn you'd like it too."

"What are they talking about?" Jada whispers to Zoey.

"I'm not sure," Zoey whispers back. "Except it sounds like Rayna's either pasta or dressing."

"She definitely is," I say, not bothering to pretend I don't hear them. "She's that kind of pasta." I point at the rotini noodles, which look like corkscrews. "All twisted up. And the dressing is my brother, who has apparently been all over her for months."

"Oh!" Jada makes an *I'm not getting in the middle of this* grimace. Wise choice.

I throw my uneaten food in my lunch bag and toss it into my scooter basket. "You know what? I've lost my appetite."

"I'm so sorry." Rayna stands. "Be sure to watch your step, *honey*."

I gasp as she storms off. She totally stole my dramatic exit. *With* a zingy one-liner.

43

By last period, news of my brother and Rayna has spread throughout the school. Instead of asking me how I am, everyone's asking if it's true my best friend and brother are dating.

I'm kind of shocked they didn't just tell the world once I knew. Rayna seemed pretty angry at lunch, but I didn't think it had to do with me outing their relationship. I'm not about to ask her now.

When the final bell rings, I'm so ready to just go home and take a nap. I'm not in any hurry to reach the exit. I expect Rayna to have staked it out again.

But when I get there, the only person waiting is Adam, and he's not wearing the friendly face he's had on the last several days. I'm surprised to find myself disappointed.

I roll to a stop and wait for him to explode. It doesn't take long.

"Pasta salad? You compared my relationship with Rayna to pasta salad?" His voice ticks up, and two passing juniors snicker.

I click my tongue. "All I did was make an observation about it being a weird dish. Rayna's technically the one who started comparing everyone to food."

"Really?" He crosses his arms. "You're going with 'she started it'? Because you won't win, Mags."

According to whom? "I think it depends on what the prize is."

"Why?" He throws his hands up. "Why are you so against us being together?"

I can't believe he doesn't already know the answer. But he appears genuinely confused. Boys are such idiots sometimes.

"Because you are the biggest jerk in the world. And you've treated me like crap for *years*." He doesn't flinch or show any surprise at this accusation, so I continue. "Why would I want my best friend to be with someone who treats me that way? Or expect you to behave any differently toward her? And why would she"—my voice breaks—"want to be with someone who's always made my life hell?"

By the end of my speech, Adam has his mouth covered with his hand.

It's into this awkward moment that Carson steps.

"Maggie! It's so great to see you back. How are you . . . ?" His last word trails off as he finally catches onto the palpable tension between me and Adam.

"Uh, sorry," he says, backing away.

It's funny. I never thought Carson would save me from anything, and he's done it twice.

"No, it's fine." Because I've said my piece, and Carson's interruption reminds me we're in the middle of a school hallway. He obviously wasn't paying attention to our argument, but others could. I have enough gossip going around about me without adding in our family feud.

Carson stops moving away and looks uncertainly between us.

"It's not fine," Adam spits. He leans toward me. "You have no idea what my life is like," he says in a low voice. "Everything isn't always about you."

Why does everyone keep saying that? It seems like how he treats me *is* about me.

Adam straightens and fixes a steady stare on Carson. "Can you take her home?"

"Uh . . ." He looks back at me, probably wondering if I'll accept a ride from him. Considering my alternatives are riding with Adam or six miles home on the scooter, I shrug.

"Sure," he says.

"Good. I'll be home later." Adam turns away like I've offended *him*. I watch him stride off, trying to figure out how that encounter turned into yet another thing that's somehow my fault. Rayna and Adam seem to think everything is.

Carson clears his throat. "So . . . are you ready to go?"

I refocus on Carson, who doesn't seem very comfortable with agreeing to drive me. "If you have somewhere to be, I can get another ride."

Calling Mom or Dad is out of the question because I'm definitely not making the Adam situation worse. Clara doesn't have a car, but some of my school theater friends do, and since the play ended, they don't have rehearsal.

"It's all good. I have golf practice, but I can drop you on the way."

"That can't possibly be on your way." I pull out my phone. "I'll find—"

Carson places his hand over mine, and it surprises me so much I stop scrolling through my contacts. "Maggie, seriously, let me help you. I promise you won't make me late."

I stare at his hand, still over mine, and he drops it. "If you're really sure."

"I am. Come on."

He leads the way outside, and now I don't know what to say. He's being nice again, and instead of the past seven months, which should be more recent for me, I'm remembering what seems like our last few interactions. Carson humming after he met me. Trying to impress me at the dunk tank. Putting Theo before himself. And how he helped me when I broke my foot.

"I never thanked you before. I should have."

He glances at me, surprised. "But you did. You sent me a message?"

I don't know what he's talking about for a second, and then it registers. "Not for the *balloons*. For helping me that day. I wasn't very nice to you."

"Oh. Well." He shrugs. "You were in pain."

It's a nice out, but it has nothing to do with why I blew him off. "I should have thanked you then. So I'm doing it now. Thank you."

We've reached his car, an older SUV. He tosses his keys between his hands as he considers me. "You're welcome."

I appreciate how he leaves it at that. Maybe because neither of us have treated the other very well in the past.

He opens the passenger door and waits until I'm inside before taking away the scooter. He lifts it right off the ground like it weighs nothing. I watch in the mirrors as he carries it to the back and shifts around golf clubs and other equipment to make room.

He slams the hatch shut, and I quickly turn my eyes forward as he slides in beside me. "Do you need my address?"

Carson turns the key in the ignition. "Nope. I know where you live."

Of course he does. He sent me balloons. "Right. I'm just tired."

"I bet. Is it hurting?" He nods at my foot as he pulls out of the parking lot.

"Just throbbing a bit." I lay my head back and my eyes drift closed, even though there are things I'd like to ask Carson, mostly about Theo. It just doesn't seem the right time for it. He lets me rest, and the ride isn't long anyway. He pulls into my driveway ten minutes later and brings my scooter around.

"Thanks." I push myself up out of the car, but as I'm shifting my hand to the scooter, I lose my balance and my foot goes over the side of it. I land hard on my foot, putting all my weight on it. I cry out, and Carson grabs me around the waist. I lean into him, taking in a huge gulp of air.

"Are you okay? Does it hurt?"

His arm is warm around my middle; I feel that more than my foot, which is odd. Shouldn't there be pain shooting up my foot? I'm not supposed to put any weight on it, and I just *fell* on it.

What if I reinjured it? What if I knocked the screw loose? What if I just put my recovery back by weeks?

My breath comes in shorter gasps, and tears prick my eyes.

"Hey." Carson's arm tightens around me as he shifts, carefully turning so he can see my face. "Was it that bad, putting weight on it?"

He looks so concerned, so not the Carson I know. It feels strange to confide in him, but also right in this moment.

I wipe away a tear. "No. But Dr. Rowland was so firm about not putting weight on it, and I've been so careful. Not even a

224

second for balance—until now. And it was only a moment, but I landed with *force*, like I jumped onto it."

Carson lifts his free hand, and I think he's about to touch my cheek or brush my hair back; I'm not sure how I feel about that. He still has his arm tight around my waist, and I'm surprised by how *not* uncomfortable that is. But he doesn't touch me; he waves his hand awkwardly. "I'm sure this happens to everyone at some point. It was an accident."

He's probably right. I inhale and a sense of calm slides through me. "I think I'm okay now."

"Good."

But it still takes him a few extra beats to release me. Once he does, the band around my waist where his arm had been feels cool. Repositioned on the scooter, I push toward the front door, with Carson beside me.

"Are you going to need a ride tomorrow?" he asks.

Adam. Or Carson.

"Yes, I think I will."

Except I have no idea what it means that for the past five minutes, I completely forgot about Theo. Or that I didn't want Carson to let me go.

44

Adam may have had a point about staying home from school. One day back, and I'm exhausted. *Plus*, I still have homework. How am I going to add Future Stars into the mix if it's this hard? At least I have the *Into the Woods* soundtrack to keep me company while I do my trig.

But trig is so boring . . .

I pick up my phone to distract myself, but the first thing I notice is a new notification on the Best Day app. Yes! My messages to Grace paid off!

This means I can finally get the information I need about Theo and put all this confusion about Carson behind me.

I grab my earbuds, because even though people are *supposed* to knock before they come into my room, it doesn't always happen. Especially since my surgery.

I open the app, and the Skee-Ball scene is available in **BACKSTAGE PASS**. *That's* what I've been waiting for.

I click on it, but it's blank. "What?"

I return to the menu and select **SCENE ELEVEN: SKEE-BALL** again. Still blank.

"Grace? Where's the Skee-Ball backstage pass?"

"I apologize," she says. "That one's corrupted. We've been

trying to recover it for the past week. But the rest are now available."

I moan. "That sucks!"

But it's okay. There's still the improv show. We had fun there too.

I'm taken aback when the video starts with a view of me walking away. It looks like this is *before* the improv show, when I left to use the bathroom and Theo stayed at our seats. His thoughts start right in.

"Hmm. Her legs seem longer than they should be based on her height, so smooth and tight. Probably from dancing."

I grimace. I thought I'd want to hear Theo's thoughts about my appearance, but that's kind of icky. Makes me reexamine how Clara and I were looking at Fireman Curmitoz too. I'd rather hear Theo reflecting on that moment at the end of Skee-Ball or something we'd laughed about.

Video me glances back at Theo, and his hand enters the camera in a lazy wave.

"The day hasn't turned out so bad," his thoughts continue. *"Therese was adorable in her show, and Maggie's totally hooked. It's too bad she wasn't into Carson, but it was obvious he wasn't getting anywhere with her, so someone might as well. She's not as hot as Isabel, but she's a decent substitute."*

"A decent substitute?" I nearly shout, then cover my mouth with my hand. I don't want Mom running into the room. "A decent substitute?" I echo more quietly.

Also, I'm starting to actually feel bad for Carson. Which is awkward, since I'm the cause of it.

"Usually it's no big deal tuning out my phone," Theo thinks, *"but*

today has been excruciating! Now that Maggie's in the bathroom—which will take way longer than it should—I can finally check it."

The view turns down to his phone, and the first notification on his lock screen makes him half rise out of his seat and look from side to side. Almost like he's making sure I haven't returned.

Easy enough to see why.

"Isabel," he thinks in a voice that's almost reverent.

Ugh.

"Stupid," he thinks. *"It's only a message. She didn't show up like she was supposed to."*

Theo settles back into his seat, then unlocks the phone. His thumb visibly shakes as he opens the message.

This is all wrong! I'm in the bathroom. We just had the most amazing time at Skee-Ball, where he had me practically begging for a kiss, and he's trembling over another girl!

Sorry I couldn't make it, the text says.

"That's it?" Theo thinks incredulously. *"No explanation. Not even a sad emoji. What does that mean?"*

Theo types, Where are you?

"Too needy," he thinks and deletes it.

Are you okay?

"No, that also comes across the wrong way," he thinks. He starts three more responses before he finally writes, No big deal. Catch you later?

The screen stays frozen on the text for a solid minute. It's agonizing. Who knew boys stressed just as much about finding the right words? But I don't feel too sorry for him, as the view tips up, catches me returning, and Theo finally clicks the arrow.

He tucks the phone out of view as I reach the end of the row, and the video ends.

There's a lump in my throat when I ask, "Is there no memory of that day worth saving? Did he ever want *me*?"

"From my understanding, you were with him for seven months. This is just one day."

"And you're ruining it!" Tears prick my eyes.

It wasn't a magical day at all. If it wouldn't be so much effort, I'd go rip the August 6 calendar entry off the wall right now.

"Are you finished, Maggie?" Grace asks gently.

Am I? After he said I was a "decent substitute"? It certainly doesn't make me want to win him back anymore! He's like that giant unicorn we gave away to the little girl at the carnival—better in someone else's hands. Katelyn is welcome to him.

But I also can't stop myself from watching the other backstage passes. I have to get the full picture.

"No. You're not going away again until I've seen the rest."

"Fair enough."

Nothing about this is fair, but I'm all in now.

45

I may be all in, but the app is still glitchy. There's nothing during the actual improv show or on the bear ride. I knew Theo was playing me then, but it was adorable.

The next video is the Ferris wheel. I brace myself to have that memory ruined too.

It starts by the game concourse.

"It's been cool hanging with her today," Theo thinks as he looks down at me. *"I wouldn't mind seeing her again. But I've gotta bail for now. I've counted four notifications on my phone, and at least one of them has to be Isabel. What if she said she's on her way to the carnival and she sees me with Maggie?"*

Gross.

The view drifts toward the Ferris wheel, which has a long line. "Do you want to wait?" Theo asks aloud.

"I *love* the Ferris wheel."

"She looks so excited about it I don't want to disappoint her," he thinks. *"But I have to check my phone first."*

Then he proceeds to give me the line about seeing if there's an emergency at home.

I don't need his excited thoughts about Isabel texting. I can see it. Same time, same place tomorrow?

"*Yes, yes, yes! Still in the game!*" he thinks.

The screen shifts to me. I've turned away to give him privacy while he checks on his "family."

Works for me. See ya then, he replies.

"*Isabel didn't ditch me!*" he thinks. "*At least not forever. She must have had a good reason for not making it today, which she'll explain tomorrow. Now I can hang with Maggie as long as she wants.*

"*It's not like I made any sort of commitment to Isabel. Maggie's here, and she's obviously into me. Why shouldn't I enjoy that? Even after today, maybe I could see Maggie and Isabel. At least until I decide which one is better.*

"*I do feel bad about Carson, though. Especially if Isabel's still in the picture. But Maggie made it clear earlier she didn't want anything to do with Carson, so it's not really a guy code violation.*"

The camera follows us into the gondola, and I am *seething* at these revelations. On my behalf. On Isabel's. On Carson's. How did I not see this side of Theo?

We settle into the gondola, and Theo surveys the surroundings. He thinks, "*This Ferris wheel was an excellent idea after all. The sides and canopy actually provide a decent amount of privacy.*"

The view stays focused on me the entire ride to the top. I guess that's something.

When the gondola stops at the top to reload more cars at the bottom, Theo peeks out—to make sure no one can see?—before he turns back to me.

My smile makes it clear I want him to kiss me. Why did I make things so easy for him?

"So, Maggie Scott," he says, "has this been an amazing day or what?"

"The best," I say in a way-too-familiar voice for the first date. I see what Grace meant about changing the day. I have a feeling this last part is not going to be like it was the first time around.

"She must really want me!" Theo thinks.

His next words are fuzzy, like he doesn't even know what he said.

Video me smirks at him (because I heard what he said; it was lame), but I don't back away.

For the next few minutes, the screen is just black, I guess because Theo closed his eyes while we were kissing. His thoughts are like *"lips, tongue, hair, skin"* and at this point I want to mute him.

I tune back in when he offers to buy me dinner. The me onscreen looks away and turns him down.

"Why's she playing hard to get now?" Theo thinks. *"After that kiss? Did I put her off somehow? It seemed great to me, but maybe it wasn't great for her."*

Like he has anything to worry about.

I watch as I type my number into his phone and hand it back to him, wondering if this video is ever going to end.

Just as he takes the phone back, a new text comes in. From Isabel. Of course. It's a thumbs-up emoji in response to his last text.

"What if that had come through while Maggie had my phone?" he thinks. *"But it didn't, and I'll see her tomorrow."*

The never-ending video follows us off the Ferris wheel as Theo's gaze looks back and forth around the crowd. *"That kiss was hot, but I can't kiss Maggie again where everyone can see, since I'm meeting Isabel here tomorrow. But I am glad I met her. No matter what happens with Isabel, this one's not going anywhere."*

The video ends.

"This one?" I gasp aloud. "*This* one? Like I'm interchangeable with any other girl? How could I not notice what an arrogant jerk Theo was?"

Grace doesn't answer.

"Did he still go out with her the next day?"

"This simulation only covers August sixth of last year," Grace says.

I don't believe her. It doesn't make sense that Grace could have such detailed intel on *this* day and it just cuts off abruptly. After all, she always knows what I'm doing *now*. "You know. I'm sure you do. And I have a right to know if Theo was cheating on me."

"Is it cheating on you?" Grace poses thoughtfully. "Or on Isabel?"

I inhale gustily. "You . . ."

For the past seven months, it's been firmly planted in my mind and heart that Theo and I felt the same way the day we met. In reality, I was a consolation prize when he didn't get the jumbo reward he'd been anticipating. What I don't know is if he still tried to win the jumbo again later or decided he was happy with what he already got. I can't know for sure unless I ask him, and I can't imagine doing that—especially not now.

"It's not like Isabel was his *girlfriend*," I finally respond.

"Does that matter? You consider it cheating if he saw her the day after your date."

I swallow. In my mind, we were dating from that moment on, even if it wasn't actually the case. Theo made no promises at Bridgeport Days. All he did was ask for my number. As I think back, we didn't have a discussion about exclusivity until at least a month later, after we'd been on several dates.

I probably have no right to be upset about Isabel, even if he did see her the next day. It's all about my perspective. I thought he was just as enthralled with me as I was with him. It's a knife twisting in my heart to realize he still wanted another girl more.

"That's it, then, right, Grace?"

"If you've reviewed everything you'd like to, I will deactivate act two."

That doesn't sound quite as final as I'd like.

"Yes. I'm done."

"Goodbye, Maggie."

As I'm watching, the app pixelates and disappears from my phone. I slide across all the screens, do a search for Best Day app, and it's completely gone.

Good.

I'm done with that day.

And I'm finally ready to let Theo go. But where does that leave me? Even though I don't want him back anymore, now I have even *less* closure than before. I have more questions for Theo, and I won't be able to move on completely until I track down the answers.

46

It's one thing to *want* answers and another to actually get them. As with my mom, the only way to find out for sure if Theo was cheating on me (or Isabel) is to ask him.

I don't have the guts to confront him about it right now, especially with Katelyn glued to his side.

Which brings me to my next option: Carson knew about Isabel that day. If Theo kept seeing her afterward, he might know about that too. But it isn't so easy to bring up Theo with Carson either, especially with the new knowledge I have about *him*.

By Thursday, I've gotten into a routine, riding with Carson to and from school. He's so different from the person I remember while I was dating Theo that I'm starting to wonder if he had an out-of-body experience too, except his just happened sooner.

I also appreciate how his rides help me avoid Adam and Rayna. Adam has stopped being extra nice, but he hasn't returned to total jerk mode either. We're now just two people who live in the same house but don't acknowledge each other, which is fine by me.

Mom was curious why Adam wasn't driving me anymore, but she hasn't pried into it or our ongoing silent war—at least not with me.

School's going all right too. Each day has been better. Yesterday I didn't fall asleep when I got home, so that was a huge step. Today I feel pretty energized. Maybe next week I can go back to rehearsal.

"Oh, hey," Carson says once we're in the car, "I won't be able to take you home after school tomorrow. We have a tournament Saturday, and we're staying after to study up on the competition."

"It's okay. I actually won't need a ride in the morning either. I have a follow-up appointment. Maybe I'll be allowed to walk again." I cross my fingers.

"That would be awesome!"

"Yeah. So today's the usual kind of practice?"

"Depends what you mean by practice."

"I mean hitting golf balls. Isn't that what you usually do?"

He chuckles. "Did you pay attention at all when Theo talked about golf?"

It's the first time he's mentioned Theo during any of our rides. It's not like him giving me rides has changed their friendship. He still sits with Theo every day at lunch, jokes around with him.

I wonder if Theo knows we've been hanging out. If he cares.

Carson's just given me an opening to ask my questions about Theo and Isabel, but I'm not ready to spoil the easiness between us. Aside from Clara, it's the most comfortable relationship I have right now. So bizarre.

Carson's expression shifts, as if he's just realized he brought up Theo too, so I quickly act offended. "Of course I listened! And studied up. I know Rickie Fowler makes the most interesting fashion choices on the tour. And that they give out ugly green and yellow jackets that look like they're from the last millennium. Oh!" I point at him and smirk. "And that you're supposed to stay quiet while golfers are teeing off."

He rolls his lips around like he's holding back a smile. "I wonder who told you that."

I raise an eyebrow. "Kind of a jerk actually."

"Yeah." He hasn't apologized for his past behavior or explained it, and I'm okay with that for now. I'm not ready to dig into our history, and maybe that's also why I don't ask him about Theo and Isabel. Because if I do, it might lead to the reasons he left me with Theo in the first place.

"So you don't have regular practice today?" It seems safer to return the discussion to golf.

"No, our coach has a meeting. I thought about playing a round on my own, but I'm gonna go work on my putting instead."

"That doesn't count as hitting balls?" I ask archly.

"Have you played miniature golf?" he shoots back.

"Sure."

"Do you *hit* the ball?"

This seems like a technicality. "Is that where you're going? To play mini golf?" A hint of excitement enters my voice.

"Why? Do you want to go?" He sounds skeptical, and at first I think it's because of our history, but then I notice he's looking down at my foot.

Yeah, that's a complication. But I could try. It would be better than just going home and sitting again. "I think I could make it work."

His mouth turns down, like he's weighing the pros and cons. "Okay, but I hope you're not a sore loser."

I chuckle. "Bring it on, Carson."

.+ .+ .+ +.

Carson takes us to what must be the only outdoor mini golf course open on a Thursday afternoon in April. It's in the sixties today, so I'm not worried about the weather, but as I examine the course, I'm a bit concerned about navigating it with the scooter. I wait outside while he goes in the office to pay. He returns a few minutes later with two clubs and balls.

He hands me a blue ball. "It's almost the same color as your eyes."

The words come out so casually I don't know whether he means them as a compliment, so all I end up saying is "Thanks."

"How do you want to do this?" He gestures at the first hole, which is thankfully flat.

"I have a plan."

He nods. "Show me what you've got."

I roll into position, arranging the scooter sideways with my knee still propped on it, and set down my ball. But the way I'm standing, the scooter's in the way of the club. So I move it until it's facing backward. I'm waiting for Carson to make some sort of comment, but when I glance back, he's watching with a small smile. Sometimes silence is the best gift.

Finally in a position to putt, I study the course ahead. This first hole is a pretty straight shot, with a small hill in the middle. If I miss the hill, it will send me off to the side, but if I catch it, my ball might go right in the hole. Making sure I'm well balanced, I swing back gently and tap the ball. It rolls straight for the hill, glides over it, heads for the hole—and pops right over it.

"Seriously?"

"Happens all the time." Carson steps forward with his club and ball, so I carefully twist onto the scooter and out of his way.

I wait to the side as he gets into a professional golfer's stance and expertly hits the ball. It sails at perfect speed directly into the hole. "Not to you, apparently," I grumble.

He turns around, smirking. "Not often, but that's because I practice. A lot."

"It's basically your life, huh?" I say as I move toward my ball. I don't bother positioning the scooter. The ball's so close to the hole I tap it in one-handed.

"Sort of like you and theater, right?" He stoops down to retrieve our balls. "You put the work in, and it pays off in your performance."

That does put it in perspective. I've never really thought of sports as being anything like what I do, but I can understand passion. If Carson feels the same exhilaration playing golf that I experience inhabiting a character onstage, I get why he's so committed to it.

We move on to the next hole, and I have a better handle on how to position myself this time. "So do you want to be a pro golfer?"

He waits until I hit the ball down the line, bouncing it off the ninety-degree angle, to answer. "That's my dream job, but obviously not very many people make it."

"You're really good, though. Aren't you, like, ranked at the state level?"

He rests on his putter, looking at me in surprise. "You know about that?"

I shrug. "Theo's really proud of you."

It's one of the things that always drove me crazy, how he'd go on and on about "his man Carson" and how boss he was at golf. But it was also one of the sweet things about Theo, because he truly admired his friend. There was maybe some envy, but not the overly competitive type.

"He's a good friend."

He certainly does care about Carson, and yet the day we all met, Theo put himself first.

There's a question in Carson's eyes, but I'm not totally sure what he's asking. Whether I'm still hung up on Theo? Now I've gone and brought him up, when earlier I didn't want to. Maybe it *is* time to ask my questions.

"Does he know we've been hanging out?"

I'm surprised this is the first question that came out of my mouth. Carson avoids it momentarily, bending over to hit the ball. It bounces off the barrier and stops a few inches from the hole. I don't comment on the miss.

As we move toward our balls, he says, "I haven't mentioned it, but I haven't hidden it either. I'm sure people have seen us."

I'm not sure what to do with that. Does "people" include Theo? It's weird Carson wouldn't mention to his best friend that he's driving his ex around. "You think he'd have a problem with it?"

He meets my gaze. "He broke up with you, so why would he?"

"Ouch." I cover my heart.

"Sorry." He pushes the bill of his cap up so that his hair peeks out above his forehead. "I just . . . I never . . ."

I never . . . wanted you to be with Theo.

I never . . . meant to be such a jerk to you.

I never . . . thought you were a good couple.

I never . . . what?

But I don't prompt him to finish the sentence. Because I'm not ready for that yet. Instead I ask, "Who's Isabel?"

I wasn't paying attention to what Carson was doing, so I didn't notice he was putting. He jerks the club, and the ball bounces out of the green onto the gravel.

"Isabel?" he repeats in a strangled voice. Red creeps up past his neck and jawline, finally filling his cheeks with a rosy blush. "I don't know who you're talking about."

I lower my chin. "Your skin says otherwise."

He touches his cheek. "I—I—it's hot out here."

"It's sixty-something degrees. It's only hot if you're my menopausal grandma."

The red creeps all the way to his hairline. "I can't, Maggie. I like hanging out with you, but you can't ask me that. Please."

He looks seriously pained, like I've punched him in the solar plexus. A part of me wants to push, to badger him until he spills every detail he knows about Theo and Isabel. But another part doesn't want to spoil whatever is happening between us. I don't understand that part. Because this is *Carson*. Who just a few weeks ago I would have cheerfully put on a plane to Siberia and completely forgotten his existence. It's unreal how your opinion of someone can change so quickly.

"Fine." I look into the gravel. "Better get your ball."

Carson tries to bring back the lightheartedness from earlier in the game, but it's hard now that I put Theo in the middle of it.

Halfway through I get tired and go sit on a bench with my leg propped up. Carson offers to take me home, but I insist he finish practicing.

I guess I did learn one thing at least. Carson definitely knows about Isabel, and what he knows makes him very uncomfortable.

47

The next day, Dr. Rowland clears me to walk, but there are conditions—only in the boot, and only one hour at first. Then I can add another hour each day until I'm basically walking all the time. I'm nervous to put weight on my foot after so many weeks of being told *not* to, but Dr. Rowland shows us the X-rays and assures me everything is healing exactly as it should. The screw is perfectly in place (*so* relieved I didn't mess anything up the day I lost my balance).

As soon as Mom drops me at home, I retrieve the walking boot and strap it onto my foot. Since she had to return to work for a meeting, she added the condition that Adam had to watch "in case I fall." Of course he's nowhere to be seen, even though he should be home from school by now. I consider just getting up without him, but I promised Mom, and I don't want to risk her restricting my walking privileges more than Dr. Rowland suggested.

I have to call Adam four times before he finally ambles into the living room. "What?" He leans against the wall with his arms crossed.

"What took you so long? I could have been dying."

"You're not."

So not helpful. "Mom says you have to watch me walk in case, I don't know, I stumble down the invisible stairs in this living room."

He snorts. "I'm watching."

I've been so focused on *not* putting any weight on the foot, now that I can, I'm a little nervous.

"Still watching," Adam says.

I glare at him, then look down at my feet. Here goes nothing. I push up to standing, and pain shoots up my leg from the right side of my foot. I cry out involuntarily and reach for the scooter, but it's too far away.

Adam races across the room and grips my arm. "What? What is it?"

I lean into him. "It hurts," I whimper. "Why does it hurt? It didn't really hurt to walk on it before the surgery."

"I don't know." He actually sounds concerned. "Try taking a step maybe."

I do, and another spike of pain hits. It's not like the pain from right after surgery—I hope I never feel anything like that again—but I'm supposed to do this for an *hour* today?

"Let's see if we can make it to your room."

We do, but tears are coursing down my cheeks, and I wonder if Dr. Rowland is wrong about my foot healing properly.

I send Clara a message about the pain, and fifteen minutes later, she arrives, just like Rayna used to.

I miss her.

"Have you tried again?" Clara asks.

"No." I've stayed propped on my bed with the ice pack Adam got for me. I haven't seen him again since, although I give him credit for helping me. "It's settled. I'm never going to dance again. Never going to stride across the stage. My foot is ruined forever!"

"Well, you definitely haven't lost your dramatic flair." Clara purses her lips. "I think you should try again. I'm sure it will get better the more you walk on it."

I eye the walking boot. "I really don't want to."

"Come on! You can do it!"

She looks so earnest, with her hands clasped together under her chin. Maybe I was a little overdramatic. "Fine."

I discard the ice and hook my foot back in, then brace myself as I slide off the side of the bed. This time, I'm ready for the impact, and it still really hurts, but it doesn't bring tears to my eyes.

"How is it?" Clara's standing right beside me, ready to serve as a human crutch.

"We'll see." I step forward, and it's painful but bearable.

"You're lopsided," Clara observes.

"Yeah, this boot is tall. I've gotta find some shoes to even myself out."

"It probably doesn't help to walk around uneven."

She has a point. I head for the closet, Clara my shadow.

She peeks inside, and her eyes widen. "Was there a tornado inside your closet?"

I flush. "Um, I sort of just toss them in there."

"How do you find anything?" She brightens like a light bulb's just gone off. "Let's have some fun."

"Okay," I say, but it comes out like a question.

She rushes over to my desk and pushes my chair toward the closet. "Sit."

"Woof," I say as I do.

"Ha." She taps her lips, examining my mess of shoes. "We'll make a sort of fashion show and organize at the same time."

I'm starting to get the gist of her idea. If she wants to clean my closet, she can have at it. I won't burst her bubble by telling her I'll only mess it up again. "My phone's on the nightstand."

"Perfect." She gets it for me, then studies the boot for height. "Let's start with everyday wear."

She digs in my closet and returns with a tennis shoe. I put it on my left foot and take a few steps. Clara starts a live video on my phone. "I'm here with Maggie Scott. She's back in this *lovely* boot, which comes in a rather high platform, but unfortunately it isn't part of a pair."

I snort. "Thank God for that!"

"So we are attempting to find a shoe to complement it. Much like Prince Charming placing a glass slipper on Cinderella's foot, we seek a perfect fit."

The mention of Prince Charming reminds me how Carson put my flip-flop back on the day I broke my foot. I shake away the image as Clara skims the phone up from the boot to my face. I probably should have checked my makeup before we started this, considering I was crying earlier.

"What shall it be?" I pout. "I'm all out of glass slippers."

Clara peers at the phone. "Alexis suggests a wedge."

She hands me the phone so I can track her progress in the closet.

Did I tell you I was wearing the flip-flops you gave me when I broke my foot? I reply to Alexis.

Noooo! she answers.

Clara returns, triumphantly holding up a red sandal with a wedge heel, and trades it for the phone.

I strap on the shoe. "Hmm. It's almost the right height, but the boot is flat, whereas this shoe is slanted, so I still feel uneven."

More suggestions come in (my troupe friends are especially into it), and we're having so much fun I lose track of how long we've had the live feed going.

Until a comment comes through from my mom: Your hour is up.

"Oops!" Clara says. "Looks like this Cinderella's curfew is well before midnight. Thank you for joining us."

At her prompt, I smile and wave like we're signing off from a talk show. She puts down the phone, and I'm still smiling. "That was hilarious." I lean around her to look in the closet. "But you did not succeed in cleaning up my shoes."

They're actually more of a mess now, completely separated from their pairs, spread all over the floor.

Grinning, Clara uses her foot to shove all the shoes against the wall. "You only need the left ones anyway, right?"

"True enough. I'm so glad you came over."

"Me too. But I can't stay much longer. David and I are going to his little brother's basketball game."

"Do I detect a hint of rancor in your tone?"

She sighs. "I love David, but sometimes there's a little too much together time with his family."

Huh. Guess everything isn't perfect between Clara and David. "Have you told him that?"

"No. It's just"—she casts her eyes at the ceiling—"easier to go along than cause issues."

That sounds like the story of Clara's life. She's the eternal peacemaker. I wiggle on my seat a bit, wondering if she's stayed silent when *I've* made her uncomfortable. She's the one person I didn't hear from in the Best Day app.

"It's okay," she says brightly. "We'll go out afterward, just the two of us. He always lets me pick after these sorts of things. I'm thinking . . . the high ropes course at Amp Up."

My mouth forms an O. "Isn't David afraid of heights?"

She holds her thumb and pointer finger an inch apart. "Maybe a little."

"Where did this streak of evil come from? I'm impressed!"

"You would be," a new voice says from the doorway.

I don't need to turn to recognize it, but I still do.

"What are you doing here, Rayna?"

Rayna pushes away from the doorframe. "Didn't your mom tell you? She invited me for dinner."

I gasp. At the doctor this afternoon, Mom did mention having company and asked me to be on my best behavior. It suddenly makes a lot more sense.

Clara grabs her phone and jacket. "And that's my cue to leave."

She's out the door before I can beg her to stay as my sorely needed backup.

Rayna walks inside like she still belongs here. It hurts because I really miss her, but I still don't know how to forgive her for lying to me.

"Your mom texted me herself. Said you would all love to see me."

I laugh bitterly. "They do love you."

Obviously my parents have no trouble forgiving her.

She picks up the *Life's Little Inspiration Calendar*, which today says, "In life we never lose friends; we only learn who the true ones are."

Ouch, Grandma.

Rayna sets it back on my desk without addressing it and says, "How long are you going to punish me?"

"Punish you? That's what you think this is?"

She scans the room like she's searching for a different solution before zeroing in on me again. "Pretty much."

"You really don't get it, Rayna. Imagine if I'd . . ." It's actually hard to come up with a good analogy here. She doesn't have an awful brother or even someone she really dislikes. Her main concern is school—that's it! "Imagine if there were a test we both had to take, and this test would determine what college we got into. But unknown to you, I cheated on the test and achieved a higher score, which allowed me to move ahead of you. And then, I *never told you*, just let you think you'd somehow failed."

She stares at me, her chin tucked into her neck. "That . . . I can't . . . Where did you even come up with a plot like that?"

I point at her. "You'd have a really hard time forgiving me if I did that, wouldn't you?"

"That doesn't make any sense," she says, towering over me.

"You're just deflecting now."

"You'd do a lot of things, but you're not a cheater," Rayna says.

Wow. "What does *that* mean? I'd do a lot of things?"

She waves a hand. "Forget it. You're obviously not up for talking to me right now."

She storms out the room, completely spoiling the good mood I was in after Clara's visit. I hobble over to the bed and plop onto it, hoping Clara's evening goes better than mine.

48

I don't leave my room until Dad wheels the scooter in for me at six o'clock. "Dinner's ready. Your chariot awaits, Cinderella."

"You saw that, huh?"

"Yep." He smirks. "My favorite was the sneaker with the reversible sequins."

"Those were for a dance recital. I'm not wearing them in public."

"Your loss." He gets serious. "Are you going to be good tonight?"

"No, Dad. I'm going to launch broccoli across the table at Rayna and Adam. Because I'm really a two-year-old, thanks."

"That's not what I mean." For once Dad sounds serious. "I know this situation isn't ideal. It would have been better if they hadn't hidden it from you. But they obviously care about each other, so what good does it do to fight it?"

It's interesting how everyone has their own interpretation of my reaction to Adam and Rayna's relationship. I'm pouting. I'm angry. I'm being a baby. None of them seem to get how *hurt* I am. And it's not the kind of hurt a surgeon can stick a screw in and give me a set of instructions on how long it will take to heal.

But I'm also done trying to explain that. "I'll behave."

As I follow Dad to the dining room, I decide what character will be most effective tonight. Ignoring Rayna hasn't worked. Neither has shouting at her. Maybe it's time to try something new to get through to her.

Rayna's come over for dinner millions of times, and we always sit the same way at our six-person table—the two of us on one side, Mom and Dad at each end, and Adam across from me. Tonight, Rayna's sitting beside Adam, leaving me alone. I expected it, but it still causes a twinge. I don't let it show as I slide into my seat.

"Good evening, everyone." I make sure to encompass Rayna and Adam in my smile. "This looks delicious, Mom."

She's gone homestyle for Rayna's visit, with ham glazed in brown sugar and cinnamon, homemade baked mac 'n' cheese, baked beans, and buttery biscuits. I wonder if she made Rayna's favorite dessert too.

"Thank you, Maggie."

I wouldn't describe Mom's expression as suspicious exactly, but she also doesn't appear to believe I'm sincere. As we're all settled, she turns to Dad. "Jim, would you say the blessing?"

Dad nods, and we all bow our heads while he thanks God for our food and then gets really pointed about it. "And thank you for bringing us all together tonight so we can enjoy each other's company and mend our differences. Amen."

I do *not* say "amen" to that, but I smile so brightly he blinks.

We start passing the food around, filling our plates, and there's no need to talk for a few minutes. But of course my parents can't leave it at that. Mom is the first to push a thumb into the bruise.

"I heard the prom theme is 'A Global Affair.' What does that mean exactly?"

Rayna glances at me, and I don't let my smile falter, even as I stuff a bite of cheesy noodles into my mouth. Prom's now two weeks away. Mom clearly doesn't realize how touchy of a subject this is for me, but Rayna does. It occurs to me that the day I broke my foot, Rayna was speaking from her own experience about boyfriends and prom. She thought Theo already expected to go with me because Adam expected *her* to go with *him* and had been asking her repeatedly. If Grace hadn't already shown me how flawed my relationship with Theo was, this would just be further proof.

I guess Theo will be taking Katelyn to prom now, although I haven't seen her broadcasting an invite from him yet.

Rayna sets down her fork to answer Mom. "They're going to have stations decorated for different parts of the world with desserts and photo ops. Somebody said they'd even have experts there to give dance lessons from those countries."

"Oh, that sounds like fun!" Mom rests her chin on her hand, apparently forgetting about her dinner. "I've always wanted to go to France. And Italy."

Dad chuckles. "Maybe we should volunteer as chaperones so I can give your mom a taste of Europe."

"That's a wonderful idea!" I swirl my fork in the air, super careful to remove all traces of sarcasm from my voice. "The four of you can learn the paso doble at the Spanish station. I've always wanted to learn ballroom. Doesn't that sound like fun, Adam?"

He chokes and has to take a drink of water. "No." He looks between Mom and Dad. "You are not chaperoning the prom." He turns to Rayna. "And I'm not dancing."

"At all?" She gapes at him, while I cheer internally.

"Well, uh, dancing's not really my thing." A dull flush creeps up his neck.

I wonder what Carson's position on dancing is. Theo and I went to homecoming together. He danced almost every dance with me. But Carson didn't go, so I don't know if he has any moves.

"What's the point of going to the prom if you're not going to dance?" Rayna presses.

It's like we have a front row seat to their breakup. I wish I had some popcorn.

"If you really want to dance, I'll try," Adam grumbles.

What? That's not the Adam I know. Is it possible . . . Does he really care about Rayna?

"Maggie could give you some tips," Dad suggests.

Adam and Rayna both turn toward me, sporting identical expressions of skepticism. I'm still thrown by Adam agreeing to dance, but I'm determined to keep up my act.

"Oh, absolutely." I nod for emphasis. "You can put some of those soccer moves to use on the dance floor."

In goes another delicious bite, just to show I'm a totally gracious host, like Mom and Dad requested.

Adam finally turns his narrowed eyes from me to Dad. "And the other thing?"

Dad sighs gustily. "I won't offer to chaperone. Although your mom would've looked hot."

"Ew," Adam and I say together in a rare moment of agreement.

But I quickly back off. "Mom, I'm sure you'd look great. I just can't handle Dad saying that kind of stuff."

She pats my hand. "Understood." She focuses on Rayna again. "So have you picked out a dress yet?"

Seriously, are we going to talk about this for the whole dinner? It's like Mom's pushing her thumb into the screw in my foot. I guess part of it's my fault for not telling her how much prom meant to me. I just figured after Theo made a big gesture, that would be the time to gush about it. After everything that happened, it was too humiliating to mention what I'd expected that day.

"My mom took me out last weekend," Rayna says, "but we didn't find anything yet."

I bet. Rayna hates shopping with her mom. They have completely different tastes, and Rayna tends to cave and let her mom pick out things she hates. That would really suck for a prom dress.

I so want to offer advice on what type of dress she should buy, but that would go beyond my good hostess act. I shake my head sadly. "It's hard to find the right dress."

"You should shop with a friend." Mom's verbal hint comes with an overly obvious head bob in Rayna's direction as well.

"Oh, I'm doing that tomorrow, Mrs. Scott."

I almost give myself whiplash twisting back toward Rayna.

"Clara offered to go with me. She's sweet that way."

It takes two tries for me to swallow the bite of ham stuck in the back of my mouth, but I finally succeed. "She sure is," I say enthusiastically. "I bet she'll help you find the perfect global dress."

After that, Mom gives up. She doesn't broach any other topics directly related to Adam and Rayna. Instead, we discuss school, Rayna's entry for the upcoming district science fair, and the schedule for Adam's next soccer tournament. Nobody asks about my activities since they're on hold for now, but hopefully I'll at least be returning to Future Stars soon.

By the time Mom serves dessert—totally Rayna's favorite, strawberry shortcake—I'm exhausted by my act and just want to go back to being myself. I've never disliked acting before, but I'm not usually using my skills on my former best friend.

She wants to know how long I'm going to punish her?

It's starting to feel like I'm punishing myself.

49

On Saturday, I watch Rayna's feed for prom dress pictures or even a picture of her out with Clara, but there's nothing. She actually hasn't posted anything recently at all. Not even a picture of her and Adam to make their relationship official. I wonder what she's waiting for.

I click over to Adam's profile, and it's just his usual stream of soccer, soccer, stupid meme, soccer.

They both like to say it's not all about me.

But is it?

I check on Clara and burst out laughing. She has a picture of David clinging to a huge barrel twenty feet off the ground. He looks terrified.

You really made him go to the high ropes course? I text her.

Oh, yeah, she answers. But then I fed him Baskin-Robbins, so he was all good.

I debate whether to acknowledge I know she's with Rayna today. On one hand, it might be putting her even more in the middle. But staying quiet might make her feel she's in the awkward position of keeping secrets from us. I don't want to make things worse for her either way. She's been amazing through all this. I decide on a generic message that will let her know I'm aware she's out with Rayna without asking her to tell me anything. She knows Rayna was at my house last night. So there's a good chance she's heard about the prom discussion anyway.

Hope you have fun shopping today!

She sends back a smiley face and a shopping bag.

I close out of the message and open up Instagram. There's a new picture from Carson (who I now follow). He's posing with Theo, Theo's dad, and another man I assume must be his own dad. Carson and Theo are both dressed in polos and khakis, holding golf clubs. I like the photo, not caring if Theo notices.

Actually, it wouldn't hurt to *ask* Carson about it. We're sort of friends now.

How'd your tournament go?

I wait impatiently for him to reply. It must be ten whole minutes.

Great! Our team took first place.

Congrats! What did you shoot?

70.

The dots appear, then, Do you know what that means?

Wow. He really doesn't think I was paying attention when I came along with Theo.

The only appropriate response to that is a raised eyebrow emoji.

I guess that means you do.

I nod, but he's still typing something else.

Or you're bluffing.

He wants me to prove it? It's on.

I don't know which course you were playing, but 70 should at least be a couple strokes under par.

It's a par 72, he shoots back.

257

Okay, then. 2 under par.

I feel like there's a word for that. Birdie or something? Although that might only be for a single hole instead of the overall game. I'm not going to screw up now by throwing out the wrong term.

You've impressed me.

A shiver runs through me at the simple statement. I don't know why. I get compliments all the time after a show. Not gonna lie—I thrive on them. But there's something different about Carson praising me.

Maybe it's because of how my perspective of him has changed. The first time we met, he didn't make an impression on me at all, but then I took a second look . . .

I still don't know how to respond to the text. Because I could be putting a totally wrong interpretation on his words. I need to see whether he's grinning, focused entirely on the phone while he texts me, or typing off answers distractedly while he hangs with Theo.

That thought puts a total damper on the conversation.

I can just imagine how Grace would present it in act two.

The video begins with Carson's phone in view, Theo standing beside him.

"Who are you texting?" Theo asks.

"Maggie. She asked about the tournament."

"Ugh," says Theo. "Don't tell her I'm here."

"She asked about the score."

Theo snorts. "She won't know what that means. She never paid attention."

"*He would know*," Carson thinks, and proceeds to give Maggie a hard time.

End video.

Except . . . I don't know why he'd say I impressed him if that was going on in the background.

Is he on the other end, wondering why I haven't replied? Probably not. Boys are so clueless.

Finally I decide on I'm impressed by your score.

It's kind of lame, but at least it's something. And it doesn't expose me at all.

My phone rings, and I nearly drop it when I see Carson's asking me to accept a video call. Did I put on makeup today? Pretty sure I did. I click Accept, and I'm relieved when my own image looks okay.

"Hey," I say casually, despite the *thump-thump-thump* of my heart.

"Hi," he says. "How's the walking?"

"Better than scooting." It actually is today. It still hurts, but I've gotten more used to it. "I'm allowed to add one hour every day, so my mom's making me set a timer whenever I get up. It's pretty annoying."

She doesn't need to know I've forgotten a couple of times.

"How much are you at now?" he asks.

"Um." I swipe over to the stopwatch. "One hour, two minutes, twenty-three seconds."

"That's exact. So . . ." He pauses, and it takes monumental effort for me to refrain from filling the silence. I'm rewarded when he finally says, "What about driving?"

I thought you'd never ask. "Well . . . my mom would prefer I hold off."

Now who's the liar? Although, Mom was definitely hesitant

when Dr. Rowland said it would be okay. I feel the teensiest bit bad misleading Carson, but not enough to take it back.

"No need to wear you out when you're just getting back on your stride."

"Ha." The foot/walking jokes are getting old, but somehow I don't mind it from Carson. Something about how he says it. Or maybe it's more to do with how I view him now.

"So . . . I'd better go. Kind of gross from the tournament."

You wouldn't think golf's a sweaty sport, but it turns out it is. Although, he doesn't look that bad to me, his skin flushed and his eyes bright from his win.

"'Kay. See you Monday." A delighted shiver runs through me as I confirm it.

"Yep. See you then."

I hang up, a silly smile on my face.

"What are *you* so happy about?" Adam says.

I didn't hear him come in. He's filthy, all decked out in his blue-and-white soccer uniform, minus the cleats and shin guards.

I'm not talking to Adam about Carson, but—a memory tugs at me from the app, about Adam and soccer. "Did you win?"

He looks surprised I asked but recovers quickly. "Six to two."

"Nice."

"You must be in a good mood."

Like I've never congratulated him on winning a game.

Okay, so I probably haven't without prompting from Mom and Dad. At least recently. I wonder if Mom and Dad were there to watch, but I don't ask as I don't want to change *his* mood.

I shrug, and he lets it go. "I'm gonna hit the shower." But then he turns around. "No, I actually want to say something."

Oh, great.

"Maggie, I know we haven't always gotten along. And a lot of that's my fault." He scratches his neck. "I got into a habit over the years with you, and it's been really hard to break."

I drop my chin. "Torturing me is a *habit*?"

"A bad one?" He says it like he's not completely convinced.

If this is supposed to be his form of an apology, he really needs to work on it.

"Anyway"—he waves his hand like his never-ending snide comments and grumpy attitude about my shows are inconsequential—"I'm trying to be better."

I snort.

"I really am. It's important to Rayna. And maybe you're trying too. Despite your whole *everything in the world revolves around me* attitude."

I throw out my hands. "This is you trying?"

"So if you are," he continues, completely ignoring my skepticism, "you should really talk to Rayna about why she went to crazy lengths to keep our relationship a secret from you. Because whether you believe it or not, it had more to do with you than Rayna."

With that parting comment, he finally leaves for his shower. Easy enough to wash away the dirt. Not so easy to get rid of all the questions he left swirling through my mind.

I'm still thinking about what Adam said when Rayna sends me a picture of herself in a dress. It's simple but very Rayna, canary yellow satin with spaghetti straps and a rhinestone-embellished waist. And are those—I zoom in—pockets? I'm about to type this very question to her in response when I remember that I'm still not talking to her.

Tears prick my eyes. Oh, that was tricky. Sending me a picture, knowing I'd want more details. I set the phone down and wiggle my fingers to keep myself from responding.

She looks fabulous. Adam does not deserve Rayna in that dress.

Except . . . he said he would dance with her. He defended her to me. He said he was trying to be nicer to me *for her.* So maybe he does.

I'm angry with her.

It hurts that she lied to me.

But I miss her most of all, and I hate that she went out and bought that gorgeous dress without me.

It's like she said. Who am I punishing by refusing to forgive her?

I honestly don't know if I *can* forgive her, but I can at least listen. I have a feeling that was the point of the whole "best" day scenario anyway—to understand that my perspective is just one of many.

"If you're listening, Grace, I got the point. I should pay more attention to what's going on around me. You can go find someone else to Ghost of Christmas Past now."

Also, I suppose, to ask the people in my life why they chose to do the things they did. Starting with Rayna.

So I pick up the phone and reply. Come show it to me?

50

In much less time than I expected, Rayna's at my bedroom door, a garment bag over her arm. "You wanted to see my dress?"

I nod, and she moves toward my closet, fixing the hanger over the door. The plastic rustles as she lifts it up. The yellow is even more vibrant in person. I can totally picture her in it, with some low-heeled sandals, because she'll never attempt walking in anything over two inches. Maybe with some dangling chandelier earrings.

"That's going to look fabulous on you," I say around the knot in my throat. "Does it have pockets?"

"Yep." She smiles, making her dimple pop, and slips her hand inside one to show me.

"Nice." I mean it. The dress is exactly what I would have picked for Rayna if I'd been there.

But I wasn't.

"So." She slips the plastic back over the dress and turns to face me.

"So . . . it sucked you went shopping for a prom dress without me."

"It sucked *going* shopping without you—not that I don't love Clara," she rushes to add.

Poor Clara. We both love her, but she's always been the slightest bit outside our circle, coming into it after we'd already formed so many inside jokes and memories. I wonder if she feels that, or if she's so inside her own circle with David that she doesn't mind.

I scoot over on my bed and motion for Rayna to join me. We've spent many hours leaning against my wall, talking through everything from frustrating teachers to what we'd wear for the last day of school. It seems appropriate for us to hash this Adam thing out here too.

I study her familiar features. I've always thought Rayna and I could tell each other anything. But apparently she didn't feel that way about me.

I twirl the fringe from a pillow around my finger. "Tell me about how you and Adam got together."

It's what any best friend who didn't have issues with the guy would ask. And I have a feeling that this answer might hold clues to Rayna's subsequent choices.

"You sure you're ready for that?"

I'm absolutely not ready for a play-by-play of Rayna falling for my brother, but I think it's time to stop avoiding it. I can't make a real decision about whether to forgive her until I know why she did it.

"Yes." I do my best not to sound grudging.

"Okay." She hesitates, winding a curl of hair around her finger. "It started when we were at your summer production. I ended up sitting next to Adam, which had happened before, but this time none of our other friends were there, and we started talking. Like, about real stuff."

I nod for her to continue.

"He asked about the data science camp I was doing that week, and he had really incisive questions."

"*Adam* had good questions for you about *data science*?" It had taken every ounce of concentration for me to make sense of what Rayna was doing that week.

"He did." She grins like only Rayna could over science. "And asked if he could see my capstone project at the end of the week. You had a cast party after the last show, and he seemed genuinely interested, so I agreed to meet up with him."

"Your first date with Adam was for a data presentation?"

This is so not the Adam I know. He must've been really into her to sacrifice a Friday night to science. I feel a twinge of guilt that I never asked to see her presentation. She comes to every single one of my shows.

Rayna purses her lips. "It wasn't a date at that point. But I definitely started looking at him a different way. I'd always seen him as your annoying older brother." She holds up a hand. "I know it's way more than that to you. But isn't it always when you live with someone?"

When I don't respond to that understatement, she continues. "He was so attentive to my presentation, and he asked great follow-up questions, and then we talked about what we both want to do later. I always thought soccer was his life, but really it's just his ticket to a scholarship. Someday he hopes to be an engineer."

"Adam wants to be an *engineer*?" I try to imagine Adam designing anything other than the perfect sandwich, which I've heard him wax eloquent about. "What kind?"

"Chemical. He loves chemistry but isn't sure exactly where he'd want to focus yet."

"Chemistry?" I expected this conversation to leave me dumbfounded, but in a completely different way. She can't be talking about my brother.

She shakes her head sadly. "You don't know him at all."

That's what he said too.

"I guess not." But whose fault is that? The lack of conversation goes in both directions. "So you talked science"—still can't fathom that—"and then what?"

"Well . . . it was really nice, hanging out with Adam, but I honestly thought it was just a one-off, so I didn't bother mentioning it to you. Then a couple of weeks later, I came over and you weren't home. I don't even know why. And we ended up hanging out again. Somehow, it turned into a thing. And I knew you would freak if I told you about it. Adam didn't think you'd be happy about it either. We actually discussed it."

"Great." Now I have an image of them laughing over my reaction to them hanging out.

"Not like that." She shakes a finger at me. "I was worried. I knew you wouldn't understand. But Adam . . ." She bites her lip. "Adam said you'd probably convince me never to see him again."

"I—" I stop myself from protesting because it's probably true. My gut reaction would have been to talk her out of seeing Adam. It's *still* my first instinct, even after what she just told me. There are too many years of bad blood between us. "You could have tried telling me about this science bond you had."

She traces a seam on my comforter. "It was . . . exciting to have a secret relationship. Until it wasn't."

"What do you mean by that?"

"I don't like lying to you, Maggie. Or to anyone. But Adam

and I dug our way so far into it that I didn't know how to tell you. I kept thinking, 'This will end and then she'll never have to know.' But it didn't. I just fell for him even more."

Ugh. I can't ask for the details I'd usually ask at this point. The details I've spilled to her about my relationship with Theo.

"Seems like you could have worked on getting Adam to be nicer to me so you could ease into the truth."

She winces. "It's the one thing he wouldn't listen to me about. He said if he started being nicer you'd be suspicious. I really don't understand what's wrong with you two. He's not like that with me at all. And if you pay attention, he treats your mom really well."

I guess that's true.

It makes me cringe to ask, but I do it anyway. "How is he with you?"

She relaxes against the wall. "He sends me messages every morning, telling me to have a great day. He always remembers if I have something stressful to do, like a test, and wishes me luck. In the fall, if he didn't have soccer, he came to watch me at band practice. And he never"—she casts a significant look at me—"complains about his sister, even though he has a very complicated relationship with her."

"Hmm." She makes Adam sound like a perfect boyfriend. It's very hard to reconcile that boy with the brother I know. It also makes me see my own relationship in an uncomfortable light. On the surface, there were a lot of good things with Theo, but we never went much deeper. Rayna knows my brother wants to study chemical engineering. Theo and I dated for seven months, and I have a clearer idea of what Carson wants to do with his life than Theo.

But my sainted brother aside, I still have a lot of questions.

"How does he have time to do all of that? How do *you*? You're with me all the time."

Or she was. I wonder: if I hadn't been given the opportunity to relive my "best" day, would I have interpreted that conversation I overheard between them the same way? Or would I have assumed it was just Adam being a pest? Every other comment he made to Rayna about how great she looked, I brushed aside with an annoyed eye roll. If I hadn't heard Rayna lying to me at Bridgeport Days, I probably would've blown the prom invite off too.

"Well . . . you remember when we were talking about Theo? After you broke up?"

"You mean after he dumped me?" I gesture at my foot. "How could I forget?"

"And we were talking about all your drama commitments . . ."

Where is she going with this? "I'm not following."

"You're super busy a lot of the time. It made it very easy to plan things with Adam. After a while it just felt like you had your thing and I had mine."

"Except you knew about my thing," I can't help but point out. We'll keep coming back to that no matter how much we talk about it. "I don't think you understand how much it *hurt* to realize you've been hiding something so big for so long."

Rayna clasps my hands. "I'm sorry, Maggie. I don't know if I'd choose differently if I went back. How can anyone know one choice is better than the other for sure? But I'm sorry now, and I hope you'll forgive me."

I'm pretty sure you can know that *lying* is the wrong choice. And thanks to the Best Day app, I was able to look back and see that Theo was not the best choice. But it's not like Grace gave me the opportunity to change that choice—just to use the information for moving forward now. Which is what Rayna's asking me to do.

I want to, but I'm not quite there. "Adam said keeping the relationship secret had more to do with me than you."

"Did he?" She exhales. "I wouldn't say it had *more* to do with you. At the beginning, I was definitely worried about you interfering, but later, I wanted to keep it to myself."

"Because you thought I'd make it about me?"

"Man, he's really inside your head." She glares at the door. "We'll keep working on that. Adam doesn't understand why you're upset because you've never been close, but I do. And I want to fix it."

Is it wrong I'm a little happy I might cause an argument between them?

Wrong, but also satisfying.

"Okay. I'm not all the way at forgiveness, but it's been awful without you."

Rayna tackle-hugs me. "I know. So awful."

"Just . . . no PDA in front of me, okay?"

She laughs and pulls back. "Got it."

"Girls night soon? We can even"—I swallow—"talk about all your prom plans."

"I'd love that." She squeezes my hand, and while I don't feel like we're back to normal, it's a step in the right direction.

51

When Carson picks me up Monday morning, he zeroes in on my feet. "So you went with tennis shoes."

"Huh?" I glance down, then flush warmly. "You saw that?" For some reason, I didn't really think about Carson watching the video Clara and I made.

He smiles. "Sure did."

The actual ride to school is filled with a recap of our weekends, but all throughout the day, I think about how Carson was stalking my feed on Friday the way I was stalking his on Saturday. This dynamic between us is so different from how we used to treat each other, and not for the first time I wonder what he's thinking.

Grace really messed me up, putting ideas in my head about everyone. It's hard to trust anything anyone says out loud when you've been inside their heads, even for a few moments.

At lunch, Rayna's prom dress is the main topic of discussion.

"Did she try it on for you?" Clara asks me.

"Yes, and she looks radiant. Luminous. Dazzling!"

Jada blinks across the table, her dark eyes bemused. "Guess you guys made up?"

"Isn't it great?" Clara dips a fry into ketchup.

"Yeees," Zoey drags out dramatically. "One of you was going to have to leave the table if it went on much longer."

We laugh, but I'm not sure she's joking. I didn't realize how hard our fight was on the people around us.

"I think prom would be fun, but just with a group of friends," Jada says. "Dating doesn't really interest me."

That's how I always thought Rayna felt, and then she surprised me with Adam.

"Maybe we can do it that way next year," I say, since we're all sophomores anyway. Rayna's the only one who got asked.

"Ooh, are you talking about *prom*?" Katelyn leans between me and Clara. "Who's going? Because I know poor Maggie won't be dancing."

Did Theo tell her I thought he was going to ask me to the prom? Or is this just a dig at my injury? Either way, I won't let her get to me.

"Katelyn, I am so touched by your concern." I place my hand over my heart. "You might not have noticed, but I'm back to walking, which means there's a good chance I'll be dancing again by prom."

Clara and Rayna both look at me like I've lost it, but thankfully Katelyn's focused on me.

"Wow. That's . . ." Katelyn works very hard to smile brightly, proof she's nowhere near as good an actor as me. "I'm so happy for you."

"I knew you would be. Not that I have any plans to go." I wave toward Rayna. "But Rayna is. With my brother. You know—star of the soccer team? She just got the most gorgeous dress."

Rayna quickly pastes on a smile when Katelyn turns her

saccharine sweetness in her direction. "Those rumors are true then? About you and Adam? I haven't seen it declared officially, so I didn't believe it."

"Some of us don't need to declare everything to the world to believe it's real," Rayna replies.

Katelyn takes the hit without flinching.

"Will I see you there? At the prom?" Rayna adds.

Katelyn darts a glance at me. "Possibly."

Interesting.

"Do be sure to keep us updated," I say. "And tell Theo I said hi."

I glance over at his table, and for the first time in weeks, he's actually watching us, uneasy. How lovely. I wave, and he quickly looks back down at his lunch tray. Carson's beside him, as usual. Even from across the room, I can see the approval in his smile.

"I will." Katelyn flounces away, and I return to my own lunch.

"Do you think he'll ask her?" Clara asks hesitantly.

I swirl my fork in my spaghetti. It was really nice to go through the lunch line again today.

Rayna, Jada, and Zoey all lean in for my response. "If he does, stay tuned for a live report on all available channels."

52

It's only been about a month since Rayna, Clara, and I went out together, but it feels like much longer. The truce Rayna and I struck is still so new. It's like we're walking through a laser field, trying not to get singed.

We started out the evening with a movie. Easy enough; no talking involved there. But now we're at Cheeburger Cheeburger, waiting for our burgers and shakes, and the silence has extended beyond a comfortable minute.

"Are you all set for next weekend?" I tap the table, where Rayna has her hand splayed. She tends to bite her nails when she's studying, so they're all ragged. "I hope you have an appointment for a manicure."

"Um." She looks down. "I hadn't really thought about it. I was maybe going to paint them myself."

"We can come over and do it," Clara offers.

"Sure," I agree. "What about your hair?"

She reaches up to touch it. "I was just going to put it in a twist myself somehow. Is that not okay?"

It will probably fall out after one dance. I look accusingly at Clara. "I thought you had this under control."

"I helped her with the dress and shoes. I thought she'd be okay from there."

"Really? This is Rayna we're talking about."

"Um, guys, I'm still here," Rayna says in a disgruntled voice, but she's suppressing a smile.

"I can help with your hair. We're always doing each other's hair before shows." I make a picture frame with my thumbs and pointer fingers. "I'm thinking you should do half up, half down."

"Good idea," Clara says. "And if you don't want to go to a salon, I can come do your nails."

"I'd rather not." Rayna scrunches her nose. "Those places stink."

"We'll have you all set. But I probably need to make sure Adam's presentable too."

"Oh, he'll love that," Rayna says.

"He has no choice. If he wants to date my best friend, we have to learn to get along." The idea makes me shudder inside, but I'm trying.

Clara beams at me like a proud teacher whose student has just exceeded all her expectations.

Then her expression turns mischievous. She leans her elbow on the table and props her chin on her fist. "Now that we have Rayna all figured out, what is going on with you and Carson Lockwood?"

My place mat is very interesting. There's a maze on it. I don't need a crayon to follow the path, just to focus mentally and—

"Maggie!"

"What?" I blink up at her.

"Clara asked you a very interesting question," Rayna chimes

274

in. "About your former worst enemy Carson. Who you now seem to be spending a lot of time with. And who sent you balloons."

"It's complicated."

Rayna cocks her head. They aren't going to leave me alone until I spill. I might as well make it good.

"What if I told you that back when I met Theo, it was actually Carson who liked me first?"

Clara doesn't react, but Rayna's appropriately shocked. "Seriously? And Theo still went after you?"

"I don't totally understand what happened between the guys." I press my finger into a drop of water on my place mat. "But from the time Carson left us that day, I never doubted Theo was the one for me." At least not until Grace showed me Theo's side of the day. "While Carson acted like a total jerk."

"Probably because he felt rejected," Clara says sadly.

"What?" I frown.

"Oh. Of course." Rayna nods.

"You're saying Carson was a jerk to me because I didn't notice him?"

Clara's about to answer, but our server brings our food and milkshakes, so she waits. It gives me time to process the idea. It seems like a pretty extreme reaction when he didn't make any outright move that day.

As soon as the server leaves, Clara leans forward. "Just imagine how awkward it would have been for him. Theo already knew Carson was attracted to you; then Theo starts dating you for real, and Carson is left with the certain knowledge you chose the other guy."

"Except I didn't know there was a choice."

"And if you had?" Rayna swirls her straw in her milkshake, an eyebrow raised.

Even though I just reexperienced that day, I don't know the answer to that question. "I barely remember meeting Carson that day. I only had eyes for Theo. I guess if Theo had backed off . . . but he didn't."

"So what you're saying is, Carson didn't stand a chance against Theo," Rayna concludes.

I wince, but it's probably true. Carson didn't make any impression on me at all. But on second impression . . .

"And now?" Clara asks. "If you had to choose?"

I flick my fingers. "It's not a choice anymore. Theo's with Katelyn. We're over."

Rayna blinks. "I missed a lot the last few weeks."

I guess the last time we discussed Theo, winning him back was my primary goal.

"Does Carson believe you and Theo are really done?" Clara muses.

Rayna points at her. "I have noticed he doesn't talk to Maggie in front of Theo. He's probably still insecure."

I squirm, since this very detail has bothered me too. "I'm not totally sure Theo knows we're hanging out. Or at least that Carson's talked to him about it. It's sort of weird actually."

"Definitely insecure," Rayna says.

"So if you like him . . ." Clara lifts her brows like she's waiting for me to answer, and I shrug helplessly. "Then you have to find a way to make it clear you aren't still harboring feelings for Theo."

I scrunch my nose. I might have complicated that by asking him about Isabel.

"What?" Rayna asks.

I don't want to explain the Isabel situation. "Nothing. I'm hungry."

I take a huge bite of my burger. Clara and Rayna obviously want to push me for more, but I shake my head and keep chewing, making it clear the topic of Carson is now off-limits.

The truth is, I do like him. But there's also so much history between us, plus the complication of Theo. We may have started over in many respects, but there are still a lot of unanswered questions before we can truly move forward.

53

The following Wednesday, I exit Dr. Rowland's office building with Mom, "upgraded" from the walking boot to the surgical shoe. Mom apparently anticipated this, as she brought it along.

"I can't believe this!" I fume. "How is this a step up?"

"It's only for two more weeks," Mom says. "Then you can wear athletic shoes!"

"Oh, yay!" I say sarcastically, then attempt an unconvincing smile at her disappointed frown. It's hard to stay positive when these supposed improvements don't allow me to do anything new.

I walk around experimentally, and I'm uneven again. The surgical shoe isn't as tall as the boot. Guess I should have Clara over for part two of Cinderella's Glass Slipper. Actually, Rayna could join in now too. We'll make it a party. "I thought I'd be able to start dancing again."

Mom hums sympathetically. "I'm sorry, sweetheart. Healing takes time."

"I know that, but we're not even going back for another month. My dance recital's in six weeks, so even if she clears me then, they won't be able to put me back into the dances."

"I'm sorry it's not what you hoped for." She pulls me in for a quick hug. "But at least you can move your ankle now. And I know it's not the same, but you can go back to Future Stars rehearsals, even tonight if you want."

That *is* something. "Mom, I—"

Her phone rings, and she glances down at it, frowning. "I need to take this."

"Okay."

She walks away before she picks up. It's probably a work call, but what if it has to do with her health? I've never been able to bring myself to ask her outright if she had cancer, and it's been eating away at me. This could be my opportunity to find out more.

If I follow, she'll hear me clunking on the sidewalk. Moving as quietly as I can in her direction, I'm able to catch a few words of her side of the conversation: ". . . be there Thursday at three . . . building A, right?" And then she's hanging up, and I stop abruptly.

She turns around, and her eyes widen at how close I am.

"Everything okay?" I ask.

She quickly rearranges her expression into a calm mask. "Just confirming a meeting."

A meeting, huh? Or an appointment? I intend to find out.

54

The moment I walk into Future Stars rehearsal that night, I get tackle-hugged from multiple directions.

"Maggie!" Alexis squeals in my left ear. "I thought you were never coming back."

"You can't leave us like that again," Tyrone says in my right.

They're both dressed to dance, in jazz shoes, leggings, and tanks. It gives me a twinge, since I can't do the choreography, but at least I'm here.

"Someone get Maggie a chair," Yvonne says as she comes into the rehearsal room. Her auburn hair is in a messy bun, with tendrils escaping against her creamy temples. She's wearing a bright pink Susan G. Komen T-shirt. "We have a lot of material to cover. The concert's in just over two weeks."

Good thing I've still been practicing the music.

Hailey brings me a chair. "Great to see you back."

"Thanks! Hey, what did you decide about *Footloose*?"

She shrugs. "I passed on the ensemble. Going for *Hairspray*."

I figured she would. "Let me know how it goes!"

Hailey salutes me as she heads back to join Elana on the other side of the room.

Alexis and Tyrone sit on the floor on either side of me and start stretching. Alexis twists her dark hair up into a tight bun. "So, Maggie, about *Footloose*, I was wondering . . ."

And then nothing.

"I've never seen her lose a line like this," I say, sharing an amused look with Tyrone.

She huffs. "Fine. I know you were going for Rusty before you got hurt, so if you say no, I get it. But would you be up for brainstorming some character ideas? I just didn't expect to get this part, and I'm kind of nervous."

Oh. Actually, I have a lot of thoughts about the character and specifically how Alexis could use her strengths best. Maybe Mrs. Pintado had a point after *A Midsummer Night's Dream*.

"You know, I would."

"Great." She relaxes. "We'll figure out a time."

I find I'm looking forward to it.

And then, a minute before it's time to start, Katelyn strides in. When she sees me, she stops and does a classic double take. Priceless.

"Hey, Katelyn, aren't you happy to see me?"

"Overjoyed," she replies, but it sounds like she's choking. She recovers and moves to a spot away from everyone else.

Tyrone leans forward with his chin on his fist. "What real-life drama did I miss?"

He must not follow Katelyn's socials, or he'd know about her and Theo, including that he finally asked her to prom. She even put up a poll asking people to vote on which dress she should wear. It felt very similar to my shoe feed. I wonder how many other things in my life she wants to copy. There's a set of stairs I can show her to if she wants to get really method . . .

I shake my head, because Yvonne just played a chord on the piano, which means it's time for vocal warm-ups. *That* I can do.

And for the next two hours, I lose myself in the music.

55

"Thanks for coming with me," I tell Carson as we trail my mom's car into the hospital parking lot on Thursday afternoon. He had to skip golf practice, which is a huge deal for him. I don't know what excuse he gave, but I'm grateful he's here.

"Are you kidding?" Carson grins. "You're fulfilling my child-hood dream of becoming James Bond."

I scan his car, which is old enough he still has to plug his phone in to listen to his playlist. "You're gonna need to upgrade if you wanna be 007."

He pats the dashboard. "She's a faithful companion but not the most high tech. I could—"

"Look! She's parking."

Mom pulls into a space in the ground floor of the parking garage, and of course there aren't any other spots in sight.

"What do you want to do?" Carson asks.

"Is it too obvious to follow her?"

"In the car?" Carson smirks. "Yes. But it looks like there's only one door from this garage into the hospital. So I can just drop you off and go park, and you sneak in behind her."

"That could work."

He drives past Mom toward the hospital entrance and lets me

out. There's a post near the entrance; I slip behind it and gag. A pile of cigarette butts ring the bottom of the post, and various liquids have stained the concrete. It smells like someone might have even peed in the area.

I hear footsteps approaching, but I don't peek out. I don't want to risk Mom seeing me. When the doors swish open, I take a quick look and see her disappearing through them. I wait an extra moment and slip out from behind the post. She's moved completely inside the doors, but I miscalculated, because there are stairs and an elevator right inside. How am I supposed to tell where she went?

"Boo!"

I'm so startled I jump and land off-balance. Carson has to catch me. I hold a hand over my heart; I swear I can feel it pulsing out of my chest.

"What are you *doing*?"

"Sorry." He bites his lip. "Where'd your mom go?" He squints inside the doors.

"I don't know. She disappeared fast, so I think maybe she took the stairs. But I'm afraid she'll see me."

"Don't worry. She's less likely to recognize me. I'll go."

True. Mom's seen Carson before, considering he's Theo's best friend. But not recently. The day I broke my foot, he kept his distance after I got so ticked at him for helping. And he picks me up after she leaves for work and drops me off before she gets home.

"Go." I shove him toward the door, and he bounds inside.

Now what am I supposed to do?

I stand there aimlessly while a couple of other people walk into the building, giving me questioning looks. A few minutes later, my phone buzzes in my pocket. It's a text from Carson: The coast is clear.

I head inside and take the elevator up to the lobby. Carson's waiting by the doors when I emerge.

"I spotted the subject at the green elevators over there."

The subject? "You're really getting into this."

He grins. "She got into the second elevator and was the only passenger. It stopped on the sixth floor."

"Okay." I nod. "Thanks, Carson."

When I head for the elevators, he grabs my forearm. "What are you doing?"

"Finding out what's on the sixth floor."

"She might see you." He's still holding my arm. His fingers are gentle; I find I don't want to pull free. "Maybe check the directory first?"

When I concede, he releases me, leaving my skin cold where he was touching me. We walk toward the plaque on the elevator wall. I run a finger down the numbers and stop on six. There are only four things listed, but I'm already sure which one Mom's here for.

"The Breast Wellness Center," I say around a knot in my throat.

"What makes you think so?" Carson asks quietly. "There's a dermatologist and a—"

"No." I shake my head firmly as the exact words Mom used in the simulation solidify in my mind. "It's something to do with a cyst. It's the Breast Wellness Center."

"A cyst?" Carson scrunches his eyebrows. "I thought we were following her because you had a feeling. A cyst is pretty specific."

Oops. I didn't give Carson many details when I asked him to chauffeur me on this mission. He gave up his afternoon anyway.

"Did you overhear something?"

I don't want to lie to him, but he'd never believe the truth. "Sort of."

"Are we going up to the Breast Wellness Center?"

I picture myself marching in there and confronting my mom. I want to know what's going on, but maybe *before* she finds out herself isn't the best time. I'm not even sure if I want to confront her here. Now that I know a little more, I might have the guts to ask her at home.

"I don't think so."

"Okay."

He's being so patient.

"I'll wait with you," he adds.

I scan the lobby and spot a group of empty couches near a vending machine. "Let's sit."

He follows me willingly, and we choose two armchairs catty-cornered to each other.

I cross my legs, then uncross them, unsure how to fill the time on what's basically a stakeout. "So . . . Theo's taking Katelyn to the prom now, huh?"

He pales, which should be impossible for him, and sits back in his chair. "That's what you want to talk about?"

Not really. But apparently I can't help bringing Theo up to Carson. We each have our issues. Like Carson's of not knowing how to say *anything* when we met.

Carson runs his thumb along a pen mark on his jeans. "Theo really did care about you."

His voice is quiet—and sad.

"I thought he did. But he sure hasn't acted like I meant anything to him since we broke up," I say bitterly.

"He—" Carson lets out a frustrated breath. "I can't do this with you. Theo's my best friend, and you're— Things have just gotten really confused."

I can't tell if he's trying to make excuses for Theo or say something completely different.

"Does he know we're hanging out?" I ask again.

He meets my gaze. "We don't talk about you."

It's the same thing he said that day in the hall, when I asked if he'd told Theo I broke my foot. I thought he was being hurtful then, but maybe it's something else. "You mean . . . never?"

Carson shakes his head. "Ever since the day we all met, Theo and I have had an unspoken agreement not to. Even when I've had really strong opinions about . . . things."

Things like Isabel? And Katelyn?

"But you're his best friend. Who else do you talk to about . . ."

. . . your girlfriend?

Or boyfriend? If you're Rayna, no one. She just kept Adam a secret for eight months. Is that what's happening here? Am I now Carson's secret?

But does that mean Theo didn't talk to anyone about us? Because he knew Carson had feelings for me when we first met? But then . . . is that why Theo's been such a jerk since? Because he has no one to give him better advice about how to handle a breakup? I don't know what to think.

"Theo has other friends," Carson says.

"Not like you."

Carson concedes with a defeated shrug and rests his elbows on his knees.

I copy his position, which brings us close together.

"Maybe you're too good of a friend." I want him to understand my meaning, that I know he stepped aside that day, recognizing I was into Theo. That I see him now for who he really is instead of the jerk he hid behind for the past seven months.

He shifts closer so our faces are only inches apart. "I'm not, Maggie. If you knew . . ."

"What should I know? Tell me."

But I don't really want him to talk. His lips are so close, and he doesn't need to use words. I can't believe it, but I want Carson Lockwood to kiss me.

His lips curve. "I—"

"Maggie?"

Carson leaps to his feet much more quickly than I react, disoriented by the interruption. I start to push up myself but don't quite have my balance and rock back into the chair. I twist toward the voice and smile weakly.

"Hi, Mom."

56

"What are you doing here?" Mom looks confused rather than angry, but that could quickly change, considering I was snooping in her business. She shifts her gaze to Carson. "Aren't you Carson?"

He snaps to attention and extends his hand. "Yes, ma'am. Nice to meet you officially, Mrs. Scott."

She smiles as she shakes his hand. "Likewise. Thank you for giving Maggie a ride the last few weeks."

"My pleasure." He stuffs his hands in his pockets.

"Mm-hmm." Her eyes shift between us. "But I'm still wondering why you gave her a ride *here*. Because I don't really believe you brought her to the hospital for a date."

"Mom!" Heat blazes in my cheeks, but she casts me a wry look that clearly states *I saw what you were up to.*

"Uh, no." Carson clears his throat, his own face a dull red.

Mom might have officially ruined any chance I have of moving things forward with Carson.

"Maggie?" Mom lifts her eyebrows, awaiting my explanation.

I know when to give up—and when to fess up. "We followed you."

"Why?" She doesn't appear worried by my statement.

"To find out what's wrong with you. Clearly something is, since you're going to the Breast Wellness Center." I motion toward the elevators.

"I see."

Then why isn't she more concerned?

Mom smiles warmly at Carson, who's bouncing his knee like he's ready to make a run for it. "Thank you again for your help. I'll take Maggie home."

He bobs his head. "Right. See you tomorrow, Maggie."

He barely looks at me as he flees for the stairs back to the garage.

I wish I could go with him. Mom doesn't seem mad, but she's awfully good at hiding her frustration in front of others. She was probably just waiting for him to leave to let loose on me.

I jump when she wraps an arm around my shoulder. "Why don't we go get some coffee?"

I peek up at her. "You aren't going to yell at me for sneaking up on you?"

She smirks. "I think I was the one who did the sneaking."

True. I'll have to think more later about how close I came to kissing Carson. Or maybe how close he came to kissing *me*. I'm not sure which way things were headed.

Neither of us says anything as we walk out to the car. I'm waiting until I can look her in the eye; maybe she is too. When we get to Mom's car, my backpack is sitting on the trunk. I glance around; Carson's SUV is idling at the end of the row. He gives a small wave as he pulls away.

"What a thoughtful boy." Mom watches him drive off with a pensive expression.

I make a noncommittal noise. I'm not letting her turn this conversation into boy talk, even if the idea of hashing it out with her is strangely appealing.

Mom picks a local coffee shop a few blocks from the hospital and even orders us both cookies.

I take mine gingerly. "I'm starting to think you aren't angry?"

She presses her lips together and exhales through her nose. "Let's find a seat."

She leads me to a quiet corner and sits with both hands cupped around her coffee. I'd think she was trying to warm them, but it's actually pretty toasty in here.

"I'm not sure why you felt like you should follow me, but I want to assure you first off that there's nothing to worry about."

"Okay," I say slowly, still not completely reassured.

"Last summer, I went in for my regular mammogram, and it showed an irregularity."

This sounds like how those stories of women having to get their breasts removed start. Or having to undergo months of chemo. I can't imagine Mom with no hair. "What sort of irregularity?"

"A cyst, they said, but there are lots of types of cysts. Some you have to worry about, and others are nothing at all."

Even though I've had multiple proofs Grace showed me the truth, this one hits hardest. Because it's not only about Mom keeping information from me; it's also an actual health crisis that could take *her* away from me.

"What kind is yours?" I ask in a small voice, feeling like a three-year-old who wants nothing more than to crawl into her mother's lap.

Mom nudges the cookie toward me. "Take a bite."

Seriously? She thinks I can eat at a time like this? She cocks an eyebrow, clearly waiting for me to comply. I bite off a small piece and chew, but it tastes like sandpaper in my mouth. I quickly take a gulp of my coffee to wash it down.

"Good." Mom breaks off a piece of her own cookie but doesn't eat it. "Last August, I went in for an ultrasound to check the cyst. The doctor said she wasn't currently concerned about it but that she wanted me to come back in for a follow-up in four months."

She plops the cookie in her mouth, like she isn't worried at all. If it were me, I'd be a total wreck.

That must have been after August 6, since she *was* worried about it that day. Four months later would've been . . . December. What an awful time of year to be thinking about a lump on your breast. "What happened when you went back?"

She swallows. "No change. Which was a good sign. But the doctor still wasn't ready to clear me completely, so she asked me to come back again in another four months. That was today's appointment."

I scoot forward in my chair. "And?"

Mom runs her fingers through her hair. "And today she finally said that since there's been no change in the cyst over eight months, she's satisfied it's benign and I can return to regular mammograms. I haven't even had a chance to tell your dad yet. He's probably sent me ten messages asking," she says with a significant look at me.

I'm not convinced. "That's it? Just an ultrasound? They don't do a biopsy to test it?"

Mom reaches across the table to squeeze my fingers. "If they were truly concerned about it, they'd order additional tests. This is good news, Maggie. That's why we're celebrating."

She picks up her cookie and takes another big bite, as if this settles it. Maybe in her mind it does, but I'm not completely satisfied. I guess about her being okay. If she feels confident in what the doctor told her, then it doesn't make sense for me to question them. Although, I got all worked up and then had the worry yanked away like a magic trick. It's something else.

"What's bothering you, sweetheart?"

Here I am, spoiling Mom's clean bill of health celebration, but I can't help it.

"Why did you keep it a secret from us?" I frown. "Unless Adam knew?"

She breaks her cookie into several small pieces. "No, he doesn't."

That's something, at least. I couldn't handle it if Adam was in on one more secret.

"But we might have told him."

"What?" I set my coffee down so forcefully it sloshes. "Why?"

"Maggie . . ." She appears to be arguing with herself, and I'm afraid to say anything in case I tip her in the direction of continuing to freeze me out. Her shoulders slump and she meets my eyes. "When all this started, you were in the middle of that summer production, the one where they brought all the kids from different camps to watch every day."

I fail to see what that has to do with anything. "So?"

She lifts her hands. "So we were afraid if you knew, it would distract you."

Her repeated use of "we" makes it clear Dad was in on this

decision to keep me in the dark. "You were worried about *distract-ing* me? When you thought you might have cancer? That's way more important!"

"We would have told you if it had been cancer."

I'm starting to doubt that's true. *Nobody* tells me anything. "What about when you had that first ultrasound? I was done with the summer production in August."

She smiles gently. "Yes, but you'd just found out about *Frozen*. And before you ask"—she puts up her palm—"the second ultrasound was the week of your show. I definitely didn't want you worried about me during tech week."

"Are you *kidding*? Mom, you're way more important than a show."

She's still smiling, but in a fixed way. "When you broke your foot, what was the first thing you worried about?"

I squirm in my seat, afraid of where she's going with this. "I don't see what that has to do with whether you told me you possibly had cancer."

Mom twists her lips to the side. "Maggie, for the past . . . seven or eight years, all you've cared about is being in shows. You have the most focused drive, and I love that about you."

"It's not *all* I care about." Is that really what she believes? "You're my mom. I would have been there for you."

She's wearing the same skeptical expression as before. What have I done to give my mom the impression I don't care? No, not just an impression. A deep-seated belief.

"I'm here now, Mom. Doesn't that prove how much I care?"

She falters. "I know you love us, Maggie. I've never questioned that. It's just . . . would you be so focused on me today if you were in a show?"

Wow. My throat is clogged. There's no way I'm choking down more of that cookie. I push it toward Mom.

"I'm really sorry I made you feel like you came second, Mom. I know there's nothing I can do right now to prove I mean it, but I'm going to be better in the future."

"That's all any of us can ever do. I think you also need to realize that part of us loving *you* is deciding what we think you need to know and when. In this case, that wasn't when I first found out." She pats my hand. "And I really am fine. I'd better call your dad and give him the update."

As she pulls out her phone, I sink back into my seat and ponder what she shared. If my parents think I care more about my own ambitions than them, what vibes have I been giving off to the other people in my life? Am I as bad as Katelyn?

But I have friends, plus other people who care about me. That wouldn't be true if I were completely self-absorbed.

I don't know what to do with this information Mom dumped on me. It would've been much easier if she'd said she hid it to protect me, but she had to add that tidbit about distracting me. I hate that Mom doubted the depth of my feelings, and I vow to immediately start showing her how much I love her.

51

Dad's waiting for us when we get home. As soon as we walk through the door, he sweeps Mom into his arms and buries his face in her neck. I avert my gaze.

They murmur together for a few moments, and then Dad releases her and turns to me. "Sounds like you had an eventful afternoon, Maggie Mae."

Mom talked to him in front of me, and even though I was lost in my own thoughts, I don't think she told him about the Carson incident. So I assume he's just referring to me following her.

"I wanted to know what was going on with Mom."

His brow crinkles. "What I don't understand is why you suspected anything in the first place."

I cast around for a plausible explanation and fall back on the same one I used with Carson. "Something I overheard."

He's still frowning. "I thought we—"

"It doesn't matter," Mom says firmly.

Thank you, Mom.

"Is Adam home?" she asks.

"Yes." Dad's brow clears. "I'll go get him."

I link my arm with Mom's, all in as a supportive family member. "Yes, let's get Adam."

By the time we reach the living room, Dad and Adam are already waiting.

Adam sits quietly through Mom's explanation about the cyst, but his jaw's tight, a muscle ticking near his throat.

At the end, he says, "And you're only telling us this now because Maggie caught you at the doctor's office?"

I wish she'd left that part out, but I guess it couldn't be avoided.

"If she hadn't, would you have ever told us?" he presses.

"Probably not," Mom says gently. "Your dad and I discussed it and decided not to. Of course, if there had been something real to worry about, we would have shared that with you."

She's careful not to say the C-word.

Adam scowls at me. "Why do you have to stick your nose in everything? There's no reason we had to know anything about this."

I flinch at his tone and scoot closer to Mom. "Don't you care how worried Mom's been about this? It's super scary!"

"If she were that worried about it, she would have told us. Right, Mom?"

I look over, expecting her to tear into him, but she's gazing at Adam with the same empathy she showed me in the coffee shop. "Yes, Adam."

But it's not right at all. She was worried. Dad too. The way he held her so tight when she walked in the door—his relief was palpable.

Adam stands and leans over to kiss Mom on the cheek. "I'm glad you're okay."

"Me too." She watches him leave the room with a bittersweet smile.

"That's it?" I look between my parents. "That was so rude! And you think *I* don't care."

Dad looks startled for a moment; then awareness dawns on his face. "You and Adam process things very differently."

You bet we do. "I'm going to talk to him."

I squeeze Mom's arm and get up, hobbling toward the hall.

"You should leave him alone," Dad calls.

I ignore him and don't make out Mom's response.

Adam's door is closed, but I ignore that too, twisting the handle and barging in without knocking. He swivels around at my entrance, and even though it's dark in his room with his blackout curtains pulled closed, I catch the anguish on his face before he masks it.

He marches toward me and stabs a finger at my chest. "You ruin everything."

I stumble backward. "What? Because I followed Mom to find out what was wrong with her? I was worried!"

He keeps advancing until I can smell the apple he must have eaten as a snack. "*You* were worried. Once again everything is about you. Mom had reasons for keeping her own health issues to herself. It wasn't any of your business!"

It seems to me like Adam's the one who's focused on me, but I don't dare say it. Especially when I know something he doesn't—that Mom might have told him sooner if it weren't for me. Would he feel differently if Mom had told him about all this last August?

I have no idea, and it actually *is* my fault he didn't have the chance to find out then. So instead of arguing like I normally would, I hold his gaze and simply say, "I'm sorry."

"Yeah, you—wait. You're sorry?" He deflates at the hole I've poked in his righteous indignation.

I came in here, prepared to attack him for not taking Mom's health seriously enough. But I don't think that's what's going on at all. He does care; like Dad said, Adam just has a different way of handling it.

"Yes," I confirm. Because it's possibly the first time I've said that to him in years. "I'm not sorry that I followed Mom because I was really worried, but I am sorry I didn't consider how that would affect you."

"Wow." Adam steps back.

Maybe I shouldn't have added that last part, but it's the truth.

"Rayna was right. There is something different about you."

I rankle a bit at the evidence they're still talking about me. But then, of course they are. I have to get used to it. And, yes, maybe there is something different about me lately. I got dumped, broke my foot, missed out on two shows, haven't been able to dance or do most of the other activities I love, and then discovered I'd totally misunderstood most of the people around me. How could I *not* be different?

"The past few weeks have been intense."

"Tell me about it." He runs his hand through his hair. "It would mean a lot to Rayna if we both tried harder—for real."

I know what he means. Not just saying we will but actually doing it. Which, unfortunately, involves spending time together. I sigh. "Give me a ride tomorrow?"

He smiles over his grimace. "Yeah."

58

Prom prep is surprisingly fun, considering I'd dreamed of going myself and instead I'm an observer. Clara and I treat Rayna like our personal doll, picking out every accessory, giving her a mani-pedi, and styling her hair according to our specifications. We take her preferences into account, but she doesn't have much input. Rayna's not fussy about her appearance, which apparently works just fine for my brother.

I give him props for that.

I put Mom on his case, and when he arrives to pick up Rayna, I'm pleased to see he's properly attired and groomed.

Okay, I admit it. He looks handsome. They're about to take pictures when I notice his tie is crooked. "Wait!"

I dart forward and reach for it. Adam's eyes widen.

"Don't worry. I'm not going to strangle you."

He relaxes as I smooth the tie. "Never thought you were."

"Liar." I smirk.

I rejoin Clara in the background while Rayna's parents take a bunch of pictures, but then I realize Mom and Dad will want them too, so I snap a few.

"You ready?" Adam smiles down at Rayna, his expression

incredibly tender. I suppose I really will have to start getting along with him.

"In a sec. I just need a picture with my girls," Rayna says.

"You're too glamorous for us," Clara protests.

"As if!" Rayna scoffs.

But it's true. Tonight, Rayna outshines us both.

We all lean together for the photos, and my smile isn't practiced or extra bright for the camera. It's the relaxed smile of a girl who truly has her best friend back. I'm grateful to have her here beside me now, even if I have to accept my annoying brother as her boyfriend.

I turn and hug her. "You have the most magical time, Rayna," I say against her ear. "I can't wait to hear about the world tour, especially the food stations."

She pulls back to wiggle her eyebrows. "You don't want to hear about after?"

I give her a pained look. "I want to hear about it all."

She laughs and nudges Clara. "I'll call you about that part."

"Thank you," I say with heartfelt emotion. I turn to my brother. "I hope you have a wonderful time. See you later."

He nods and holds his hand out for Rayna. Clara and I follow them outside.

"Have fun with David," I call to Clara as I walk to my car.

Fortunately for David, their plans have nothing to do with his siblings tonight.

I'd be lying if I didn't admit to some nostalgic feelings when I was watching Adam and Rayna together. I expected to go with Theo, and now he's going with—ugh—Katelyn instead. I don't want to be with Theo anymore, but I still want to know about Isabel. It's awful to think he might have been seeing another girl when we first started dating, that those early weeks together were also a lie. I also just want to understand where we went wrong. His explanation is very hazy to me. I think I was in shock while he was telling me he wanted to break up.

When I get home, I sit in the driveway for several moments, trying to decide what to do.

A knock on the window startles me, and I nearly fall over into the passenger seat when I turn and see Carson standing on my street.

I motion for him to back up so I can get out of the car. "Hey. What's up?"

What's up? Really smooth.

"You're driving!"

"Oh. Yes." Today was actually the first time since I broke my foot.

"I was driving in the lane next to you for the past five minutes, and you looked completely spaced out, so I followed you home. Do you always drive on autopilot?"

That must have been super attractive. I gather my wits. "You could've honked."

He scrunches his face. "Have you noticed how honking's just not accepted these days? It's like, if you honk at someone, all the other drivers give you nasty looks. *Especially* if it's to get the attention of a pretty girl in the next lane."

I suppress a grin. "I see your point."

"So is this why you don't need a ride from me anymore?" He leans against my car. "I missed you yesterday."

I blink, trying to organize everything that's happened since I saw him at the hospital on Thursday.

"Sorry. No, I'm still not driving to school. My brother and I had a talk Thursday night, and we're trying to get along for Rayna's sake." I guess my text to Carson saying I didn't need a ride Friday didn't make that clear. "So I'm riding with him for now, but I appreciate how much you helped me."

This doesn't seem as significant as what I want to say.

"I wanted to." Carson drags his shoe along the pavement. "What about your mom? Is she okay?" He looks up quickly. "Not that you need to tell me anything private."

"No, it's fine," I assure him. "She was getting some tests, but everything came up negative. She's all good."

He smiles broadly. "That's the best news I've heard all day."

Remembering my conversation with the girls last week, I peek over at him. "You could've asked me at school. My lunch table's not so far away from yours."

"I—" He clears his throat. "Yeah. I could have."

That's it. No explanation of why he didn't or even a suggestion that he might talk to me another time in front of Theo. It ignites a devilish streak in me.

"I just got back from Rayna's. We got her all ready for the prom and sent her off with Adam. It's a big night."

He swallows. "Yep."

"You weren't interested in going? Doubling with Theo and Katelyn?"

His gaze whips over to me, and I curse myself for mentioning Theo. I should've stopped at the first question.

He must see the dismay on my face. "I'm not a fan of Katelyn."

I recover, relaxing against the car. "Still, you could've avoided her."

"Maybe. If there was someone I wanted to take."

Ouch. "Well, that's clear enough."

I push away from the car, but before I can take a step, he grabs my wrist and turns me toward him. "Wait, Maggie. That's not what I meant."

I keep my eyes steady on his. "What then?"

"I meant"—he breaks eye contact for a moment, looking up at the sky before refocusing on me—"if the person I wanted to take was available."

Obviously he missed the *kiss me* signal I was sending off the other day, when I leaned toward him in the hospital lounge area. "I'm thinking she's available."

He grins slowly. "You think she's available next Saturday night?"

We'd better be talking about the same thing now. "I do think so."

"Okay then." He releases my wrist and steps back. Why? I thought we were having a moment.

"Until next Saturday then."

Next Saturday? What about all the days in between? Carson is still the most frustrating boy in the world!

"That's it?" I can't help but ask.

He ambles toward his car. "I've got plans to make."

He's got plans? Well, so do I. Before I can start anything with Carson, I need real closure with Theo. It's time he gets over this thing where he refuses to talk to me.

59

I nurse an iced mocha at a corner table in Bread Co., wondering if Theo will stand me up. Shocking enough that he even answered my text on Sunday, and then he said if I wanted to talk, it would have to be late on Tuesday, after golf practice.

I'm relieved when I see him walk through the door only five minutes after we planned to meet. His hair is matted on his forehead, and he looks sticky overall from practice. Used to be he would have cleaned himself up before meeting me; I wonder if it's intentional. He's still handsome, even when he's a sweaty mess.

"Sorry," he says as he sits across from me. "Coach had a long speech at the end of practice, or I wouldn't be stinking up the place."

"It's okay." I don't mind because I have no desire to get close to him anyway. It's such a change from how I felt before. I admit I did a little stalking on Sunday, scrolling through Katelyn's prom photos. He looked gorgeous in his tux but not necessarily like he was having a great time. I really don't understand what he's doing with her, but I'm also not getting into that topic.

"How's your foot?" He gestures under the table, and his tone is super casual, like one of those "how's the fam" questions you ask an acquaintance.

I can't help but laugh. "Seriously?"

His brows lower. "What?"

"Theo . . ." I take a moment to compose myself, swirling the ice in my cup. There are so many things I want to discuss with him, and I don't really want to start by ticking him off, but I sincerely want to understand how he so quickly reached this level of indifference.

"I don't want to in any way imply that my broken foot is your fault"—he snaps back in his chair, so I push forward—"because it was totally me not paying attention. The timing was just very unfortunate. But . . ." How to phrase it . . . ? "Even though we were broken up, it really hurt that you didn't even acknowledge I'd been injured. And injured in a way you knew would sideline me from all the things I loved most aside from you."

Theo stares at the table for several moments. It kills me to stay silent, but it's important for me to hear his point of view, so I hold in the ten additional questions threatening to burst out. Finally, I'm rewarded by him looking up at me with his beautiful brown eyes.

"I'm sorry," he says hoarsely. "I did care. I'll always care about you, Maggie. But . . ." He tips his chin back. "I just didn't feel like we had the same priorities."

I've reached the same conclusion, but I still want to understand where he's coming from. "What do you mean by that? With everything that happened after you dumped me"—he winces again—"I don't really remember what you said about *why* you were breaking up with me. It seemed awfully sudden."

"Maggie, you . . ." He exhales through his nose and shakes his head. "When we got together, you were so much fun. You came to watch me play golf. You hung out with my family and played with Therese. And then . . ."

I lean forward, catch a whiff of him, and sit back again. "Then what?"

"Then your theater troupe started up for the fall and you weren't around as much. But you still made an effort to come to my stuff. Until *Frozen* rehearsals began."

He spits out *Frozen* like it's a nasty word.

"I had no idea you hated it so much."

He deflates. "It's not that I hated the musical itself. It just took so much of your time."

This is basically what Rayna said. "Why didn't you talk to me about it?"

"When I did see you, you were so excited about it. I could tell how much you loved it."

I'm about to answer when he adds in a mutter, "And that you'd always love that more than me. More than any guy really."

I know I was in a daze the day Theo broke up with me, but I'm pretty sure I'd remember if he said *that*. The thing is, I can't deny his point. I told him I loved him, and I did, but as I look back on our relationship, I wasn't *in love* with Theo. Not the way I'm in love with the theater.

But honestly, I don't see anything wrong with that. We're in high school. Even though I had our path charted out for the next couple of years, I wasn't under any illusions we'd try the long-distance thing once Theo went off to college. I feel like Carson would understand that, considering his passion for golf.

It's just evidence Theo was never the right fit for me. Still, it never occurred to me I hurt Theo's feelings with my ambition. "Why didn't you break up with me sooner then?"

He smiles wryly. "Once the show was over, the old Maggie returned. The one who made me the center of her world."

The comment makes me uneasy, especially as I recall my conversation with Rayna right after the breakup. My first instinct when I broke my foot was to make Theo my main priority. It sounds like that was my pattern throughout our relationship: Theo, show, Theo, show.

"And then I started working on the spring play at school."

He wags a finger. "Don't forget your spring showcase with your troupe."

I had forgotten about that; it happened the first week of March. I guess I was busy leading up to that. I performed a dance duet with another girl, along with singing a solo and the ensemble pieces. "Was that the final straw for you?"

He grimaces. "Do you remember me asking you to go to that trivia night with my parents?"

It sounds vaguely familiar, but I can't recall any of the details. "What was it for?"

He waves a hand. "A charity my dad's on the board for. But the point is, I asked you to go with me, and you blew me off because you had to rehearse. On a Friday night."

I wince, suddenly remembering the night he's talking about. My dance partner said she could rehearse then or the next morning, and I didn't want to go out Saturday morning, so I canceled on Theo at the last minute.

In hindsight, that wasn't cool. And yet, I don't remember even hesitating. What does that say about me? Theo's right; he wasn't at the top of my priority list.

"I'm sorry about that. I should have been more thoughtful about you."

"Thanks." He looks surprised. "You're different. Maybe . . ."

He trails off, leaving me to fill in the blanks.

Maybe I should've talked to you more before I dumped you so hastily?

Maybe I made a mistake?

Maybe you aren't the insensitive girl I thought you were?

Who knows? It's pointless to try to read his mind now. I've already discovered I was way off base when I assumed I understood him before.

"I've had a lot of time to think the past few weeks," I say. "And to talk through things with people."

He opens his mouth again, and I wonder if he's going to ask about Carson. I came to this meeting intending to bring him up myself, especially since Carson continues to pretend there's nothing between us at school. But then I think about how he's told me twice that they don't talk about me, and it feels wrong to get in the middle of their friendship. If I've learned nothing else from what's happened with Rayna, I definitely understand how complicated friendship is.

I have no such reservations getting other answers. I'll take responsibility for not being as attentive as I could have been, but it wasn't all one-sided. If Theo expected more from me, he could have told me. I might have been wrapped up in rehearsals, but the threat of losing him would have caught my attention. I'd like to think I would have at least made an effort.

"There's something else I need to know about." I take a deep breath. "Isabel."

He blanches. "Where did you hear that name?" His face falls. "From Carson?"

It's the closest he's come to acknowledging I've been talking to Carson. "Carson would never betray you." That's how we got into this relationship in the first place.

"I wasn't sure I should come talk to you. He convinced me to."

I blink, completely thrown off track. "You told Carson we were meeting up today?"

"Yeah. He wanted— Well, that doesn't matter." He flushes, making me even more curious what Carson said to him. "The point is, he said I should be honest with you. I'm glad you guys are finally friends."

Friends. Whatever they discussed, it wasn't our upcoming date. I feel a trickle of frustration toward both of them.

I push that aside, because Theo apparently came here to be honest, so it's the perfect time to push for answers. "About Isabel— suffice it to say I know the day we met I was your second choice."

"Uhh . . ."

I think I broke him. I wave a hand in front of his face. "Theo?"

He blinks several times. "Okay." He closes his eyes and inhales, then opens them and meets my gaze. "I'm not proud of the way I acted when we first met."

I resist the urge to shoot a sarcastic comeback his way.

"There was this girl, Isabel. She worked at the movie theater with me, and she was really ho—er, nice."

"Uh-huh." I've heard about Isabel's hotness ad nauseam.

"We flirted for months at work, and she finally agreed to meet me at Bridgeport Days."

"So that was supposed to be your first date?" It's what I'd gathered, but I hadn't been one hundred percent sure.

"Yeah. But then she stood me up, and I was really bummed, but I met you instead. And I had a great time, except . . ." He scratches his head. "I just kept thinking . . . you were great, but I'd been talking to Isabel for months, so I should at least give her a chance. So I still met up with her at Bridgeport Days the next afternoon."

My heart speeds up. "And?"

"We had a good time. I was really conflicted, you know?"

It's hard to empathize with him when I'm one of the two girls in question.

"But when she kissed me, it felt wrong somehow, and that's when I knew I would rather be with you."

He beams at me, as if this solves everything.

"You *kissed* her?"

He shrugs. "It's not like we were officially together or anything."

In my heart we were. "I thought the day we met was magical. I would never have looked at another guy after that."

Theo squirms. "I don't know what to say."

I guess it is unfair, putting my expectations on him. He came to our relationship already interested in someone else. But he picked me.

"It doesn't really matter now," I say. "I just wanted to know."

"Does it make things better now that you do?"

"Not really. But it's been bugging me."

"Now what?"

"You mean for us?" I wave my pointer finger between us. "I think . . . we can at least acknowledge each other now. It's good to have everything out there. On both sides."

"It kinda is." He taps his knuckles together. "So . . . I'll see you around?"

"Yeah. See you around."

60

I sink back into my chair. It's reassuring Theo wasn't cheating on me when we first started dating. But also uncomfortable to learn he felt like *I* was cheating on him with my activities. We clearly did not talk enough.

"Is this chair open?"

I'm so lost in my thoughts it takes me a moment to focus. "Clara." I smile, but when she starts to sit, I point at the chair diagonal to me. "Use that one."

She gives me a weird look but complies. "Did I just see Theo leaving?"

"Yep. That's why you don't want to sit in that chair. He was gross."

"Not sure I've ever heard you say that before."

I make a surprised sound in the back of my throat.

"So you're not getting back together?" she asks.

"What? No!" I can't believe that's her first reaction.

"Then why was he here?"

"To talk." I swirl my straw in my now watered-down mocha. "We needed a post-breakup convo. For closure."

"That's very mature of you." Even though she says it in her polite Clara way, I still sense her skepticism.

"Why do you sound so surprised?"

"Because Theo's acted like the worst sort of jerk since you broke up. Seems more like you'd be plotting revenge than asking for explanations."

Hmm. Is that what I would have done before?

"I just wanted to understand why he broke up with me in the first place so I could move on."

"Were you satisfied with the answer?"

"It was . . . enlightening."

About both of us. Seems that's what I'm discovering with every new conversation—how different others' perceptions are of me than I thought.

"Interesting." Clara props her chin on her fist. "Care to share?"

I cover my mouth with my fingertips, debating how much I should tell her. She's wise in a way I doubt I'll ever be, and she's truly kind.

"In the past few days, I've learned that I'm a pretty crappy daughter, friend, and girlfriend. Oh"—I raise a finger—"and sister. Although I never really tried at that last one anyway."

Clara frowns. "I'm sure that's not true."

"Clara." I press my lips together. "Honestly, how often have I really asked about *you* in the past?"

"Hey, you're being too tough on yourself." She scoots her chair closer to me. "Nobody's perfect when it comes to paying attention to everyone else. We all miss things sometimes. But you've been a good friend to me. You've come to watch me sing at church. You've listened to me go on and on about David, especially when I first liked him and wasn't sure where he stood."

"Oh, that was agony," I tease.

"My point is, don't beat yourself up so much. Could you do better? Sure, but we all can. And if you've had some insight into how, that's amazing. Use it."

Clara should consider a future as a motivational speaker. "How?"

"Whatever it is you were doing before, don't do it anymore. Make yourself a list, like—a better-Maggie list!"

She looks so pleased with her suggestion, and it's not a bad idea, really. "I bet you don't need a better-Clara list."

"Are you kidding? You have no idea the sort of thoughts swirling around in this brain." She taps her temple. "I work very hard not to let them escape into very bad behavior."

"You, behaving badly," I scoff. "Impossible."

She turns serious. "Maggie, I told you. Nobody's perfect. Especially not me."

"Okay," I say, taken aback. "So I'll make a better-Maggie list."

"Great." Clara pushes back her chair. "Gotta go."

"'Bye," I call as she strides away.

A better-Maggie list. What would that entail? I pull out my phone and almost drop it on the table. I have a new text message from an unknown number.

Click here to activate Act Three:

There's another new link that I assume will reactivate the Best Day app. But why? I finished the day. What could possibly be on there now?

I shouldn't click. I *won't* click.

Maybe just to see what it is?

No.

I'm making a better-Maggie list, like Clara suggested. And thanks to this reminder, I'll use what I learned in the Best Day app as a starting point. Only like Clara said, these will be tasks I have to keep working at forever instead of things I can check off and forget.

Take that, Grace!

First, my family. Mom believed I put drama before family. What are some practical ways I can show love to my parents? If I don't have actual daily tasks to check off, I will totally lose sight of this goal. I brainstorm several.

- Ask Mom and Dad about their days, listen to their answers, and include at least one follow-up question
- Schedule non-drama-related time with each parent once a month (Kitaro for Dad!)
- Be nice to Adam

I already committed to that last point for Rayna, but I know it's not specific enough. So I add another bullet to make sure Mom and Dad give equal attention to Adam's activities, even though I'm not sure how I'm supposed to do that. Unless . . . oh, man. *I* have to show an interest in Adam's activities.

- Attend Adam's soccer games, at least two per month

I think two is a huge concession. At least I'll be able to hang out with Rayna.

Ah, Rayna. There's a lot of work left to repair our friendship, and much of it needs to happen on my end. It's hard to figure out actionable items for that.

- Ask Rayna about science stuff, listen to answers, and ask at least one follow-up question

Hey, it's apparently what got her interested in Adam. It's

similar to what I wrote for my parents, but that's a key part of my problem—that I haven't been sincerely listening to the people in my life. I've got to pay better attention.

- **Ask Clara, Alexis, Tyrone, and other friends about what's going on in their lives**

Getting to know Clara even better has been an unexpected side effect of this whole thing, and Alexis has always been so confident I never would have expected her to ask for character help. It makes me wonder who else in my life I haven't been taking a close enough look at.

Aside from the obvious one. After our conversation, I have closure with Theo and can make a fresh start with Carson. From a better-Maggie standpoint, I think it's about finding an appropriate balance between my relationships and drama activities. I don't know what may happen with Carson, but like with Theo, it's starting at a time when I'm not in a show. So . . .

- **Be honest with Carson about my drama commitments**
- **When I'm able to act again, check priorities**

This point is important to me, because in Theo's eyes, I let him down more than once. I don't want to be so consumed by ambition that I neglect the people who are important in my life. So I guess this bullet applies to my family, Rayna, and anyone else I care about.

I still want to give my best effort when I perform, but there has to be balance.

I type **BALANCE** out three times, right in the middle of my list.

Funny how it took putting me physically off-balance to make me realize the rest of my life needed rebalancing too.

I resolutely close out my phone without activating the Best Day app. I've learned a lot from it, but I also can figure things out on my own now, without Grace.

As Liza Minnelli says, "I think that's the greatest gift one can have: point of view."

I've gained enough perspective to move forward, and that's what I plan to do.

61

The next afternoon, I'm sitting on the couch scrolling through various notifications on my phone when I receive an interesting email.

Dear Maggie,

I heard about your unfortunate accident in March, and I was very sorry you weren't able to audition for our summer production of *Footloose*. I hope you're healing well! I've been in your position before, and I know how frustrating it is to be sidelined from the stage.

I received supporting emails from both your school drama teacher, Lorelei Pintado, and Yvonne Mescall at Metro Theater Arts praising your talent for building up other actors. Yvonne said you might be a fit for our assistant director internship this summer. While you would not be on the stage, you would be involved in prep meetings and all other aspects of the production, including coordination with set design, costumes, music, choreography, and actor relations. If this sounds like something that would interest you, please

reply at your earliest convenience, and we can set up a time
to discuss it further.

Sincerely,
Solomon Cross

Wow. Directing.

"What's put such a thoughtful expression on your face?" Mom
says as she comes in and sits beside me.

I pass her the phone with the email. She skims through it and
makes a "huh" sound in the back of her throat. "Well?" She hands
the phone back to me. "*Are* you interested?"

I haven't really wrapped my mind around the idea yet.
"Maybe."

"It sure is nice of Yvonne to suggest you."

"Yeah, it is." I never really thought of myself as having that
much of an impact on others. Although, I did help Riley get ready
for *A Midsummer Night's Dream*, and I felt really proud of the way
her performance turned out. So maybe it would be rewarding to
do that on a bigger scale.

I think of Felix, running around before the play, making sure
everything was ready to go. I also remember how happy I was,
even no longer a member of the cast, to see how well the show
went. I imagine that satisfaction must have been exponentially
higher for Felix, who was instrumental to organizing it all.

Did Yvonne overhear me talking with Alexis, or is her rec-
ommendation based on something else she's seen me do in the
troupe? I could ask her about it at rehearsal tonight, but sitting
here with Mom actually brings to mind another memory Grace

showed me. I thought I had let it go, but I guess it's still been bugging me.

"Mom, do you find out the casting before we do? When there's a show at MTA?"

"Not usually," Mom hedges.

"But sometimes?" I press. "Like for *Frozen*?"

Her eyebrows pop up. "That was a bit of a unique case." She purses her lips, like she's trying to decide what to tell me. "It wasn't Yvonne who initiated it, but me."

"Why?" It bothered me when it first came up, and it still does, that Mom apparently thought I couldn't be professional about the part I got.

She sighs. "Partially because of what was going on with me at the time. I was already very emotional."

Oh. It hadn't occurred to me it might be about *Mom*.

"I'd been talking to Yvonne about that anyway. Since she had breast cancer several years ago."

That's right. I wasn't in the troupe yet when Yvonne underwent her treatment, but every year she participates in the Susan G. Komen Race for the Cure. She had on one of the old T-shirts that first night I returned to rehearsal.

"So we were chatting more than usual during the casting of *Frozen*, and it came up that you thought you'd be cast as the queen, so when she decided to cast Katelyn as the queen and you as Oaken, she gave me a heads-up. Because"—she shrugs apologetically—"I had a total mom fail moment and told her about your reaction when Katelyn got the part you wanted in the school play."

Everything clicks into place. When I relived August 6 and looked at the cast list, I was reviewing it through the lens of having loved playing Oaken. I didn't care about Katelyn playing the queen, even though it had come up earlier in the day that I'd originally seen myself playing that part.

But in hindsight, I can understand why my mom would have been concerned, considering my ongoing feud with Katelyn—and also the other casting she mentioned earlier that year. There were tears. Maybe even something thrown across the room, I don't remember what. I guess that would have been fresh in Mom's memory. It's also possible that if I hadn't met Theo that day, I would have cared more about Katelyn getting the queen.

"I'm sorry, Maggie." Mom squeezes my hand. "I overstepped, and although Yvonne and I remain friends, I really try to maintain an appropriate distance and not get in the middle of things."

It just goes to show that even when you're inside someone else's head, you still aren't getting the full picture. I'm glad I asked Mom about it.

"It's all right, Mom."

"So what about this internship?" Mom releases my hand and taps the phone. She tilts her head, a very un-Mom-like grin spreading across her face. "Did I hear Katelyn's in the show?"

I smile back. "I see where you're going with this. If I'm the assistant director, I'll kind of be her boss." I rub my chin. "It's a definite consideration."

She wags her finger. "As long as you don't abuse it."

It's tempting, but that would definitely violate my efforts to be a better Maggie. "I think I can handle working with Katelyn—*without* going on a crazy power trip."

Mom brightens. "Then you are interested."

"It's at least worth having the discussion about it. What else will I be doing then? Even if Dr. Rowland clears me for activities, I doubt there's another show I can do this summer. I probably need to go easy on my foot at first anyway."

Mom hugs me. "That's very wise, Maggie."

I'm not sure that word has ever been used to describe me before, but I'll take it.

62

On the way to school Thursday morning, I ask Adam when his next soccer game is.

"Why?" he asks suspiciously.

"Don't worry. I'm not going to put dog poop in your cleats or anything."

He recoils. "Now I'll have to sniff my shoes before I put them on."

"Seriously. I want to come."

"The dog poop is more believable."

I scrunch my nose. "As if I'd go anywhere near that stuff. There's a reason I never begged for a puppy. Too much work."

He laughs. "Agreed. I have a game Saturday. At ten."

"Cool. I'll be there."

He no longer looks suspicious, but I've definitely unnerved him. It's kind of fun actually. I didn't expect this side effect.

I'm in a great mood when I walk into school. I want to tell Clara all about how I'm implementing my better-Maggie list (including *not* cheating by peeking into people's thoughts with an app), but I have a feeling that's not the point.

When I sit down at lunch, I glance toward Carson's table.

I texted him last night that I had some news, but he never replied. He doesn't look up from the table, so I'm unable to catch his eye.

Rayna sits beside me and bumps my shoulder. "Are you really going to Adam's game Saturday?"

"Yep."

Clara grins from my other side. "Maybe David and I will come too. Could be fun."

"Really?" Rayna's lip trembles.

It seems a bit of an overreaction. "Um, what's with the emotion?"

She blinks. "It's just . . . you said you'd try, but this is huge."

"I helped you get ready for prom."

"This is different. This is something that matters to *Adam*."

"Hey." I give her a side hug. "We're not going to become one of those super-tight sibling duos overnight, but we're working on it."

She inhales. "It means a lot."

I don't really know what to do with an emotional Rayna, so I just give her an extra squeeze and start eating my lunch.

Excited whispering starts behind us, signaling some sort of public scene. We all turn in our seats and discover the source of the drama is Theo and Katelyn.

"You're seriously dumping me less than a week after the prom?" Katelyn shouts. She's standing over him, her fists clenched.

Theo answers, but in a normal tone, so even with the lunch crowd all listening in riveted silence, I don't hear what he says.

"I've never been so insulted in my life!" Katelyn replies at full volume.

Theo answers again, and then Katelyn grabs her tray and flounces away. People start murmuring, until Katelyn turns back. We all pause, waiting to see what she'll do next. I notice her eyes flicker to her audience, making me wonder if she's playing this up for dramatic effect.

Katelyn narrows her eyes and smirks. The room quiets even more as she says in a carrying voice, "Just a tip. Before you date someone else, you might want to ask Parker Tau for some kissing advice, because he's better at it than you."

A collective gasp runs through the room. Most theater gossip is not widely known among the student population, but the story of Parker Tau—who thankfully isn't in this lunch period—got turned into a meme (poor guy) after someone snapped a photo of his stage kiss with Katelyn last spring. He didn't understand the definition of "stage kiss" and basically tried to devour her. Since they hadn't practiced it until the show, Katelyn had no choice but to endure it, but it was the one time she lost character for a split second, and that's the moment caught in the photo. So the insult hits its mark with Theo.

He stands, his palms planted firmly on the table, and glares at Katelyn. Carson half rises beside him and murmurs something. Theo gives the most infinitesimal shake of his head, obviously deciding to ignore Carson's advice.

"Katelyn," he says, and this time his voice carries. "My only mistake was thinking you would be any sort of replacement for Maggie. She's ten times the actress you are and ten times the girlfriend."

At this, half the eyes in the room turn to me, and I'm frozen in my seat.

"Oh, crap," I say under my breath and swivel around so my back's to the crowd.

Rayna leans into my shoulder. "What was *that*?"

I turned so quickly I didn't have time to see Carson's reaction to Theo's statement, but this isn't good. Why did he do that? Even with Katelyn goading him, he didn't need to drag *me* into it.

"Maggie?" Rayna presses. "Last I heard, Theo was still ignoring you. That"—she hooks her thumb over her shoulder—"is quite an about-face."

"I met up with Theo Tuesday. I'll fill you in later." I gather my lunch. "I've gotta get out of here."

I can feel the eyes boring into my back, the people dying for details about why Theo's suddenly my biggest fan again.

I keep my head down as I rush for the door. I can tell from the growing murmurings something else is going down, but I refuse to look back and see what it is.

As I push through the door, a hand grasps my arm. "YOU!"

Oh, seriously, no. I spare Katelyn a disgusted look before shaking her off and pushing through the door. She follows me through to the hallway and lets the door slam shut.

Katelyn checks to make sure we're alone and shakes her hair out. "That was entertaining."

"Not for me."

She rolls her eyes. "There was no way I was letting him dump me quietly. It's not like it was a real relationship anyway. I needed my moment."

I blink. "What do you mean, not a real relationship?"

She raises an eyebrow. "He didn't tell you at your little coffee date?"

I try to compose myself. "You didn't come up."

"It was all an act so you wouldn't turn him back into your leading man again once you were sidelined from performing," she says. "It's what you always do, after all."

I'm uncomfortable with the realization someone I so intensely dislike understands me so well. Does that mean Katelyn and I are more alike than I thought?

"But how did you get involved?" Because they were already "dating" by the next day, when Rayna came to my house trying to convince me to give up on Theo.

"A perfect coincidence." She smiles. "I happened to be nearby when Carson called to tell him about your injury."

My heart tip-taps. Carson *did* tell Theo. He broke their pact not to talk about me because he was worried.

"By the way," Katelyn continues, oblivious, "it's not as much fun to win by default. So could you fix that already?" She twirls her finger at my foot.

Nice. "I'm getting there."

"So will you take my leftovers now?" She gestures at the lunchroom doors.

"You mean Theo?" I snort. "Not likely."

Also, more like she was taking *my* leftovers.

"I don't blame you. He's pretty but not the brightest." She starts to walk away and then looks back at me. "But I lied about the kissing. He was really fantastic at that."

I wonder how many times she practiced that line. It's a good thing I no longer care who Theo kisses.

63

At the end of the day, I text Adam to please wait an extra few minutes for me so I can catch Carson. I can't wait to tell him about the internship opportunity, but when I spot him, I immediately notice something's off. He's staring at the floor, his steps unusually heavy.

"Hey, Carson." I fall into step beside him. "Rough day? Please don't tell me someone else has been tapped as the next James Bond and once again crushed your dreams."

As soon as he looks up at me, my smile drops. It's exactly like I feared that first day when he helped me with my foot—Mr. Hyde has taken back over from Dr. Jekyll. His scowl is so fierce I stumble backward. "What's wrong?"

"Nothing."

The word is so opposite of what he's emoting I'd laugh if I weren't so distressed by his complete transformation. At one time I was used to *grumpy, stay out of my space* Carson, but I'm not anymore. I want the other Carson back.

"Whatever it is, I'm here. I—" I reach a hand toward him, but he jerks away like I'm revolting. It finally gets through that maybe his mood is about *me*.

"Are you . . . mad at me?" He certainly seems like it, with an edge of . . . hurt?

"I don't know why you think I'd have any sort of feelings about you at all."

The words are worse than a slap, bringing instant tears to my eyes. I blink them back, still trying to find a source for this return to the old Carson I thought was gone for good.

"I don't know what's got your boxers twisted, but there's no reason to take it out on me."

He laughs harshly. "I told you. It has nothing to do with you. I don't care about *you*."

Well that couldn't be any clearer. "I guess our date is off then."

For a moment he looks stricken, and then his face settles back into the scowl. "I don't think it would be a good idea under the circumstances."

"What circumstances?" I fling my arms out. "Your return to the dark side?"

The corner of his mouth twitches, and for a moment I see a glimpse of the Carson I've gotten to know, but it's quickly gone.

"*I'm* not the only one returning to old habits," he says and strides off.

"What does that mean?" I call after him, but he doesn't respond.

Wait. Did *Carson* buy into that scene in the cafeteria? I can't believe he would go back to blowing me off just because of a stupid comment Theo made.

I know it's wrong to rely on Grace, but if I hadn't gone back to visit the day we all met, I wouldn't even know there was a better side to Carson. And while a lot of what I learned was hard, it's mostly turned out to be things I needed to know to move on.

So I scroll back through my texts until I find the one with the link, and, once again, I click.

The app loads on my phone, and I only hesitate a moment before opening it. There it is: **MAGGIE SCOTT ACT THREE**.

But I went through everything for the whole day. What's left?

I shouldn't look. I so shouldn't. It's like Kelli O'Hara says: "I don't read reviews, because if you believe the good ones, you have to believe the bad."

And all of these scenes have ended up being like reviews of me—mostly negative ones. Or at least reviews that showed me how unaware I was of what was happening in the lives around me.

"What are you doing?"

I jump into the bank of lockers behind me, pressing my phone against my chest.

"Whoa." Adam throws up his hands. "You never came out, so I came to find you."

"Right. Sorry. Let's go."

He stopped me. Good.

But as we start walking toward the doors, I glance down at my phone. My thumb must have slipped across the Backstage Pass option when I jumped backward. I can't help but look. There are two scenes listed, but they aren't part of the original day at all.

The first one is **MARCH 28: THEO AT THE PARK**. That's the

day I broke my foot. The second one is from Sunday—**CARSON CONFRONTS THEO.**

Oh, no.

I grip the phone tightly as we walk to the car. Once inside, I look down at the scene titles again.

"You okay?" Adam asks.

I laugh in the back of my throat. "Not really."

"Is it about what happened at lunch?"

Not surprised he heard about it, considering the show Katelyn put on. Or maybe he talked to Rayna. "Sort of."

"Are you getting back with Theo?"

Why does everyone keep asking that? "Definitely not."

"So his friend then. The one who's been giving you a ride."

I grunt. I do *not* want to have this conversation with Adam. Unfortunately, the person I want to discuss it with just blew me off.

Taking the hint, Adam is silent the rest of the way home. I rush to my room and pull up the app. The temptation to play the videos is so strong it's like a magnet is pulling my thumb toward the first scene.

But then I think about my list. Using the Best Day app isn't the way to a better Maggie. Sure, if I watch the videos, I'll get more insight into Theo and Carson, but it won't be the full picture.

With my mom, there was so much behind why she didn't tell me about her health scare *and* the whole *Frozen* casting thing. And even Rayna's story about connecting with Adam went in directions I never could have imagined on my own. So, yes, I could watch these and get inside Theo's or Carson's head. But I'd probably just be left with more questions.

No. I'm done with the app. I close it and hold my thumb on

the yellow Best Day square until the Edit Home Screen option comes up. The app jiggles on my screen; I tap the minus symbol in the corner.

A message asks if I want to delete the app or just remove it from my home screen. I almost expect Grace to start talking, but she doesn't chime in while I make my decision.

"Goodbye, Grace," I say as I click Delete App.

And just like that, it's gone.

64

On Saturday, I dig around in my closet for an outfit in Adam's team colors, deciding on a blue-and-white-striped shirt and medium wash jeans. I tie my hair back with a blue ribbon and write "Go Storm!" on my cheek.

My parents are suitably impressed when I meet them in the kitchen.

"Auditioning for the role of soccer groupie, we have Maggie Scott!" Dad intones.

I curtsy. "In the bag."

"Okay then. We're off," Mom says.

Adam had to be at the game early, so it's just me and the parentals. They're equipped with a cooler of supplies and bag chairs. I think wistfully of cushy theater seats, but I can adapt. As Dad said, I will slip into the role of soccer fan and make everyone believe I'm loving it. It's vital to the better-Maggie list.

Rayna, Clara, and David have already snagged a spot near the middle of the field.

As we approach, Rayna does a double take. "Whoa. I have to get a picture of this."

"I'm not as fangirl as you."

Rayna has an actual Storm T-shirt to go with her face paint. She shrugs. "I *am* the girlfriend."

I lean in close and motion for her to snap the picture.

It's the first selfie we've taken of just the two of us since we reconciled, and it seems significant that it's so blatantly supporting Adam.

"Make sure you tag him when you post it," I tell her.

She raises her eyebrows. "We still haven't made it public on social."

That doesn't seem right. "You haven't? What about prom?"

"Didn't post them."

It's easy to miss things that *aren't* posted when you're focused on the things that are. "Why not?"

She opens her mouth but doesn't say anything.

"Still because of me?" I ask wryly.

She scrunches her face. "Sort of? But I'm also kind of afraid."

I hug her. "I get that. But you're serious about Adam, right?"

Gag. I hope she appreciates how good of an actor I am.

"Yes." She still looks uncertain, but I know it's not about her feelings.

"Then go for it. He'll appreciate it."

I can't believe I'm giving Rayna relationship advice that will help Adam, but this is where we are.

"Okay. I'll do it." She starts captioning the photo from today, and I go join Clara and David.

Clara hands me a bag of Twizzlers, and I happily take one. "You sure know the way to a girl's heart."

David reaches around to snatch the bag. "All mine."

"I had no idea you felt so strongly about licorice."

A whistle blows, drawing our attention to the field.

"The game's about to start!" Rayna says with an excitement she usually reserves for data science.

"Talk about a soccer groupie." I smirk at Rayna.

She smiles archly, keeping one eye on the field. "I seem to recall you paying a fair amount of attention to golf at one point."

I shrug, and Rayna spares me her full-on attention. "You never did tell me the deal with Theo."

"Oh, it's even more interesting than Theo," I blurt out, and Clara leans in too. David stays focused on the game.

I've completely distracted Rayna and Clara from Adam, which was not my intention. "Maybe we should talk about this later? We're supposed to be watching Adam."

Rayna's eyes widen. "You *are* making an effort. But as soon as he subs out, I want details."

For the entire first quarter, I get a rundown from Rayna and David on soccer—rules I used to know but have forgotten after not coming for a couple of years. When Adam dribbles the ball down the field and misses a shot, I groan with everyone else. He doesn't get another chance by the time the quarter ends and another player takes his place.

"Okay, now spill," Rayna says.

They're going to *love* this. "Theo and Katelyn were never actually together."

"What?" Rayna bursts out so loudly one of the players from the opposing team glares at us. She seams her lips together but socks me in the shoulder.

"Okay, okay." I laugh. It really is too good. "But you guys have to swear not to tell anyone else about this."

Clara mimics turning a key before her pursed lips.

"I can keep a secret," Rayna says.

I side-eye her. "Too soon."

"Just saying."

"Mm-hmm." I gather my thoughts. "I met with Theo to get some closure, and Rayna, you were right about him feeling neglected. I really wish he would've *talked* to me about it, but apparently he has issues with that. Which, in the end, is why we weren't a good fit."

"Communication is very important," Clara says. "David and I talk about everything. Right, David?"

He turns toward us and grins easily at Clara. "Absolutely everything. The sky. Global warming. Animal rights. The cultural implications of *Stranger Things*."

I gape at him. "Were you actually listening to us?"

"Don't worry, I have no interest in spreading anything around about Theo."

He turns back toward the game, leaving us to our bubble, but I feel like it's already been punctured.

"Go on," Clara urges. "You really don't have to worry about David."

It's not that I'm concerned about him gossiping, more that he's there at all. But I guess it's too late for that.

"The cultural implications of *Stranger Things*?"

"Later," Clara insists.

"Okay." I try to remember where I was before that odd turn.

"Anyway, after that scene in the lunchroom, Katelyn followed me out and told me they decided to fake-date so I wouldn't convince him to get back together while he was my entire focus."

"That's extreme," Rayna says, but wisely doesn't comment on how this was my plan.

"Sounds like a movie plot," Clara says.

It does seem familiar, now that she mentions it. "Could be."

"Do you think she was hoping he'd fall for her? That's what always seems to happen in books with fake-dating scenarios," Rayna muses.

"Originally I did, but you know what else she said?"

"Yes!" David jumps to his feet, and we quickly turn toward the game. Someone from Adam's team just made a goal, so we all cheer.

It takes a few minutes for everything to settle down, and then I continue. "She wanted to make sure I knew she'd lied about Theo being a bad kisser."

Clara sits back. "So it was just more of the Katelyn witch show."

I laugh. It's the closest Clara will ever get to the word Riley used for Katelyn. "Pretty much. Although she did say she wanted my foot to heal."

Being allowed to wear real shoes is not as exciting as I hoped. It's hard to fit my foot in my tennis shoe, and when I walk, I still feel like I'm uneven. It was the first time my foot was allowed to bend in six weeks, and I could feel all the tendons in the top of it stretching.

I so want to try dancing, but as odd as my foot feels just from walking around, I understand why Dr. Rowland said I have to wait. At least I won't be wearing the ugly surgical shoe for our concert Friday night.

"You believe her?" Rayna asks.

I tuck my knees into my chair and wrap my arms around them. "Sort of. But mostly I believe she enjoyed stringing along my ex and making a big show of it."

"The breakup was definitely a big show," Rayna says.

I hum in the back of my throat. "I still think I win. Breaking my foot and all."

"Since you're keeping score," Clara says.

"Always." I smile.

"Glad to see better Maggie is still Maggie."

"Better Maggie?" Rayna tilts her head.

"Just something Clara and I discussed."

Rayna still looks thoughtful, and I think it's because she wants to ask about better Maggie, but then she says, "What about what Theo said in the breakup scene? Was that planned?"

I backtrack. "The breakup scene with Katelyn? I got the impression he sprang it on her."

"Then I'm not sure the plan totally worked."

"You might be right," Clara adds. "Isn't tonight your date with Carson?"

All the intrigue of the previous conversation turns to a horrible taste in my mouth. "He canceled."

"When?" Clara asks.

"When he turned back into Mr. Hyde the other day."

"David?" Clara says, and he turns back to us.

"Of course he's being a jerk. That's his MO when Theo's in the picture, and he obviously thinks his BF's back with you again."

"That's the most ridiculous—" I stop.

It *is* ridiculous, but both Clara and Adam jumped to the conclusion I might get back together with Theo. Carson might too, especially since he knows I met up with Theo before his very public breakup with Katelyn.

"It seems like a possibility, after the way Theo talked about you to Katelyn—in front of half the school," David explains.

I drop my chin. "Did I miss something? Do you go to our school now?"

Not that it surprises me Clara's filled him in, but he's talking like he witnessed it firsthand.

"The point is, based on his previous behavior, Carson will never ask you out again, not while he thinks he's encroaching on Theo's territory," David lectures like he's presenting on boy theory to a class of uneducated girls.

"I'm not a *territory*!" I spit out.

It's not my fault Theo used me in his act with Katelyn. I'm sure it was just to get back at her for the kiss comment.

"I don't appreciate this analogy either," Clara says, her eyes narrowed on David. "It makes me feel like you're about to mark us with your pee."

"I'd never!" David presses a hand over his heart. "How about a flag?"

She smacks his arm. "You're awful."

Rayna compresses her lips. "So what are you going to do about Carson?"

I want to show him he has nothing to worry about when it comes to Theo, but at the same time, he screwed up too. It's not right for him to treat me that way.

"Nothing for the moment. Besides, I have other things to focus on. Like a potential directing internship. A concert. And this game." I gesture toward the field, where Adam is running back on.

Today is about the ongoing improvement of Maggie, and that means showing my brother and everyone else I can put him first.

65

I don't hear anything from Carson over the weekend, and I admit I'm disappointed. I hoped Thursday was a fluke. That Carson would get past his insecurity and text me.

I really wanted to tell him about the *Footloose* opportunity. I got used to talking to him about things over the past several weeks. Of course I filled Rayna and Clara in after the game. They both think it's a fantastic idea. I also video chatted with Alexis, Tyrone, and Elana. I wasn't quite ready to talk about it at rehearsal last Wednesday, but if I'm seriously considering it, I wanted their opinions first. They're all in, especially Alexis, who reminded me she already "hired" me as her character consultant.

Strangely, I end up talking to Adam about it on the way to school. Even though I'm in regular shoes and don't have any limits on walking, I'm still riding with him. Our improved relationship is a work in progress.

"I think you should do it," Adam says. "When I broke my arm and wasn't allowed to play, I went to all the games and cheered my team on. That way I was still a part of it."

"I hadn't thought of it that way. Did it bother you, not being able to get out there with everyone else?"

"Sure. But my team needed me." He glances over. "I know it's not exactly the same. But you still have friends in that show. Maybe you can make a difference for them. Besides"—he shrugs—"it's better than sitting at home."

"True. I've done enough of that."

When we arrive at school, Adam actually walks in with me. We don't have anything else to say, but it's a companionable silence. Rayna meets us inside, and it doesn't even bother me when they hold hands in the hall. After she posted the photo of us at the game Saturday, she also posted pictures of her and Adam from prom and made their relationship official.

"Hey, Maggie!" My heart skips a beat at the masculine voice, but when I turn around, a smile already blooming, it's Theo.

I keep my smile in place, but it's not as natural now. Adam and Rayna stop with me, Rayna casting a quick glance at her watch.

I'm not going to just blow him off, not after he gave me that whole spiel about how I didn't pay attention to him before.

"Hi, Theo. What's up?"

He stops before me, his thumbs looped in his backpack straps. "I was just wondering. You have that end-of-year concert this Friday, right?"

"Um, yeah?" I gave him a list of all my events earlier in the year. Just like all his golf tournaments are on my calendar. I haven't bothered deleting them yet.

"Will you be there?"

This keeps getting stranger. "I'll be singing, yes."

"Cool. Break a, er, good lu—I mean, cool." He waves and heads off down the hall.

We all watch him, confused.

"Why did Theo want to know about your concert?" Rayna asks.

Adam shakes his head. "Dude. I want nothing to do with this."

He leaves in the same direction as Theo, and honestly? I'm with him. Theo Kallis is no longer a puzzle I want to figure out.

66

On Wednesday I do a video call with the *Footloose* director, and the internship sounds pretty great. It will be different working behind the scenes, but I'm looking forward to it. I already told him yes, even though I expect Dr. Rowland to have good news for me at my next appointment. Even if she says I can start dancing again, I think this is the better choice for me this summer.

That night, as soon as I get to dress rehearsal, I pull Alexis, Tyrone, and Elana aside to tell them I'm definitely taking the internship. They're all thrilled. Katelyn coasts in right before rehearsal; she can be surprised the first day of *Footloose*.

By Friday, I'm anxious to perform, even if I will be singing from a stool stage left while everyone else dances. It's not as much of a blow as missing an actual show, but I'd still rather be using all my talents.

Soon, I hope.

Alexis sidles up beside me. "Ready?"

"All set."

"I think I saw your boyfriend out there," Tyrone says, joining us. He smooths down the gold lapels on his jacket. "Or is it Katelyn's boyfriend now?"

He arches an eyebrow playfully. I knew he'd snoop after I didn't talk before, but I don't really care if he knows either.

Still, what is Theo doing here? "He's no one's boyfriend now."

With everything else going on this week, I forgot he asked about the concert.

"Interesting," Tyrone drawls.

I swat his shoulder. "It's really not," I say with a smile.

But I can't help searching for him when we take the stage, and I almost miss our first entrance when I find not only Theo in the audience, but Carson right beside him too.

✦ ✦ ✦ ✦

After the bows, I wind through the crowd in the lobby to find my family, keeping an eye out for Theo and Carson as well. I don't know what to think about their presence here. Did they finally talk? Did Theo ask about the concert because Carson was too afraid to do it himself after the way he treated me last week?

Before I spot them, my family finds me. Mom and Dad envelop me in hugs. "Wonderful job, sweetheart," Mom says. "Now how's your foot?"

"Okay. I might ice it later."

"See? Nothing to worry about," Dad says. "Let's go get ice cream!"

"Dad's solution to everything." Adam shakes his head.

While they keep chatting, Rayna pulls away from Adam and leans in close. "Your boys are here."

I don't really like the way that sounds. "Where are they?"

"Right behind you."

I whirl around, hoping I'll see the Carson I rode home with

346

every day. The one who helped me sneak into the hospital and played mini golf with me.

Instead, I'm faced with an armful of gerbera daisies. My favorite flower.

But the wrong boy is holding them.

For a moment, I look back and forth between Theo and Carson, unsure what to do. I want to shout at Carson for not telling Theo he asked me out. To shake Theo for being so blind.

Then Theo thrusts the flowers forward, leaving me little choice but to accept them.

"You were fantastic up there, Maggie," he says.

"Thank you." I glance over at Carson again. He isn't wearing a cap today, so he can't hide that way, but he still won't meet my gaze.

"Really loved it," Carson murmurs.

Before I can respond to Carson, Theo steps closer to me. "Maggie, can I talk to you a minute?"

My confusion must show on my face because he adds, "Alone?"

I really don't want to, especially with Carson here. I'd rather talk to *him*, clear up whatever is going through his head. But that's probably not happening until Theo says his piece. "Sure."

I lead him down a side hallway.

"Okay." Theo takes a deep breath. "The thing is . . . I've been thinking a lot since the other day when we talked. I can tell you've really changed, and I'd like to give things another shot. I miss you, superstar."

What? Even with all the signs pointing toward something like this, I can't really believe it's happening.

Theo reaches for my free hand, and I'm so shocked I let him

take it. But there's no tingle anymore. No jolt of excitement at his touch.

Out of the corner of my eye, I see Carson watching us from the lobby, but now it seems overly reactive to jerk away from Theo. How do I get out of this?

"I can see I've surprised you," Theo says.

I stare down at our clasped hands, and a dozen memories flash through my mind. Afternoons making hilarious stop-motion videos with Therese. Helping me run lines even though he obviously resented the time my drama activities took from him. There was a lot of good with Theo.

When we broke up, I was devastated. But the way he reacted afterward, even if it was an act devised with Katelyn, showed me how wrong we are for each other. Whatever I felt for him is gone.

"I'm sorry, Theo. You're right. I have changed. I'll always care about you, but as a friend. We can't go back to what we had."

"Ouch." He squeezes my hand, then releases it. "Well, I'm glad I at least tried."

He backs away, a self-pitying grin on his face, then turns and strides away.

It takes a moment to process what just happened. I clasp the flowers to my chest, crinkling the tissue paper. I feel like a weight has been lifted. I thought I was through with Theo before, but back then it was his choice. Now it's mine, and that's so much more satisfying.

Except . . . wait. Theo brought Carson along with him *to ask me to get back together*. I have to catch Carson before he leaves.

I head toward where I last saw them. Rayna intercepts me near the exit.

"What happened?" she asks.

"I'll explain later. Did you see where they went?"

"That way." She points to the left. "We'll be waiting at the car!" she calls.

I wave the flowers at her as I walk as quickly as possible in the direction she pointed. Even though I cut myself off from the app and the ability to essentially eavesdrop on the thoughts of those around me, it's impossible not to stop and listen when I hear Carson and Theo talking.

"I thought she'd changed, but I guess not," Theo says.

"Seriously, Theo?" Carson responds. "You treated her like an afterthought in the beginning, hedging your bets with Isabel. And then this whole thing with Katelyn. Of course she doesn't want to get back together."

"Whoa," Theo says. I wish I could see their expressions, but they're around the corner of the building. "Why didn't you say any of this before?"

"I tried. I just—I never stopped liking her. So I couldn't bring her up to you."

Theo sighs. "I thought you'd moved on."

"Unfortunately, no."

Oh, Carson.

"Then why did you tell me to go talk to her?"

Good question.

"Because she texted you right after—"

Carson stops, but I get it. Right after he asked me out. We had the same plan, to get closure. It was just poor timing he finally decided to talk to Theo about me at the same time. We are one huge mess of miscommunication.

"After what?" Theo prompts.

"It doesn't matter. I screwed up."

"We both did," Theo says. "I wish you'd told me you were into her *before* I asked her out again."

They walk into view, and I plaster myself against the wall, causing the family of some troupe members to look at me strangely. Theo and Carson are gone by the time I look again.

67

I get into a pretty regular routine over the next week. Rayna and I are almost back to normal. I'm getting more used to not sniping at Adam, although I can't just shut that off completely.

As for Theo and Carson . . . I wish I could say the fact they had it out suddenly made Carson come declare himself, but no. He isn't scowling at me anymore, but he isn't approaching me either, so when I spot him outside the cafeteria door, I take the initiative.

"Hi," I say, wishing I had something better prepared.

"Hey," he says, avoiding my gaze just like he did at the concert.

So awkward. "Thanks for coming to see me sing."

He glances up, just quick enough to give me a glimpse of his eyes, before looking down again. "You looked great up there."

"I've mastered the art of stool balancing." Actually a tricky feat for more than an hour.

"And you'll be dancing again soon, I bet." He still won't look at me. I know the floor isn't that interesting.

"Yeah, I have an appointment on Friday. I should find out then. Maybe we can—"

"I'm sorry, Maggie. For everything," he says, then darts away.

Seriously? He ran away? It's like Theo all over again.

Well, not exactly. As for being sorry, he should be. Because he was a total jerk for months, and it wasn't cool. If he's apologizing for his more recent behavior, also necessary. But at the same time, he could stick around for my answer. He's so frustrating!

I don't try to talk to Carson again the rest of the week. Like I told him, I have something else to count down to anyway—my next appointment with Dr. Rowland. Mom scheduled it for right after school on Friday; Adam drops me off, and Mom meets me in the lobby.

It takes considerable effort for me not to skip in.

"Now, Maggie, we still need to wait for Dr. Rowland to clear you."

"I know, but I have a good feeling about it."

We go through the same rigamarole as usual—X-rays, questions about how it's feeling.

When Dr. Rowland comes in with a smile, I'm already anticipating good news.

"Well, Maggie, everything has healed quite nicely." She goes on to show us the X-rays, but I don't really care about what the bone or screw are doing as long as it's all fixed.

As soon as she stops talking, I blurt out, "Can I dance?"

She nods. "Dance, leap, whatever you want. You can return to all normal activities. Just continue to ice it if it bothers you. And you can also wear any shoes that are comfortable."

"Yes!" I throw my head back. "I love you, Dr. Rowland!"

"That's not something I hear very often." She chuckles. "I would like you to come back in three months for a checkup, but I don't anticipate any issues."

I can't get out of there fast enough. Against Mom's protests, I skip into the lobby, then perform a pirouette and a few extra jazz moves for good measure. A man walking by claps, and I bow.

Mom shakes her head. "I knew you missed dancing, but I don't think I quite realized how much."

"This has been *torture*." It's too late for me to jump back into my dance recital numbers, but that doesn't mean I can't dance for myself.

I can't wait to tell everyone. Actually. I find a ledge and set my phone to record, then repeat my dance moves. I post the video with an all-caps headline: CLEARED TO DANCE! Then I text Rayna and Clara, as well as Alexis, Tyrone, and the rest of my Future Stars friends.

However, I am very careful to watch for steps.

Carson is one of the first people to like my post, and I just want to reach through the phone and strangle him. Why can't he see that I want to be with him?

If I leave this to Carson, it will probably be another seven months before he talks to me again. It's time to take matters into my own hands. I don't know if I'll ever get him to tell me everything about the day we met. That's a lot to ask of a guy. I think the best I can hope for is to get him to talk about how he feels *now*. So that's my mission.

68

"Why are you dragging me along to this thing again?" Adam whines as we park at the country club.

I side-eye Rayna. "I invited Rayna. She asked you to come along. Maybe you'll learn something."

"Golf is so slow."

"And remember"—I give him a stern look—"no talking while they're getting ready to hit the ball."

I smile a little as I remember how Carson once lectured me about that.

We lock up the car and head toward the course itself. The tournament is in full swing. I texted Theo last night to confirm details, and *that* wasn't at all awkward. I made it very clear that I was coming to watch Carson, and he took a while to reply, but then he sent me the tee-off times and added, Don't break his heart.

Like he's one to talk.

At least Theo is acknowledging I've moved on and seems okay with it.

"How come Clara and David don't have to come?" Adam says grumpily.

I smirk at Rayna. "Now *this* is the Adam I'm used to."

She loops her arm through his. "Don't worry. I'll make it worth your while."

I curl my lip. "Ugh! We had an agreement!"

I stride ahead of them toward the first hole. Carson is getting ready to tee off, along with a guy from Farthingwood High School.

"Are you going to say anything to him?" Rayna asks.

"Nope. I'm just going to watch."

Carson looks great doing his warm-up swing. He's wearing a Bridgeport High School cap, a dark blue polo shirt, and khaki pants. The other guy is more flamboyant, in bright orange pants and a striped orange-and-teal shirt—kind of like Rickie Fowler.

The marshal signals for everyone to be quiet, and Carson gets into position. He swings, and the ball soars straight down the fairway. An older couple to the side starts cheering. I recognize Carson's parents from pictures he's posted.

We wait for the other guy to hit the ball—it veers to the right of the fairway—and then we start walking.

"When are you going to make your move?" Adam asks.

"Soon."

Carson takes his next shot, and this time I cheer too, getting Rayna and Adam to join in. Carson squints back at us, looking confused, then shakes it off. He must not recognize us.

Carson finishes the hole one stroke ahead of the other player. We keep pace with them as they move to the second hole, and he keeps glancing back, like he's still trying to figure out who we are.

"Um, you might be making things worse for him with this strategy. Maybe you should just go up there," Rayna suggests.

I definitely don't want to throw off his game. I pick up speed so that we're only about twenty feet from the tee off, and Carson's eyes widen. I wave, and he blinks. He opens his mouth, like he's about to ask me a question, but he shakes himself out of it and goes to tee off.

Unfortunately, he veers off course this time. He waits for the other guy to hit, looking back at me several times.

As he gathers his clubs to go to his ball, I keep pace with him. He glances toward the marshal and then calls out, "What are you doing here?"

"Don't you know you're supposed to stay quiet on the golf course?" I reply with a smirk.

A myriad of emotions cross his face. Surprise. Confusion. Finally a dawning understanding and cautious optimism.

I motion toward the fairway. "You can still birdie this one."

He swallows and nods as he heads for his ball.

I stay with Carson for all eighteen holes, groaning when he has an off shot and cheering when he's on. He ends the day at par.

We stand off to the side while he finalizes his score. Theo's waiting for him. He nods in our direction; Carson catches it and they talk briefly.

What would I do to have Grace in my ear right now?

Actually, no. I never want to hear anyone's thoughts ever again. As tough as it is to figure out what's going on with other people, that's what Grace taught me—that I need to pay better attention to everyone around me.

"You owe me ice cream. Or better yet—an ice cream cake!" Adam says.

I laugh. "Deal."

"Yeah?" Adam looks surprised. "Are we done here?"

"You are. Thanks." I hug Rayna. "I really appreciated the support."

"Anytime," she says. "Good luck."

They walk off hand in hand, and I quickly pull out my phone to send Carson a text.

He ambles toward me, stopping a few feet away to set down his golf bag. He takes off his hat and wipes his brow with the back of his wrist before placing it back on his head. "I can't believe you came to watch me play after I was such a jerk to you."

"You did throw that all-encompassing apology at me."

He winces. "Not my best moment."

"Yeah, but we already had a false start, and I believe in second chances. So . . . care to explain?"

He digs his golf cleat into the ground. "Since the day we all met, I've been trying to make sure you wouldn't want anything to do with me."

And people say *girls* play games. "Are you trying to tell me I'm so magnetic I need to be repelled by hateful behavior? Or is it that *you're* so magnetic? Either way, it's a pretty awful way to treat someone you actually like."

"I know. But it seemed easier to drive you away so I wouldn't like you even more. I guess I was also kind of bitter that you didn't even notice me the day we met."

Having experienced his side of things firsthand, I get that. I still think it sucks, but I understand.

He steps closer and grins. "But you are pretty magnetic. Especially when you're on stage."

"Oh, yeah?" Before Friday, the only show I remember him

coming to was *Frozen*, and his comments afterward were not complimentary.

"I've never laughed so hard as when you played Oaken."

"Right. Because I was such a great man."

He flushes. "Yet another of my stupid comments. You were brilliant. And I couldn't wait to see your Helena. I've never looked forward to car rides as much as those weeks driving you to and from school. You're funny and driven and passionate and beautiful, and I never stopped liking you, the whole time you were with Theo."

Wow. There's the shuffle step hop in my heart.

"But if all this is true, why did you cancel our date?"

He sighs heavily. "Because I thought you were getting back together with Theo. Something he said after he met up with you for coffee." He glances behind him, but Theo is gone. Just like the day all of this started outside Starbucks. "I have a lot of insecurities about you where Theo is concerned. But I should have actually asked you—or even Theo—instead of assuming things."

"Yes. You should. We could have avoided that whole situation at my concert if you'd talked to either of us, especially Theo."

"Believe me, I know," he says earnestly.

Having already experienced what he felt that first day, I imagine watching Theo try to win me back must have been a hundred times worse for him.

"It's really easy to misinterpret a situation." I pause. "I'm sorry I didn't see you. When we first met."

Color rises up his neck.

I step closer. "I think I made it obvious by coming here today, but I also sent you a text a few minutes ago, just to make it clear."

Confusion clouds his brow, but he stoops and digs his phone out of his golf case. A text seemed appropriate to me, since that's how Grace first contacted me. Also, it's harder to misunderstand words that are right there in black and white. Carson swipes into his phone, and a grin spreads across his face as he reads the message. He quickly types a reply, and my phone buzzes in my pocket. I pull it out to read, I want to be with you too.

"Now that we've settled that . . ." I shove the phone in my pocket and close the small space between us, linking my arms around his neck. "I'm thinking we should finish that conversation my mom interrupted."

His mouth drops open slightly. "Wha—? Oh. For sure."

It's not the best line to precede a first kiss, but the kiss itself delivers. His lips are soft and gentle for a few tentative seconds. Then he increases the pressure and tugs me closer, his hands anchored on my hips. My pulse picks up tempo, kicking into an upbeat number that makes my nerve endings hum. I push up onto my tiptoes, getting as close as I can. There's no game here, just two people who've screwed up in the past and finally figured out where we're supposed to be. For several delicious moments, I'm lost in Carson.

Until the chorus of "On Top of the World" bursts out of my back pocket. I'd like to ignore it, but it doesn't stop.

We pull apart, and Carson raises his eyebrows as I retrieve my phone. "You still don't know when to silence your phone?"

"I totally did!" I protest as I look down at it. I have a new text message.

Maggie Scott Curtain Call

My heart skips a beat. I twist, scanning the golf course to see if there's anyone else around. My phone signals a second message.

359

You're welcome. Regards, Grace

A moment later, the messages and the number they came from disappear. I tap at my messages, do a search. They're nowhere.

"Something important?" Carson asks.

Way more than I understood.

"Not anymore." I put the phone away. "How about some ice cream cake?"

"Ice cream cake? Best day ever!"

He has no idea.

I bump his shoulder. "You're right. Let's go make it even better."

ACKNOWLEDGMENTS

I'm so incredibly humbled to have a second book out in the world. Thank you, God, for the continued opportunity to pursue this amazing career.

As always, a book is only possible with a veritable army of people behind the author.

Thank you to my agent, Elizabeth Bewley, for telling me *this* was the right book to focus on next. Your counsel, insight, and friendship are invaluable. I couldn't imagine going through this with anyone else by my side. Thank you also to everyone else at Sterling Lord Literistic!

Allison Moore, thank you for seeing Maggie's potential and always asking the right questions to make me dig deeper and find the best solutions. You've made me a stronger writer while whipping both of my books into shape.

I'm so grateful to everyone at Bloomsbury for making my publishing dreams come true. Thank you to Camille Kellogg for guiding me through the final publication steps for this book, as well as to editorial director Sarah Shumway and the rest of the production and managing editorial team—Oona Patrick, Nick Sweeney, Jeff Curry, Laura Phillips, Rebecca McGlynn, and Nicholas Church. Thank you to the fabulous marketing and publicity team, particularly Ariana Abad, Phoebe Dyer, Faye Bi, Erica Barmash, Valentina Rice, Beth Eller, and Alona Fryman. Finally, eternal gratitude to the sales team for everything you do to put my book into readers' hands.

This book is so incredibly gorgeous. Thank you to cover artist Jacqueline Li for so perfectly capturing Maggie, Carson, and Theo and to designers Jeanette Levy and Donna Mark for their meticulous attention to detail.

Before the book goes to my agent or editor, I run it through my critique partners and beta readers. Kip Wilson, Amy Trueblood, Carla Cullen, and Beth Ellyn Summer—your feedback on this book and others is immeasurable. I'm also grateful to my local writer friends who are always up for lunch and advice, including Jamie Krakover, Julia Maranan, and Meredith Tate.

An extra-special shout-out to Abigail Johnson, Meredith Tate, Kara McDowell, and Kristy Boyce for reading this book early and offering such lovely blurbs.

Thank you to everyone who supported me through my debut year. It was challenging debuting during a pandemic, and I couldn't have done it without the support of my debut group, #the21ders, as well as my agent siblings, Pitch Wars family, and too many other friends—both near and far—to count. Thank you to all of the book bloggers, bookstagrammers, booktokers, and book reviewers who read and shared about my debut book or will about this one. Thank you to the librarians and teachers who stock my books and share them with your students, as well as those who invited me into your classrooms virtually. I'm so grateful for your support, and I hope you enjoy this book just as much.

Thank you to my local independent bookstores, the Novel Neighbor and Main Street Books, as well as my local Barnes & Noble stores, for their support. Booksellers are the absolute best!

This book was partially inspired by my own experience breaking my foot in 2019, so I have to thank my foot surgeon, Dr. Christopher Forsbach, not only for fixing my foot but also for answering my questions while I took extensive notes.

My daughter's involvement in musical theater also served as a huge inspiration for this book. Thank you to Stages Performing Arts Academy for teaching both of my kids and for all of the great shows, including the *Frozen Jr.* production that started it all.

Right as I started drafting this book in late 2019, my best friend suffered a massive stroke, and I wrote much of the draft in early 2020 sitting in her hospital room, often brainstorming with her family members. Chrissy Stricker, you continue to inspire me. And Mary and Jesse Stricker and Nancy Kuhlman, thank you for the brainstorming sessions!

I seriously have the best friends in the world. So many of you showed up at my signings, bought copies of my first book (sometimes multiple!), read it in a week, shared about it online, and just generally checked in on me to see how things were going. I would love to list all of you by name, but I would surely miss someone, and that would make me the worst friend, so let this just be an all-encompassing THANK YOU, FRIENDS! [Endless heart emojis]

Thank you to all of my family. My parents, Ladd and Karen Faszold; my brother, Christopher Faszold; my in-laws, Chuck and Barb Mason; my aunts, Mendi Baker and Robin Faszold; and to all of the Faszolds, Masons, Bakers, Hunters, Justices, Berrys, Ralls, Kelleys, and Rays. Love you all so much!

Thank you to Luke and Anna, my extraordinary kids, who could both share a stage with Maggie. Luke would rather stick to just acting (brilliantly!), while Anna is a triple threat in the traditional sense rather than my creative new definition in the dedication (although that's totally true too). You both bring me unimaginable joy, and I really will always be your biggest fan.

Finally, thank you, Greg, for listening to story ideas and reading drafts and taking care of everything in the house when I'm on deadline. On this book in particular, thanks for checking all my golf facts. Most of all, thank you for supporting this dream and always believing in me. Looking forward to many more best days with you!